The Truth Trilogy Book One

The
Roman's
Quest

Anne Baxter Campbell

First Edition

Published by
Helping Hands Press

ISBN: 978-1-62208-478-4

Printed in the United States of America

Dedication

This book is dedicated to my precious daughter. As a small child, she kept me sane. As a teenager, she challenged all the wisdom I thought I'd gathered—but she also inspired this book which I started thirty-five years ago. As an adult, she's more cherished than ever. I am so very proud of you, Renae Anne Parsons!

Acknowledgments

First and foremost, thank You, Lord God, for Your help and inspiration.

A special thanks, too, to my precious husband, Jack Campbell. He fixed meals, encouraged, listened, advised, loved me through troubling times, exhibited amazing patience—in short, he's the perfect man.

There have been so many people who have helped me along the road with my writing and with this novel. Fay Lamb, especially when she was the moderator of the American Christian Fiction Writers (ACFW) Scribes, taught me so much I can't even begin to express my huge appreciation. She was also the first editor who tackled the entire manuscript and helped polish it. Others—June Foster, Carole Towriss, Justina Prima, F. Robert McMurray, and a host of others—challenged and stretched my writing habits at every turn, too.

Among the books and so forth that I've dug nuggets from, the Bible was highest and best. The Complete Works of Josephus, the journals of Pilate, and countless Internet sites were invaluable. I spent as much time in research as in writing, and still my greatest fear is that I will have missed or misinterpreted some vital piece in history, geography, or the Bible.

Also, I want you to know: Any mistakes in the text belong squarely on my shoulders. I appreciate feedback, and if you find things that are iffy, ucky, or just plain wrong, let me know at anneb1944@aol.com. You could also let me know if you liked it. ☺

Glossary

Abba—Aramaic word for dad

Assaria—a Roman coin made from bronze, 1/10 of a denarius

Aureus—a Roman coin made from gold, worth 25 denarii

Century—a Roman army unit of 80 legionaries

Contubernium—the smallest organized unit of soldiers in the Roman army and was composed of eight legionaries, the equivalent of a modern squad.

Culina The Latin word for kitchen, or food, or victuals.

Decanus -- The decanus was the first man of an eight man contubernium unit. A normal soldier without formal command he was most likely in charge of various tent or barracks duties.

Denarius—a Roman coin made from silver, a day's wage.

Fridgidarium—a place constructed to cool oneself (Latin), usually at a Roman bath.

Ima—Jewish word for mom.

Kodrantes—the smallest unit of currency in Rome. 1/4 of an assaria.

Legionary—a professional soldier of the Roman army. Legionaries had to be Roman citizens under the age of 45.

Chapter 1

In the thirteenth year of the reign of Tiberius Caesar, in the month of Marcius

Julius Saturnius stood in the mid-morning heat, droplets of sweat trickling from the kinks of his hair onto his forehead and down the back of his neck, watching and waiting.. He'd been stationed in Jericho for a year. In that time, a young woman had stopped some young boys from tormenting a dog, comforted a little girl who had fallen, and given a loaf of bread to a beggar, but none of that is what had captured his attention. Her wide expressive eyes and the supple grace with which she moved had drawn him to watch for her daily.

Strange, but she reminded him a little of his mother, who had also been a rescuer. Their spacious dwelling in Rome had always been filled with orphans and pups.

The young woman had taken to walking to this spring with her friends almost every morning. She never ventured here alone any more to this place where the residents got their drinking water. An incident had occurred here with a soldier named Brutus. To avoid what he'd saved her from, the women were smart to come in groups. Still he found reason to be in this vicinity most days, wishing she might set aside her fear and come alone so that he might speak to her.

As if wishful thinking had made her appear, Julius straightened as the girl and her companions made their way toward the spring.

Julius watched the young woman walking toward the well. He wondered if she were married and whether she would smile on him even if she were not. He heaved a sigh. She was a Jew; he was a Roman, and Jews hated Romans. With good cause, sometimes. Brutus spent a month cleaning latrines for what he had tried to do to this beautiful one. Did she know he had pulled Brutus off her?

All his supplications and sacrifices to Venus, the goddess of love, had gone unanswered. He chuckled to himself. He would ask

Mars, but he didn't want to go to war with the beautiful young woman. He let out his breath. Even Venus could never match this Jewess' beauty and grace.

As though she heard his thoughts, she glanced up and met his gaze. She lowered long dark lashes over golden brown eyes, blushing and frowning.

Heat rose from his throat to his face.

She looked angry, and it wasn't hard to understand why. He'd been staring like one of his mother's hungry pups when she took out scraps from the table.

Why did he have to serve in Jericho and be tormented by this woman-child? He almost wished he could be transferred somewhere else.

Almost.

But then he wouldn't see her again, never watch that delicious female walk, never hear that bubbling laugh, never see those red, ripe lips smile as she walked with her friends.

No, that would be worse.

Maybe tomorrow there would be a chance to speak to her, though about what, he didn't know. He wanted to tell her…hmm…just what, exactly? He couldn't tell her what he thought: that he would like to make good use of those inviting lips.

And how could he tell her anything with forty other women always around her?

He prayed to his gods, but he doubted any of them approved of her. The Jews claimed his gods didn't exist. The Jewish God—invisible, so they said. How could they talk to a God they couldn't see? Did this God hear their thoughts?

Hmm. Would He hear a plea from Julius? *God of the Jews, if You exist, would You show me a way to meet her?*

Miriam's thoughts spun like a desert whirlwind. What was wrong with her? Just because this Roman was handsome, muscular, and broad-shouldered didn't mean she needed to act like such a fool whenever she saw him watching her.

Ah, those eyes. Such a startling blue. Here he stood almost every day, waiting by the Spring of Elisha, watching her with those dark, piercing blue eyes. She willed herself to ignore his admiring looks, yet her mutinous gaze strayed time after time to this soldier who had saved her. At least she thought he was the one. There were just two centurions in Jericho, and she caught only a glimpse of his back as he marched the evil one away. She hoped he didn't recognize her as the one dragged into the old house of Barnabab, long deserted and crumbling from disuse. No one had mentioned the attack to her parents or her friends. If anyone had seen. Nor would she tell her parents.

Be still, thumping heart, he might hear.

Or worse, one of her friends could hear and know why her heartbeat raced faster the closer they drew, realize the red in her cheeks was not from the exertion or heat, and recognize that her thoughts were drawn to a Gentile who worshipped at the shrines of false gods. She glanced up at him but pulled her gaze back before her friends could catch her.

The wind gusted, and Miriam scowled as she reached to tuck a strand of windblown hair under the blue wool scarf.

She cast a sidelong glance at the others and then raised her eyes skyward. "Adonai, please help me control these rebel thoughts."

"Miriam, you're doing it again." Her friend Mary giggled as she lifted the full jar of water to the top of her head. "You're staring into the heavens and whispering."

"Probably praying for a husband." Hannah's grin took the edge from her teasing.

"Maybe praying she won't have to marry." Mary's hand strayed to a dark bruise on her cheek.

"Has your father found one good enough for you yet, Miriam?" Tamar's eyes narrowed, and her lips turned upward in a scornful smirk.

Miriam shook her head, blushing again.

Her father had refused seven offers of marriage for her. Not strong enough, not wise enough, too old, too young. She realized her friends, and maybe the men too, knew her father found them unsuitable because she didn't want to marry any of them.

She wished her parents had stayed in Bethsaida instead of moving here to Jericho. In Bethsaida, she hadn't been the only girl with light hair. Here, unless she covered every strand, people stared at her. The men especially, but the women, too. Sometimes she wondered if the men liked her only because of her hair.

Still, how could she disappoint her abba by telling him she had eyes for a beardless Roman centurion rather than one of the Jewish men Abba wanted? It would be better to forget the Gentile. Think instead about the smell of blooming jasmine on the soft breeze, the beauty of the wildflowers on the green hillside, the feel of the baby's kicks in Hannah's belly. Anything but dwelling on the sparks that flew whenever her glance met the Roman's.

With a start she noticed her friends had left her behind. She knelt and filled the jar from the spring and rose. She turned to hasten after the others but stepped on the edge of her long outer tunic. The water spilled as she twisted to put her body between the ground and the jar. The Roman soldier jumped forward and lifted her to her feet. He continued to hold her arms, but one hand strayed upward toward her shoulder. "Are you all right?"

She froze, staring at his hand. He loosed his grip as though her arms were hot. She opened her mouth to speak, but her tongue felt like a great wad of cloth in a dry cistern. He must think her an idiot.

"Thank you, s-sir." She backed away a step and dropped her gaze to her wet tunic. Rational thought failed to move her lips, and she fought for something to say. "Uh...how is it you speak Aramaic?"

"I, um, I just thought it might be wise to learn the language of your people because I'm assigned here for a long while." He cleared his throat. "What are you called? I'm Julius, son of Legate Gaius Saturnius."

She hesitated. She shouldn't tell this Gentile her name, should she? But the scriptures said she shouldn't be discourteous to a stranger. "I'm Miriam, daughter of Micah the carpenter." She pulled the soft blue wool scarf closer around her face. "I must go...the others...." She turned to look after her friends and saw a scowling Hannah alone waited for her.

"Of course. I'm sorry to have kept you." Julius dipped the jar into the pool and handed it to her. "Here."

His deep voice shook her bones, and her heart skipped several beats when his fingers brushed hers. She hurried away, her face hot, praying she wouldn't trip again.

Miriam caught up with Hannah, and together they walked on.

Hannah's face rippled with a comical mixture of emotions: eyebrows up, then together; lips open, then tight. She leaned toward Miriam. "What will your parents think? You know how the Roman soldiers are around women. You should be more careful. Remember, they are Gentiles. Heathens." Hannah pulled away. Her scowl had vanished, replaced by wide-eyed curiosity. "What did he say?"

"Hannah, Hannah." Miriam forced a laugh. "I'll be so glad when you give birth to your little one. Maybe then you will cease mothering me. He only helped me draw the water after I fell. He didn't act like other soldiers. He spoke to me in Aramaic. Have you ever heard of any other soldiers speaking our language?"

"No, but he doesn't fool me, and neither do you. Your face could never keep a secret. I often see him watching you, and I've caught you looking at him, too, several times. His gaze never leaves you. There, see? You blushed again."

"It's the heat. I am not blushing."

"Oh, Miriam, don't give your heart to a Roman. Your father is too lenient with you, but he would never approve a Gentile who worships those awful gods of Rome. And speaking of Rome, your father would never consent to marriage to anyone who might drag you to the far end of the world."

"You make too many assumptions, Hannah. The soldier only talked to me about his lessons in Aramaic. Imagine my surprise when he didn't mention marriage."

"Speaking of marriage, Isaiah told me he saw James ben Zebedee at the river selling fish again. What excuse can your father find against him? He works hard, he honors his parents, he's pious and handsome, and he's the oldest son of a man who established one of the most prosperous fishing businesses in Judea. Add to that his obvious affection for you. He haunts your house every time he is in Jericho waiting for you to see him. Wait much longer, and you'll be too old for marriage to James. Or anyone."

"But Hannah, you know James' temper, and his voice is so loud. I heard several dead people stuck their heads out of their tombs to shush him, chiding him for interrupting their sleep. And he always smells of fish." Miriam pinched her nose.

"Better smelly James than a stinking Roman," Hannah said, her lips a thin line, her free hand on her hip. They had arrived at her house, and she moved the hand on her hip to support her stomach. A grimace crossed her face. "I need to go inside and sit a while before I prepare my starving husband's meal. This little one feels like a full-grown camel. Want to come in? Isaiah won't return for an hour or longer."

Miriam shook her head. "I need to go home. Tomorrow, perhaps I'll get your water for you." She waved before Hannah entered the house.

Miriam tried to hold her cheerful smile, but she could feel her heart sinking. Hannah was right. She was sixteen. Each year it would be harder for her father to find any willing man to parade before her. Hannah, just a year older than she, wed at fifteen. Mary, her age, had been married three years. Tamar espoused at fourteen. All her close friends were married.

Despite his prevailing odor, James was not as bad a choice as some. Although he tended to be abrupt with others, he treated her with kindness. His voice softened when he spoke to her. This time she should tell her father yes when he asked her about James. Her heart weighed heavy at the thought, and she tasted bitterness on her tongue.

"Why will my heart not heed reason? Why can I not be logical?" she whispered to the One God. "Jehovah Rohi, shepherd me, please. I cannot change my way, no matter how hard I try. My emotions won't listen to me. You have the power to move my heart from foolishness to wisdom. Help me. Help me, please."

Chapter 2

The second contubernium replaced the third in Julius' century for the night watches. A wilderness full of brigands surrounded Jericho, and he had no doubt some of them lived within the small city. Attacks on Romans and on others the Jews called Gentiles occurred too often, in town and out. Guards stationed around the city did their best to keep the peace. Two major Jewish festivals loomed, and zealots crept from behind every building, rock, and tree before and during any feast days.

Julius gave orders to the two decani. They marched their groups of eight, one contubernium to the troop quarters and one to their guard stations. With purposeful strides he made his way toward the officers' accommodations.

"Deborah!" a woman's voice cried from behind him.

Julius turned. A Jewish woman lay on the street of the marketplace. Another woman knelt by her side. No Jewish men in sight, but several women began to make their way to the two. Julius strode to the women's side. "May I help?"

"My sister. She fainted," her companion said. "I don't want to leave her to go looking for help. If you would find someone to carry her to my house...."

"I'll carry her." He lifted the woman, thinking as he did she weighed no more than a child. "Where do you live?"

Her sister put out a hand as though to stop him, shrugged, and pointed toward the north. "This way."

Julius shifted the woman's limp form so that her head rested on his shoulder.

The woman breathed a soft sigh and woke. Her eyes widened and her body stiffened.

Julius smiled with what he hoped was a comforting look. "Please don't be alarmed. You fainted, and I'm carrying you to your sister's home."

The sister patted the woman's arm. "I'm here, Deborah, and we're nearly there. In here, sir," she said, waving in the direction of a door opening into a small stone house.

Julius carried Deborah into the home and to a couch behind a low table. He heard a sharp intake of breath from behind him.

"Leah! What are you doing?" A thin man came from a dark corner of the room. He hurried toward them wringing his hands.

"Thank you, sir, for your help," Leah said, throwing a scowl in the man's direction. "If not for you, Deborah might still be lying in the hot sun."

Deborah, pale and sweating, nodded. "I thank you, too, Centurion. May the One God bless you."

Julius nodded. "I was happy to assist." He glanced toward Leah's husband. "I'm sure any man would have done the same thing, if any had been there." He shared a knowing smile with Leah. No true man would leave a woman helpless on the ground. "Now, if you will allow me, I must go."

"I…I…It is not right for a Gentile to…to…" the man sputtered.

Julius ducked out the door and chuckled to himself. The women may have been thankful, but the man didn't seem to be of the same opinion. He walked on to his quarters, a multistoried brick building where officers and their servants dwelt. His residence had two bedrooms, a kitchen, and a combined living and dining area, Spartan but livable.

His Greek slave, Cyril, cocked one eyebrow as Julius danced into the room. Julius grinned and whirled his red cloak around his head before he tossed it to the slave. He hung his helmet on a hook, and Cyril helped him peel off his armor. Julius grinned again at this man who had been with him since they were babes, more like a brother than a slave.

"You must have had a good day, O Most Noble Master," Cyril said.

Julius' dinner sat on the table, and he crossed the floor to recline on the couch. With a wave, he motioned for Cyril to join him. "I did indeed, O Most Valued Slave. Mm, this stew is good. What's in it?"

"Lamb, garlic, onions, lentils, water, spices. Quit keeping me in suspense. What made this such a wondrous day?" Cyril sat on the bench across from Julius.

"Do you remember the Jewish girl I mentioned a few days ago? Her tenacious friends left her behind, and we talked for a few moments. She gave me her name, Miriam. Ah, Miriam. Is it not the most musical name you have ever heard? Miriam-m-m. " He held a filled spoon in front of his mouth, but it stayed there uneaten for a few moments while he reflected on the image of the young woman. "She's even more alluring up close. And I'd like to get close enough to know exactly how alluring."

"I might have known your reverie involved that enticing Jewess. It is not as though you mentioned her once a few days ago. No, it is instead a fact that every other sentence you've spoken for the past six months has been about this waking vision."

"How can I help but talk about her? The way she walks, her eyes, her lips, and my imagination filling in the rest of the details. She occupies my mind every waking moment. She even walks through my dreams at night."

Cyril snorted, wiping his face and hands on a square of damp cloth. "I don't know how you can tell any difference between her and a hundred other Jewesses. With the scarves hiding their hair and oftentimes even their faces, all you might see is their eyes."

"Ah, but their eyes speak with such eloquence. And this one wears no veil. When she walks, those shapeless wrappings cannot hide her feminine curves. She's small, beautiful, and graceful, with a purely female giggle that makes me feel like laughing too." Once again, Julius ignored the food held in front of his mouth.

"Come back from the picture of bedding the woman and eat your food before the stew congeals." Cyril tapped Julius' spoon with his own.

Julius started, focused in on the spoon, and put the bite in his mouth. He managed to maintain his concentration long enough to scoop up the last morsel. They'd finished eating when a knock sounded on the heavy wooden door.

"Ho, Julius the Courageous and Cyril the Overworked." Decanus Marcus Varitor stuck his head through the doorway. "Come, I've found a marvelous place to eat and drink, complete with Egyptian dancing girls and energizing music."

Cyril remained seated on the bench, but he grinned and raised his hand in greeting. "Come in, Marcus, even though you had no invitation."

"Humble slaves shouldn't question their betters' actions. But when have you ever been humble?" Marcus looked down his stubby nose at Cyril.

"No, Marcus the Merrymaker, I won't go with you. I have more important things to do than to follow a drunken decanus through the streets of Jericho." Julius grinned, throwing his hand towel at Marcus, catching him full in the face.

Marcus threw it back.

Julius ducked, laughing. "Your aim is off, as usual."

"Think, men, what better thing could you have to do than visit this tavern with me?"

"Cyril, bring me the Aramaic scroll I brought home yesterday."

When Cyril handed Julius the scroll, Julius waved it at Marcus. "See this? I have an appointment with my greedy friend, Zacchaeus, this evening. He charges me five assaria per lesson for the privilege of teaching me Aramaic, the robber."

"Ah-hah." Marcus' hazel eyes twinkled. "We're being studious again, are we? Now, why would anyone in his right mind want to study Aramaic? Striving to impress whom? You know nothing you do impresses your father, and he probably will never come see you anyway. It's a waste of time, time which could be spent in a more diligent occupation like eating, drinking, and beholding the daringly clad and deliciously dancing slave girls of Egypt, now presenting their many attributes in the tavern by the river, for instance." He jiggled his hips in suggestive demonstration.

Julius laughed. "Who groaned only this morning that he wished never to see another skin of wine? Aramaic neither gives me a headache nor causes me to lose a meal."

Cyril picked up a rag. "And I must attend to my humble duties of cleaning up after this sloppy centurion. Julius would never forgive me if I went with you to the flesh pots while he's being so studious."

"I can see the two of you are determined to forego the pleasures of the flesh this day, my friends, since you won't risk even a small stomachache. It's a shame. Those women are worth a thousand headaches and lost lunches. They have muscles in the most amazing places." Marcus rolled his eyes. "Good-bye, then, poor slaves to duty." With a despairing shake of his copper-topped head, he opened the door to leave.

"I'll take good care of the bread you'll have no desire to eat tomorrow morning, O Marcus the Miserable. I wouldn't want to see it wasted again." Julius waved at his vanishing friend.

He turned back to Cyril. "I go to be robbed by Zacchaeus."

"Robbed indeed. If learning new languages makes you so happy, I hope your friend Zacchaeus also teaches you Egyptian, Phoenician, Greek, and Latin. Are you sure Zacchaeus is not a she, young and willing?"

"No, Cyril, not Zacchaeus; he's neither young nor old, and I've seen prettier and more cheerful wild boars. I don't need lessons in Latin or Greek, as you know. Every moment I spent learning the local language was rewarded this day when Miriam spoke to me. And I know now a jealous husband does not stand in the way, because she introduced herself as Miriam the daughter of Micah, not Miriam the wife of some fortunate fool."

Cyril crossed his arms, tipped his head to the side, and raised his eyebrows. "You'd be better off seeking satisfaction from one of Marcus' dancing girls than the Jewess. They'd sooner cut off their noses than associate with a Roman."

"I know. I know. Or at least my head knows. The rest of me hasn't reached the same conclusion. Maybe I should cultivate a smarter heart, but I think I'd rather exchange heads."

"Any man who would choose learning a language over pleasures of the flesh must be mad or smitten by one of Cupid's arrows." His face lost its humor. "Julius, don't be too smitten. If you entice her to your bed, these people could be in an uproar, and you'll find yourself beside Brutus in a prison, awaiting trial for rape and riot. Their religion forbids them to marry anyone other than another Jew, not that you thought beyond conquest."

"No, I'm not thinking marriage. I have to admit, though, enticing her to my bed is a thought worth contemplating...."

"It won't, or shouldn't, happen, Julius. Think about it. Your father wants you to marry that senator's daughter. I think your mother did, too. If you got a child on this Jewess, he might stand to inherit all you have instead of a legitimate son. You will only meet with a heart that aches worse than Marcus' head if you pursue her. You fight a losing battle."

"You're probably right. But, Cyril, something occurs to me. I asked their God for a favor today, to give me a way to meet Miriam, and what I asked for came to pass. Maybe it's a sign." He picked up his parchment scroll, waved, and left.

Chapter 3

Miriam entered her home, and she set the water jar by a ceramic basin. She threw back the cowl from her hair. "Hello, Abba."

Her father moved from the doorway of his carpenter shop into their living area. "And what causes you to have such a bright face, daughter? Have you sampled the Purim wine a little early?" His deep voice sounded as though he had scolded her, but she knew better. His severe manner did little to hide his affection.

Miriam's gaze dropped to the floor. "Hannah and I talked about her coming little one." True, they had, but guilt pushed into her conscience at the half truth.

"If you were to marry, you could have one of your own and I would have a grandchild to comfort me in my old age." He pulled her into a hug, and his callused hands smoothed her hair. "I don't suppose James would satisfy you? How much longer must I tell him you're still too young? He'll eat with us at for the Feast of Purim tomorrow, and you know he'll ask again. He's a good man, Mirie."

"I know he's a good man. I do like James. He's been good to us—to me. I don't understand why I feel so ill when I think of marrying him. Maybe our Adonai will help me. I have been praying about it."

Her father nodded. "I'll pray, too, Mirie. Keep in mind respect and liking are more important in a marriage. Love grows when those two elements are present." He turned back into the carpenter shop.

Miriam looked for her mother, expecting to find her in the kitchen. She poured water into a clay pan and began preparations for their evening meal.

When Abba stepped in from the adjoining carpenter shop about an hour later, Miriam asked, "Where's Ima? Shouldn't she be back from the market by now?"

"Yes, she should. I'll wash the sawdust off my hands and go to look for her. She said she felt tired this morning. Maybe she stopped at Leah's house to rest."

Miriam's worry must have shown on her face, because he smiled and patted her cheek. "It's only because she's had so much to do. With three families joining us for the Feast of Purim, she's working harder than usual."

Abba washed in the earthenware basin and stepped out the door. Leah, Ima's young sister, often accompanied her to the marketplace, and Miriam suspected that was where he would find her mother.

"Shalom, Amos. Have you seen my wife?" Abba said from near the doorway of their home.

"Peace be to you and to your house, Micah," Amos said. Miriam heard his panting. "Leah sent me to get you. Deborah is resting at our house. She and Leah went to the marketplace, and she fainted on the way home. Deborah fainted, that is. A Roman soldier saw her fall and carried her to our house. Will that mean Deborah is now unclean because a Roman touched her? What if she cannot participate in the Feast of Purim? Should we move the celebration to our house? Oh, no, that soldier entered our house. Now it's also unclean. What can we do?"

Miriam left her preparations for the meal and rushed outside.

"Deborah fainted?" Her father's face had paled. "What happened?" Abba gripped Amos' shoulders tight.

Amos winced.

Without answering Amos' questions or waiting for an answer to his own, Abba raced up the street to Amos and Leah's home and pushed the door open

Miriam clapped a hand to her head. —She'd forgotten her scarf. She dashed back into the house and snatched the scarf from the table, tying it around her hair as she ran to follow Abba. What had happened to Ima?

Miriam charged into the house, running headlong into Leah. Wine splashed from a cup in Leah's right hand onto Leah, Miriam, and her mother.

Abba grabbed a second cup Leah held in her left hand, spilling only a few drops on his own tunic.

Leah and Miriam landed in front of the door.

Amos strode into the house and tripped over Leah and Miriam. He missed them only by twisting to the side, but the twist landed him in the middle of the low table. The table tilted, sending a full water jug and basin flying, dousing everyone. Dripping wine and water filled the silence.

Ima snickered. Miriam and Leah glanced at each other and giggled.

Abba broke into gales of laughter.

Amos flushed red.

When the merriment faded away, Ima wiped the tears from her eyes and stood.

"I don't believe I'll need that wine after all, Leah. I feel so much better. Is it not written that a merry heart does as much good as medicine? I think I'll take my wet family home and feed them."

Amos reached down and helped Leah and Miriam to their feet.

Leah hugged her sister. "I hope you won't faint ever again, Deborah, but if you do, next time wait until you get here instead of falling at a Roman's feet."

Ima winked. "I promise," she said.

Miriam grinned at Leah. "At least we'll not need to wash before we eat, will we?" Outside the door, she wrung water from her tunic.

Abba turned to Amos, clapping a hand to his shoulder. "By the way, I don't believe our Adonai would be upset because Deborah was carried into your house by a Roman soldier. He might have been angry if the man passed her by and left her lying there, which is what most of those soldier would have done. I think He wouldn't consider Deborah or your house unclean because of this incident. I'll ask God for His blessing on this soldier for his kindness. Do you know his name?"

Chapter 4

Julius wished Zacchaeus lived closer to the city. The publican's home was at least a mile toward the river from Jericho, and the day hadn't cooled any. Sweat soaked his tunic and ran down his face. The inside of Zacchaeus' brick house or even his courtyard should be cooler than out in this sun. Zacchaeus' mother always offered Julius a cool drink too.

Zacchaeus met Julius in front of the house, but he seemed uninclined to invite Julius into the shady courtyard or into his home. "I saw you by the marketplace this morning, Centurion. You did the woman who fainted no favor." He stood, arms folded and a sneer pasted on his face. "You should have left her alone to either recover or be carried by one of the pious Jews. Now her husband, if he is a proper Jew, will be so outraged he will not allow her to participate in the Feast of Purim. If you think you will receive thanks from her or any of her kind, you are mistaken."

"Other than the woman with her, I saw no one else nearby, Zacchaeus. You saw us. Where were you? You might have helped her and saved her from my supposed contamination. I would not have left a dog to lie there in the hot sun. I didn't do it to earn the gratitude of the Jews, but I am sorry if I caused her to miss the Feast of Whatever." Julius ran his fingers though wet curls. "Is it always this hot here in the spring?"

"I was in my tax booth, but I don't know that I would have helped her. Her husband and her sister's husband have been no friends of mine. And no, we don't often have weather this hot now. This kind of heat would begin at the end of Lyar and last through the end of Tishrei."

"Lyar? Tishrei?"

"Lyar would usually correspond to your Aprilis or Maius; Tishrei to your September or October. Would you prefer to continue discussing religion and weather, or are you still interested in learning our esteemed language?"

"The language, of course, although later I would like to hear more about your religion too. It fascinates me."

"It is not *my* religion," Zacchaeus straightened to his full height, bringing himself to just below Julius' shoulder. "Just because I am of Jewish blood does not mean I believe all the nonsense about the religion. If there *is* a God, which I doubt, why would He favor the Jews, the most stiffnecked, self-righteous, and seditious people in the world, and why would He allow good people to suffer? Before my wife died, I believed. She was as pious and as good a Jew as you have seen or heard of, and she died a painful death not long after giving birth to my son, who also died."

"I'm sorry…."

"My mother, another religious and wise woman, is so bent she cannot look up to see the sky, and her hands give her daily pain. Kind and merciful God? Bah. If there is a God, He is instead cruel and without any perceptible compassion at all. I would rather worship one of your stupid, unthinking stones with their chiseled hands and sightless eyes." He stopped abruptly and drew a deep breath, his face an angry red. "If you wish me to continue these lessons, do not refer to the Jewish beliefs as *my* religion. But I warn you, you will have trouble finding another Jew so lenient as to give lessons to a Roman."

Julius' eyes narrowed at the tirade from the tax collector. For a moment, he fought the urge to draw his sword. He clenched his fists and held them at his side. He stepped backward and bowed.

"If you ever collect your scattered wits, come see me. I may come back for further lessons. I can see no reason why I should stand here while you rant like a man possessed. I would rather cease taking lessons than listen to a foul-tempered publican. Good day, Zacchaeus."

Julius marched back to his apartment, nearly running into Marcus, now out of uniform and looking much cooler in just his tunic and leather girdle. Julius started and looked up.

Marcus clapped his hand on Julius' shoulder. "Look who's all heated up on an already blistering day. Are you through with your lessons already? If so, you still have time to take me up on my previous generous offer."

"No, still not interested. I think I need to go the bathhouse. Zacchaeus was in a rotten humor. I think his stink rubbed off on me."

Marcus shrugged and grinned. "Your loss." He saluted and strode down the street alone.

Cyril stood as Julius entered their quarters. "Finished already? I expected you much later."

"No, Cyril, not even started. I am finished with that unholy tax collector, though. I'm going to the bathhouse." He grinned. "If I fail to return in two hours, you will know I drowned. Or I'm cooling in the fridgidarium or under the hands of a skillful masseuse."

"If you drown, I'll have your body packed in ice and sent to Rome to be entombed in a cool cave." Cyril made a bow of mock subservience. "Then I might be able to join Marcus in his enjoyment of the entrancing ladies from enchanting Egypt."

"You seem anxious to be rid of me. I could come back and haunt you."

"Very well, but please do your haunting behind me. With those sweet dancers in front of me, I would never notice a mere ghost."

"Give me my towel, slave, and keep a civil tongue in your mouth before I have you scourged."

Cyril chuckled, and, with another low bow, handed his master a large towel.

The next morning, Julius bounded out of bed before Cyril could wake him, alive with the prospect of perhaps seeing and maybe even talking to Miriam again.

"Never have I beheld anyone so eager for soldiering." Cyril helped Julius with his armor. "Surely, you will merit the tribune's high approval. Or could it be a young maiden's eyes you seek to catch?"

Julius grinned. "The tribune's approval will not be tossed aside if he should proffer it, but he's not nearly as tantalizing as a certain maiden. If I must make a choice, give me the maiden. Now quit harassing me, and get us something to eat. And hurry or I swear I will begin eating my short sword."

With Cyril out of the room, Julius listened for a moment to be sure he was alone, and then he faced the window where the sun was beginning to peek over the hills. Softly, he spoke. "How do I talk to You, O God of Miriam? I cannot see You to know where to face or where to bow. How can I tell if You hear me? If You are real, please, somehow show me. And if it is not too much to also ask, could You tell me how I can be worthy of Miriam? I do not know why I am so smitten by a maiden I barely know, but I cannot stop thinking of her. Her image is burned onto my heart. If You are real, please help me. I have never before felt so inadequate."

An odd sensation, a sort of…of what…? Prickling, excitement, and yet, such peace. What an odd sensation. What was this? He stood still, holding his breath, not wanting this strange and pleasant new stirring in his chest to disappear. Then an ache rose in his throat, and he began to remember wrongs he had done in his past, things no one had told him were wrong, and yet he knew how wrong they were. An overwhelming sorrow engulfed him, as though he were unclean and heavy.

With a start, Julius broke free. He shook himself. He was a soldier, not a whimpering baby. He straightened his shoulders, dashing tears from his face. What sort of fool cried over his past?

"I must be going mad, happy one moment and behaving like a struck child the next. Well, no more of that."

Cyril reentered a moment later as Julius began buckling on his sword. "Oh good, you decided not to eat the sword. I brought you some real food."

Julius picked up a bunch of grapes, popped some into his mouth. Determined to shake off his somber mood, he grinned. "You will make someone a good wife one day. Here's a reward for your efforts." He plucked off one small grape and tossed it to Cyril, who made a show of admiring the grape, ate it, then smacked his lips.

"Ah, kind master, you are too good to me. Such feasting and flattery will go to my head."

The sound of running footsteps sounded from the long hallway leading to their apartment. As the footsteps grew closer, Cyril grabbed Julius' cloak and fastened it at his master's shoulder. Julius speared a piece of bread with his knife and put it in his mouth and then switched the knife to a ready position. Marcus burst into the room, and Julius put the knife back in its sheath.

"Well, Marcus." Julius swallowed the bread with a drink of watered wine. "What earth-shaking news would give such impetus to your lazy legs? Didn't get enough excitement last night?"

Marcus grimaced. "I didn't get as far as the edge of the compound before Sextus stopped me to tell me I am assigned to the tribune to run his errands for the next couple of months. And when the tribune sends a message, he expects it to be delivered yesterday. This is the message: You're to report to him now. Maybe even to arrive an hour ago."

"Poor Marcus. Your merrymaking is over for a while. I hope you live through it. Help me hitch Warrior and Duros to my racing chariot. They're the fastest team here, and I suspect your horse is winded after your jaunt down the road." Julius grabbed his helmet and followed Marcus out the door to the stable. Warrior, Julius' eighteen-hand chestnut stallion, pranced and tossed his head as they led him to the chariot. Duros, a seventeen-hand white gelding they used to calm the more spirited stallion, walked sedately beside his energetic friend. Once hitched, the horses raced up the steep, winding road toward Jerusalem as though running free until Julius pulled them to a reluctant trot.

Chapter 5

Miriam laid awake most of the night praying, thinking, and telling herself how well-matched she would be with James. Every time she reminded herself how blessed any woman would be with a man like James to take care of and love her, the vision of a handsome Roman filled her mind. The more she tried to banish that exciting profile, the more persistently it stayed.

She fell asleep in the early morning hours only to experience one nightmare after the other. First a faceless Roman soldier struck her and carried her to a building. Then he struck her again and carried her to another building. Julius grabbed her away from the soldier, but they ran so slow, hand-in-hand. A giant James rose up out of a well and pursued them, armed with a dead fish in one hand and a scroll of the Torah in the other. Her father and mother, Leah and Amos, and her friends Hannah, Mary, and Tamar stood at the side of the road, sometimes scowling, sometimes smiling, always silent.

In the midst of the dream her father called. It seemed at first to fit into the dream, but she opened her eyes and realized he must be on the stairway just below her room. Groaning, she rolled over and rose to her feet, but she couldn't help but smile at the sunrise from the small window. She rubbed one eye and yawned as she descended from her small enclosed bedroom in a corner of the roof.

"Good morning, Abba." She yawned again and pulled at the night's tangles in her hair with a wooden comb he had carved for her.

"Your mother feels unwell," Abba said. A worried scowl darkened his features. "I want her to rest today. Can you handle the feast preparations on your own, or should I go ask Leah to help?"

"I think I can. If not, I will go beg Leah for help. What is wrong with Ima?"

"She fainted. This time she fell as she rose from the bed. I'm going after Loukas."

Miriam stared after her father as he left. Her mother had fainted again? Miriam sent a prayer up before parting the curtain that separated her parents' bedroom from the main portion of the house. For the first time, Miriam noticed how thin her mother looked, how pale her face, and how dark-rimmed her eyes. She fought back the tightening in her stomach and smiled what she hoped was a typical morning smile.

"Do you need anything, Ima?"

"No, Daughter. Come sit with me a moment." Ima patted the bed beside her. Miriam stepped to her mother's bed and sat, wondering how long she could fight back the lump in her throat.

"Miriam, what troubles you?" Ima reached for Miriam's hand.

"I worry because you've never fainted before, and now you have fainted twice in just two days." A tear slipped past her guard and rolled down her cheek. She turned her head and brushed it away, hoping her mother wouldn't notice.

"Yes, I know you're concerned for me. You have a tender heart. Even a dog scratched in a fight merits your sympathy. That's not what I mean. For a few weeks now, your eyes have been saying things that don't reach your lips. You look like a ray of sunshine one moment and a thundercloud the next. Would you tell me why?"

"Ima, I don't want to burden you with my little troubles when you're not feeling well."

"I will rest better if I know what's wrong. Maybe I can help."

Miriam hesitated. She had to talk to someone, and who better than her mother? No, not about that brutal soldier, but about Julius. Perhaps that would be enough. "I am at war with myself and with God. I know what I should do, but even the thought of it hurts."

"What is it? I have more than forty years of living behind me. Perhaps something in my past can help you with your battle."

"I yearn after a man who is not a Jew. I know what a good man James is, what a perfect husband he would make, but I can't make my heart agree. Instead, a Roman centurion captured my eyes and my soul, and I cannot force myself back to sanity. I prayed and prayed with no change at all. I don't know what to do." Miriam laid her head on Ima's lap.

Her mother stroked her hair. "I was sure it must have been something like that, little one. I know I shouldn't call you that any more. You're a young woman now, but you will always be my little one. What hurts you hurts me. You don't cease to be my little girl, even though you are old enough to marry and have babies of your own."

Miriam blew her nose on a rag and wished her eyes would stop running over.

"Now, I have a story to tell you, one I've never told anyone except my own mother. When I was fifteen, I fell in love, or so I thought, with an Egyptian merchant's son. His father brought merchandise from Egypt to sell in the marketplace, and he would mind his father's stall as his father went after more goods. He seemed to be an honest man and very handsome. Our stall in the Bethsaida marketplace was next to theirs, and I saw him every day. It took a few months before he spoke to me, though I often caught him watching me. Each time it happened, my heart would pound, and I could scarcely breathe."

"That sounds like what's been happening to me, Ima."

Ima nodded. "One day when my father was gone, I had to tend our stall alone. That day, Beljazar spoke to me. We discussed the fine weather, the goods we sold. Casual conversation but full of meaning for me. Father was gone for a week, and every day, Beljazar would talk to me. When Father returned, Beljazar stayed away, and my heart felt as though it would break.

"I confided in my mother, and she understood my feelings, but she told me something I have always remembered. She asked first if I knew whether he believed in the One God, and I told her no. That was unimportant to me. After all, many Jewish men and women married those who do not believe as we do. She said yes, they did, but God had commanded us not to, and for good reason. She asked me to look at the marriages of those who had. They had begun full of love, or at least full of lust, but after the original excitement wore off, the marriages became empty shells which held them together but no longer blessed them. Instead of pulling together, now they pulled apart. Or the one who believed in God left Him to follow the other's gods."

"Ima, I know of some marriages between Jews that aren't any better—like Mary and her husband."

"That's true. Sometimes it happens because one or both of them stray from God."

"What happened then?"

"When Beljazar's father returned, they approached my father together to ask for my hand in marriage. Father declined, and my heart felt as if it had wrenched out of my body. I cried every night and decided I hated my Father."

"I could never hate Abba."

"I didn't hate mine either. I was angry with him and thought that was hate. A year later, my father made a marriage contract with Micah's parents. I liked Micah, but I still felt the loss of Beljazar. The day before we were to be betrothed, Mother came to me. She asked me if I had any objections to Micah. The only objection I could think of was that Micah was not Beljazar. I cried for Beljazar for the last time that night. Then I set my mind to forget him and concentrate on Micah's character. A year after we betrothed, I was surprised to find I loved Micah. He was and is my best friend. I have never been sorry I married him. Our love grows stronger with each passing year, and I am fulfilled."

Ima picked up the brush and ran it through Miriam's hair. "This is what I want for you, Miriam. James is not exciting, nor does he smell like fresh-baked bread, but he is good and he loves God. Concentrate on the good things, Miriam." Tenderly, she kissed the top of Miriam's head and then leaned back on her pillows and closed her eyes.

"And so I shall, Ima." Miriam stood and shook the wrinkles from her tunic. She knew what she must do.

"Perhaps you could fix a small breakfast for us now, hmm?" Ima's eyes were closed, and Miriam thought she saw a little moisture in the corners. Miriam bent to kiss her mother's cheek and walked into the kitchen.

Abba entered as she cut some melon and cheese. Loukas, the Greek physician who had become a Jewish proselyte, followed. He guided Loukas to the bedchamber where Deborah lay.

Miriam finished preparing breakfast and made a tray ready for her mother as Loukas and Abba exited the bedroom, but her mother waved her away. Miriam placed a second tray on the table where Loukas, Micah, and she could eat their fill of melon, cheese, and bread.

"She should rest for a time, Micah. You're fortunate to have this beautiful and capable daughter who can take her duties," Loukas said.

Miriam ducked her head in awkward acknowledgment of the praise, her cheeks warm and her lashes lowered.

"How long a time?" Abba asked.

"Long enough to put the bloom back in her cheeks and to fatten her a bit." He paused. "Does she have fevers or other ill feelings?"

"An occasional fever, yes. And she is increasingly tired."

"Any strange bumps under her skin?"

"Yes, Under her right arm there is one she mentioned."

Loukas' brow furrowed. "Hmm. I will come back to see her after the Feast of Purim. Meanwhile, try giving her more meat. It might help."

Loukas stood to leave, and Miriam exchanged a worried glance with her abba. Miriam bit her lip and took her mother's tray back to the bedchamber.

Ima's eyes were closed. Miriam hesitated but then whispered. "Are you asleep?" Her mother opened her eyes. "Here is your breakfast."

"No, I am not asleep, Daughter, just resting. I'll get up soon and help prepare the Feast of Purim. Just leave the tray here beside the bed, and I will eat in a few moments."

"I will leave your breakfast here, but I can prepare the Purim meal without help. I helped you fix it often enough. Don't worry. I will do a good job of it, too. You will see." Miriam set down the tray.

She drew a shaky breath as she stepped back into the outer room, and she steeled herself. "Abba, you may tell the father of James your daughter has come of age." She picked up the water jug and walked out the door.

Chapter 6

Miriam hurried toward the well, alone this time because she had waited for Loukas to leave. She kept a fearful eye out for danger, but Julius stood there, his eyes calling to her and a smile of welcome lighting his handsome features. She concentrated on the ground beneath her feet, the pool of water, anything but those eyes.

"Hail, Miriam bat Micah. It is good to see you."

She tipped her face upward for an instant, but she ducked it again.

"Miriam, you've been weeping. Is something wrong?" He stepped forward and reached for her arms.

"No. Please let me go."

"What is it? Tell me."

"My mother is ill. I cannot stay and talk. I have to go." Her voice wavered, and she turned to draw the water. Her hands shook, and she knocked the jar from the brick wall around the pool, shattering it on the rocky ground. She knelt by the broken pottery shards and burst into tears.

He grasped her arms and lifted her to her feet. He stood so close she could feel the heat radiating from his body, and she backed away.

"The fault is mine. I startled you. I'll get you another at the marketplace. Wait here." Without waiting for her answer, he left.

She covered her face with her hands. As his hobnailed sandals pounded the ground behind her, she looked around, hoping none of the gossips in the village had seen the encounter. "Thank You, Adonai. No one was here to witness this scene. This makes twice I dropped the water jar in front of him. And I almost let him hold me. I know he wanted to. Worse, I wanted him to. What was I thinking? Forgive me, please. And God, please protect me from the other soldiers." She peered from one shadow to the next, ready to run if she saw danger.

She sat on the wall, wiping away the tears. *How like this poor jar my life is, broken in irreparable shards too.*

It seemed but a moment until Julius came running back with an ornate jar, glazed handles formed like grape vines, scalloped shell shapes decorating the lip. She jumped up, put her hands to her face in dismay. "Oh, sir, you should not have done this. It wasn't your fault. I dropped the jar. You should not have bought a new jar at all, and this one is so much more expensive. I cannot accept this."

"If you do not want it, I will break this one, too, and the shards will lie together here next to the spring." He scowled, shaking his head. "Of course you will accept it, Miriam. Do not argue with me."

"If I accept it, you must come to our house and let my father pay for it. When I tell him what happened, he will insist."

"Your father will not pay for this. It was my fault. You looked distressed, and I should not have insisted you tell me why when it was not my concern. I am truly sorry your mother is so ill. Do you have a physician for her?"

"Yes. Loukas says she only needs to rest and eat more meat. I'm sure she'll be well soon. I'm sorry. You must have thought from my actions she is near death. Another matter also worried me and both things together overwhelmed me."

"It will help if you talk about it. Come, we'll go for a walk outside the wall. I know a beautiful place in a grove of cypress where I go to sort things out. Come." His words were a command. She opened her mouth to protest, but he tucked the jar under one arm and took her arm with his other hand. She tried to pull away, but his grip and stride didn't slacken. He led her through the gate and up a grassy hillside. Panic threatened to undo her as she remembered the attack by the soldier. *But this is Julius, not that soldier,* she reminded herself.

Was that laughter she heard behind them? *The guards...they must be thinking...oh, no, not that. Please blind the eyes of people who might see us leaving together so they do not think that I...that we...O Adonai, what is he doing?*

When they came to a large outcrop of rocks surrounded by a host of wildflowers and a ring of trees, he sat her down and looked into her eyes.

"Now," he said, "Tell me what causes these lovely eyes to swim?"

Her face burned. She lowered her lashes. "There is nothing I can tell you. It cannot concern you. I should not be here alone with you. Please allow me to leave." She tried to stand, but his hands on her shoulders held her.

"Nothing you can tell me?" He spoke with a low voice as he tipped her chin up with a determined finger.

She turned her head. "I cannot talk about it. If I do, I'll begin crying again, and I've done enough for one day. Please, if we must talk, let it be of pleasant things."

"All right," he said. "If it will help you to talk of things more pleasant then let us do that." He lifted a strand of hair that strayed from her scarf. "Maybe we could talk about your beautiful hair that rivals the most glorious sunset. Or your eyes of golden honey, trimmed in lashes so long and thick and dark it looks as though you wear kohl. We could speak of how you occupy my thoughts all through each day." He pulled her to her feet, bent his face close to hers, lips barely an inch away from her own, his breath hot against her skin. His finger traced a tingling line down her cheek to her chin. "Or the roses in your cheeks, or those rich, full lips...."

"No, no." She grabbed the water jar. "No, that does not help. Oh, why did I come with you? I should have hurried home instead. I need to go…I…oh, good-bye. Good-bye, Julius." She ran down the hill, again hearing mocking laughter as she rushed past the guards at the gate.

By the time Miriam filled the jar with water and balanced it on top of her head, she had gathered herself enough that she could hope her agitation didn't show. Inside, she felt more torn than ever.

Now she knew he felt the same.

Before it had been a little easier, thinking maybe he watched all the maidens, not just her. Now she would have to find a way to put him out of her mind, out of her heart. Forever, as her mother had done with Beljazar. From now on, she would think only of James.

She walked through the door to her house. As though her thoughts had brought him, James stood with his younger brother, John, both roaring with their booming laughter at something her mother must have said. Ima reclined on pillows beside the low table, looking up at James. Her face looked thin, but her eyes twinkled.

Her mother had a talent for making their house a happy one filled with laughter. Ima could tease a professional mourner into laughter.

Her father smiled. "Ah, Miriam. We thought you might have fallen into the pool. What's this? A new jar?"

"Yes, I…I broke the other one. A…a Roman officer startled me as I drew the water. The jar fell on the rocks and shattered. He said he felt responsible, so he went to the marketplace and bought another one, and he would not come back with me for you to pay him for it. He…he seemed very kind, Abba. Did I do wrong to accept it from him?" Tears threatened her eyes again.

"No, Mirie. Do not weep. The jar was old and chipped and of no great value. He must be a soldier who is well off. This jar is not inexpensive. It was kind of him, and I will say a prayer of thanks for him. Hmm," he said. "I seem to be blessing Roman soldiers a lot lately."

Abba took her arm and turned her toward James. "Miriam, James asked if we would give our approval to allow him to marry you, and we have. We'll announce the betrothal when his parents arrive next month."

Miriam turned to James and bowed her head. Her voice shook. "I am honored."

James beamed. "I hoped this time you would accept my troth. My father couldn't come with us on this journey, but he'll be here soon with betrothal gifts and the bride price."

Abba rocked back on his heels, happy wrinkles around his eyes. "James and John have come to eat the Feast of Purim with us, Miriam, and is it not time to begin roasting that nice fat lamb for the Feast?"

"Yes, Abba, I'll begin now," Miriam said, grateful for an excuse to flee from the room.

Chapter 7

After leaving the grove, Julius hiked some distance deep in thought about his botched encounter with Miriam. He took no notice of the rough road, dodging without thinking about or smelling the dung left behind by donkeys, oxen, and horses. How could he have so misread what she was feeling? He felt sure she was as attracted to him as he was to her. Her eyes met his so often he thought she wanted his attentions. Other women liked compliments. Why did she not?

Julius looked up, startled to realize he had walked all the way to the Jordan River. A crowd gathered on the bank listening to a man standing on a sandbar. The man shouted, but over the noise of the crowd and the water, Julius couldn't understand what he said. He walked closer, curious about what drawing power this strange-looking man could have on such a crowd.

The man's beard and hair were uncombed, his coarse tunic tucked up into a loin cloth that looked as though it had been woven of camel hair. His voice sounded rough, as though he had been shouting for hours. As he drew closer to the river, he picked up words that sounded like "snakes" and "God's wrath." Julius walked up beside a soldier.

"Who is that man?"

"Most call him John the Baptizer, sir, but some insist he is the Jewish Messiah prophesied in their writings. You said to expect rioting, sir, but no one seems inclined to disorder."

Julius nodded. The tribune passed the warning to Julius during their visit, and Julius had stationed soldiers at the river.

Someone in the audience yelled, "What must we do to be saved?"

"Repent!" John waded into the muddy river. "Turn away from your sins and be baptized, and God will forgive you."

By the dozens, people waded out to him. Julius' thoughts drifted to his experience that morning when he talked to Miriam's God, and he felt drawn to be baptized, whatever that meant, with the rest of the crowd. Instead, he turned and walked back to the city, still agonizing over his encounter with Miriam.

He thought she would be an easy conquest, that she wanted him as much as he did her. No. Instead she ran from him like a frightened doe. Maybe she was more than he knew. Different from the type of woman he'd experienced before. Perhaps this was one he should treat with more esteem. She stirred his blood, though. He could not sleep through the night without dreaming of her and waking up in a sweat. He wanted her more than he could bear, yet it seemed impossible to have her. Curse these Jewish prejudices, anyway. He scowled. *Admit it, man.If you had not been so forward, she would not have run away.*

When Julius arrived back in his quarters, Cyril joked and teased in his usual manner, but Julius' mood would not to be lifted. He was not prone to remain glum for more than a few minutes. Now Cyril tried to cheer him, and all he could do was growl.

Finally, Cyril knelt before him. "Master, why are you angry? Have I done something wrong? If so, whip me and be done with it. If someone else has offended you, tell me and I will cut his tongue out. Only tell me. I don't understand what worries you."

Julius shook his head. "I wish it were so simple, Cyril. I offended myself. My spirit is sorely troubled because of my own foolishness. There is nothing you can do."

Cyril's face brightened, and he rose to his feet. "Ah, it is the Jewish beauty again. I tried to tell you they think themselves too good for any but other Jews. It is rare for one of the men to carry on a conversation with a foreigner and even more rare for a woman. Did she reject you? I wager you attempted something more than a little conversation, hmm?"

Julius' ears warmed. "I have to have her even if I have to kidnap her. There is nothing in my past to compare this to. She fills my senses, and I can think of nothing else. There must be a way to get her into my life, Cyril, and if there is, I must find it. Go find me a physician named Loukas. If he will not come to me, I will go to him. He knows her family. I will start with him."

"I am on my way." Cyril opened the door to leave, and Marcus entered.

"Was it something I said?" Marcus asked as Cyril hurried down the hall without greeting him, "Hail, Senior Centurion Julius of Caesarea." He saluted with a flourish.

"Not yet, Marcus. Not for three or four months, or maybe more if the senior centurion now in Caesarea lingers there as long as Rufus thinks he might. And you should not be talking about this news yet. You heard what the tribune said."

"I have told no one, and nobody could have heard me now but Cyril, who hurried away at such a speed he probably didn't hear it either. And if he did, we both know he would never say anything to anyone. Ah, but it must be nice to be rich and have influential parents."

"My father's influence alone is not what earned me this promotion. You could be a centurion, too, Marcus, with a little effort. Your father was one once, and Tribune Rufus would take notice if you ceased to spend every lepton you received on wine and women. For a fact, I would not be surprised to see him fall over dead if he heard that news."

"No, it's not for me. Centurions have too much responsibility and not enough fun. And I would not want to be the cause of the honorable Rufus' demise. Being in the lesser office of decanus is bad enough. My eight soldiers expect me to be of a stern character and thus stifle my activities when they are around."

"Say, Decanus Marcus," Julius asked with a curious look in his eyes, "do you think you might accompany me tomorrow? I saw a strange man out by the Jordan River today, and I would like to see what his intentions are. He may be an inciter to riot. He had the people who heard him excited. Do you think Tribune Rufus would allow you the time? I think it would only take part of the morning."

"You asked for the right time, my friend. Rufus said I should come in after the midday meal. I spend the remainder of the day, the first watch, and part of the second watch in his service. So we may go and be entertained by this rabble-rouser. If I cannot see the dancing girls, maybe I can be entertained by knocking some heads together, eh?"

"Good. I will meet you at your quarters right after breakfast."

Marcus stood, stretched, and yawned. "I am not sure I want to admit this, but I want to sleep for a while before I go back to Jerusalem. If you tell the other men, I will deny it."

"No one would believe me anyway."

Marcus opened the door to leave as Cyril strode back into the room, a little out of breath.

"We meet again." Marcus caught Cyril's shoulders and laughed.

Cyril chuckled and pushed Marcus toward the door. Marcus saluted and sauntered down the hall to this room.

Cyril turned to Julius. "I found the man you wanted. He says he cannot come here, but he bids you welcome at his house if you can come now. Otherwise, he says he must wait until tomorrow. It seems sundown today begins some sort of celebration, and he is working on preparations."

"Very well. Let's go." Cyril followed Julius through the door and out of the compound, waiting to walk beside him until they were out of sight of the guards.

"Now, tell me, where is this physician, and how did you find him so soon?" Julius asked.

"He lives down the road toward the river but a short distance. It was easy to find him. I just asked your contingent's physician." He paused. "It is puzzling, though. This physician Loukas, he looks like a Greek and speaks Greek, yet he acts like a Jew. I do not understand."

When they arrived at the physician's house, they found him waiting at the entrance. A few strands of gray decorated his short straight black hair and beard. He looked to be in his forties, short and solid. His round face was dominated by large brown eyes and a strong straight nose.

The physician held both hands out, palms up, in welcome, and gave them a warm smile. "Shalom. Come in and be comfortable. What may I do for you, my friend? Your man here said it was urgent. Are you ill? You certainly look healthy, if I may say so."

"No, good physician, my body is well, although my heart is wounded."

Loukas eyes crinkled. "Hmm, this could be a disease for which I have no cure. In truth, I suspect this disease is incurable, because the patient instead might rather become ever more ill."

Julius chuckled. "As long as it is not fatal, perhaps I may still hope I might not be cured. The reason I have come to you is maybe you know the answer to my problem, which answer might heal the wound but not the illness. I find myself much attracted to a young Jewish maiden you may know. Her name is Miriam bat Micah. She told me today you are treating her mother, which is why I came to you. I prayed to the Jewish God to help me find a way to be made acceptable to her and her family, and I think He…I know this sounds preposterous to think their God would actually speak to a Gentile, but I think He directed me to you. Does this sound plausible?

Cyril's eyes widened and his brows lifted.

Loukas nodded. "Why did you choose to ask our God for help?"

Julius thought for a moment. "I am not sure why. I suppose because I thought He would have more influence here than any of the Roman gods. It appears he does, too, because I think He answered one of my petitions."

"I do not know the answer to your question, Centurion. If you have a heart that yearns for our God, you may do as I have done. Become a Jewish proselyte."

"What is a proselyte?" Julius asked. "To win her, I would do anything and everything within my power."

"A proselyte is one who is a Gentile but who chooses to abandon any other gods he may have worshipped and instead follow the God of Israel. It would mean taking instruction in our laws and following them. There is a hurdle you must leap, though, and you must truly search your heart for the answer. You must want to follow Him even if you do not win Miriam. The Jewish God does not want a man to change his religion for the love of a woman, but rather because of the man's love for Him. There are gate proselytes, those who abide by some of the non-religious laws but do not worship God, but I think her father would not be satisfied with that for his daughter."

Julius opened his mouth to speak, but Loukas held up his hand.

"No, don't answer now. Come back and talk to me again when you have made your decision. I must warn you, though, even if you become a proselyte, Micah has been a hard one to please. Thus far, he claims no one is good enough for his daughter. All who asked have fallen far short of his expectations of the right man for her.

"Now, enough of that. We will be eating our Feast of Purim this evening. Both of you are welcome to join us, especially since you are interested in our religion. This would be a fine introduction. Come back this evening an hour before sundown."

"Thank you, sir, we would be honored."

"Joanna," he called to his wife, who entered the room. Her winged eyebrows arched in question.

"Gentlemen, this is Joanna, my wife, and the person who makes sure all meals served not only taste delicious but also are a feast for the eyes. My love, this is Julius and his man—I am sorry, but I do not know your man's name."

"This is Cyril, my slave."

"Joanna, please set a place for two more men for dinner." He turned to Julius. "Oh, may Cyril eat with us, too? On feast days, our slaves and servants join us once they have the meal on the table. Most are proselytes, too, and one is more like a member of our family than a servant. In fact, her six years are nearly finished, and we plan to set her free, adopt her, and provide her with a dowry. Then we will set about finding her a good Jewish husband."

"Of course, and thank you for the offer. Cyril has been my friend since our childhood days, and he eats with me when no others are around." He paused. "What do you mean by 'her six years'?"

"This is one of the Jewish laws. Jewish slaves serve for only six years and then they are freed in the seventh year. Some elect to stay on with their masters either as paid servants or as permanent slaves. This one, Quinta, has also become as beloved as our own child."

"Your offer for dinner is welcome, and we will be here. We have not had any such offers before from any of the Jews. This will be a new experience."

"No, I don't suppose they offered you hospitality in their home. The Jews have strong laws regarding extending hospitality to traveling strangers, offering a meal and a place to sleep, but they seldom invite Gentiles into their homes because it renders their house unclean."

Julius' eyes narrowed. "Unclean? I'd wager I bathe more often than the average Jew."

"It is a different type of unclean. Religious rather than dirt."

"Ah, I understand. Have we made your home unclean by being here? If so, I apologize."

"I adopted the Jewish religion as my own, but it is a little different for me since I am also a Gentile."

Julius inclined his head. "Thank you, Loukas. We will return this evening."

Chapter 8

When Julius and Cyrus returned, Loukas provided them with water to wash their hands and a manservant to wash their feet. Then he led them to the dining area. They reclined at the long low table while the slaves set the food on the table. Cyril's gaze followed a pretty young woman out of the room.

Julius grinned. He bent forward and murmured into Cyril's ear. "He said a good *Jewish* husband."

Cyril jumped and reddened. Loukas and Julius chuckled.

Loukas leaned toward them and spoke from behind his hand. "I told you Quinta was comely."

Quinta reentered the room with the last of the meal and sat down at the table. Cyril's gaze had dropped to his plate, and his face went from white to red and back to white as Quinta sat down across from him. Julius never thought he would ever see his dry-humored friend at a loss for words or in such confusion, and it was with great effort he restrained himself from laughing. He dared not look again at Cyril for fear he would lose control, so he thought about the ornamental rugs beneath their feet, the decorous tapestries on the wall, and the mouth-watering smell of the lamb, fresh-baked bread, and vegetables— anything to take his mind off Cyril's bemused face. Quinta was worthy of admiration, fair complexion and hair, so rare in this country. *And mm-mm, what a figure.* She wore her hair tied back, and it hung like sunny silk to her waist. She had a small up-tilted nose in a round and innocent face, and her long blonde eyelashes sometimes hid and sometimes framed wide eyes as blue as the summer sky.

Cyril had long been an admirer of beauties, some who even rivaled this one, but Julius had never seen him act so smitten before. Maybe now Cyril would be more understanding of Julius' 'ailment.'

Julius turned to his host. "Loukas, why is this meal so special? I know it's a religious festival, but I am ignorant of its significance. Would you be willing to tell us?"

"Let's give thanks for our meal so you can get started eating. Otherwise, our food will be cold before we eat."

He lifted his hands and head, closed his eyes, and began to pray. The others bowed their heads, eyes also shut. Cyril looked at Julius, who lifted his shoulders. Julius grinned and bowed his head.

After the short prayer, Loukas passed the food to his guests and continued, "Now then, the explanation. This is called the Feast of Purim. Long ago, there lived a queen named Esther in a distant land. A wicked man called Haman had tricked the king into signing a decree ordering the deaths of all the Jewish people in the land. The king didn't know his queen was a Jew. Esther asked her Uncle Mordecai to have all the Jewish people there fast and pray for three days. At the end of those days, she entered the king's chamber without permission. To do so was a crime punishable by death unless the king held out his scepter to that person. The king did extend his scepter to her, and she invited him and Haman for dinner in her quarters. Haman, who didn't know she was a Jewess, was flattered."

"I would wager a week's pay this Haman was in for some trouble," Julius said. He couldn't tell if Cyril listened or not. His friend's gaze was still fastened on the blushing young woman across from him. Quinta must have noticed his stares, judging by her suffused face.

"He was. When the king and Haman came to dine with her, the king was pleased and said she could request anything of him, even to half his kingdom. Esther asked that the king would spare her life and the lives of her people. The king asked who would dare to threaten her life, and she told him it was Haman. The king was so enraged he had to walk outside to calm himself. Haman was panic-stricken, and he hurried to Esther, pleading with her to spare his life. He tripped and fell on her just as the king reentered the room. The king ordered him taken out and hung on the gallows the man had prepared in hopes of hanging her uncle."

"It sounds like Haman got what he earned."

"This was a simplified version of a longer and more complex story, but you can see how God saved his people."

Cyril, who had at last shifted his gaze from Quinta to Loukas, opened his mouth as though to speak, then closed it, remaining silent.

Loukas glanced at Cyril. "It's permitted for you to speak, Cyril, unless Julius objects. Have you a question?"

Cyril glanced at Julius

Julius nodded.

"I don't understand why you say it was the Jewish God's intervention," Cyril said. "Surely any good man would have done just as the king did when he allowed his wife into his presence and then punished the man who would have killed her."

"Esther was not his only wife, but she was his favorite in his harem. It hadn't been so long since he banished his previous favorite for taking advantage of his preference for her. The king saved Esther's people by adding to his previous decree that the Jewish people could take arms against the people who would kill them, which is as close as he could come to wiping out the law which said the Jews would be annihilated and could not lift a sword to defend themselves. Yes, I do believe it was truly God's intervention. But I cannot help you to believe it. That decision must be your own."

Cyril leaned back on his pillows and crossed his arms. His eyes widened for a moment. Then they narrowed He shook his head slightly and returned his gaze to Quinta.

"Why did you become a proselyte, Loukas?" Julius asked.

Loukas smiled. "I found the many gods and goddesses of Greece had no voice or power. The Roman gods were no better. I had a problem none of them could solve. When I first heard about the God of the Jews, I thought He would be just another nothing, especially since I could not even see Him. I chose to go to Him for help. Later, it was Micah, Miriam's father, who convinced me to give myself wholly to God. I decided to learn more about this God of the Jews, and the more I learned the better I liked Him. So now I am a proselyte."

"And was your problem resolved?"

"Yes. In a wondrous way. Perhaps one day I will tell you more about it."

Miriam lay in her bed weeping again. Large tears rolled down her cheeks while she bit her lips to remain quiet. "O Adonai, Ima said she cried only one last time for Beljazar and went on to learn to love my father. Adonai, surely I can do the same. Please let these be the last tears. Let them wash me clean of love for a Gentile. Never have I been so miserable. I was far happier before I saw this Roman soldier. Please, Adonai, wash him from my heart before I die from the pain of it."

Julius spent a sleepless night, and when he rose in the morning he still had come to no decision. He thought he wanted to be a proselyte but did not know if he wanted to be one in order to win Miriam or because he wanted to know this God. Julius wanted to be honest with himself as well as God. How could he determine what his own heart wanted? How could he desert the gods of his youth?

He might not have been alone in his speculations. Cyril also seemed distracted. Neither of them spoke as Cyril helped him with his tunic. Julius forgot to eat breakfast and gave an absent wave of his hand as he went out the door.

As Julius walked toward Marcus' quarters, he pulled himself back to the present with an effort. Cyril knew and now understood his reveries, but Marcus, for all his flippant talk, was as sharp as his dagger. Julius didn't want Marcus to be aware of his present mood, so he shook himself mentally and grinned at his own preoccupation. Cyril must have thought he'd left his tongue in bed this morning. But Cyril didn't exactly seem like himself, either, come to think of it. Perhaps a certain maiden with flaxen locks distracted him as well.

Chuckling, Julius walked into Marcus' quarters just as the man buckled on his sword.

"Ho, Julius. It seems you're in a better mood this morning. Good. You have been much too serious lately. Old age is soon enough for somber thoughts. Youth only passes by once, so live it while it is here. Laugh, make merry, spread good cheer." Marcus tossed his helmet into the air and spun around once before catching it.

"It will be a long time before you are old, Marcus, if seriousness is a mark of old age. You have never had a serious thought in your entire life. At least none anyone can discern. I hear you laughed as you were born and will no doubt leave this world with yet another guffaw. Come, let's go see this mad prophet."

"Prophet? Is that what they call him? From what I have heard, these "prophets" often stir up people to rebellion. Let's hope that's not the intent of this one. I find myself in a marvelous humor and do not want it spoiled by a madman."

They marched out the door and headed for the east gate.

Julius had never before been drawn by the speech of anyone as he had been by this man, John the Baptizer, who wore a camelhair tunic and now sat on a rock beside the Jordan River. He and Marcus sat on their horses for a time, but soon dismounted and looped the reins over tree limbs.

The Baptizer rose from the rock and walked barefooted out into the river. He raised his hands, and as waves erase footprints from the sand, so his gesture erased the voices from the crowd. Even the breeze seemed to still as he began to speak. His strong voice carried all over the hillside where the people stood listening.

"There is a Man coming," he cried. "Prepare the way for him. Turn from your sins and let good fruit grow from your lives."

"Who are you?" shouted someone in the crowd. "Are you that Man? Are you the coming Messiah?"

"No, I am not."

Another of the crowd spoke up. "Then who are you? Tell us so we may answer those who sent us."

"I am the voice of one crying in the wilderness, telling you to make the way of the Lord straight, as Isaiah prophesied. Fill up every valley, bring the hills down low, straighten every crooked road, smooth the rough ways. Soon all shall see the salvation of the Lord."

Some Pharisees had come, apparently to try to counteract John's teachings. John pointed at them and roared his condemnation. "You generation of vipers. Who do you think you are, that you will escape God's wrath? You, too, must repent, turn from your evil ways, and do good. Do not think just because you are descendants of Abraham that you are privileged. I tell you, God could raise up more devoted rocks to be Abraham's children than you are. Even now, God has his ax at the root of the trees, and everyone who bears no edible fruit will be hewn down and cast into the fire."

A man Julius recognized as a Pharisee derided John. "If you are neither Elijah nor the Messiah, why are you baptizing?"

"I baptize with water for repentance, but there stands One you do not yet know. He is mightier than I am; I am not even worthy to unlatch His sandals. He will baptize you with the Holy Ghost and with fire. His fan is in His hand, and He will thoroughly purge His floor and gather

His wheat into His barns, but he will burn up the chaff in a fire that never goes out."

People began wading out to him, wanting to know what they should do. John said, "Share what you have with those who have needs. If you have two coats, give one to someone who has none. Share your food with those who are hungry."

As they had the first time Julius listened to him, this baptizer's words strummed a tune in Julius' heart. Apparently, the same was occurring to Marcus, who stood beside Julius. He seemed to have difficulty remaining still.

Marcus' gaze locked with his.

"Come on, my friend," Marcus said, his voice taut with emotion. "We might as well go together."

Julius followed Marcus into the water. "What should we do?" Julius asked John.

John seemed unsurprised to see two Roman soldiers asking to be baptized. "Do no violence to anyone; do not bring false charges against any; be content with your own pay." Then he dunked them as he had the others.

As they walked back to the shore, Julius noticed a lone Man standing at the edge of the water. The Baptizer must have noticed Him, too. John held out his hands toward the Man, and in a booming voice proclaimed, "Behold, the Lamb of God Who takes away the sin of the world." Julius watched as the Man walked into the river. After a short conversation too soft for him to hear, John baptized the stranger.

A soft rumbling like distant thunder rippled across the heavens, and a reverberating Voice proclaimed, **"You are My beloved Son; in You I am well pleased."** A smile spread across the Man's face, much like any son would under the praise of his father.

The Man turned and came up out of the water toward Julius and Marcus. Pausing in front of them, He looked intently first into Marcus' eyes and then into Julius' as though searching for something. Then He nodded, smiled, and walked on by. Julius wondered why he felt as though the Man knew him. Not only knew him, but knew him inside and out.

Nearly two weeks passed, and Julius felt no closer to a decision. Every time he started to go see Loukas and tell him he decided to become a proselyte, he would wonder again if his reasons were honest. In the entire two weeks, he had not seen Miriam. He wanted to talk to her about proselytes, about the man in the river who baptized, and about the quiet Man with the knowing eyes. In fact, he'd like to talk to her about a lot more than that. But more than anything, he wanted to talk about proselytes.

Each day, he waited by the well, hoping she would come, but she never came, at least not while he was there. The young women she came with before acted strange. When they saw him, they looked smug, and they nudged each other and giggled. Especially the one who was with child. She looked as though she possessed some secret knowledge that pleased her.

One evening, he walked out of the city and up to his special grove of trees on the hillside, trying to think more clearly. Would he still want to be a proselyte if he could never see Miriam again? In his heart, he still wasn't sure. The time had come to visit his favorite thinking place.

When he reached the grove, he couldn't believe his eyes. There, on the same rock, sat Miriam. His heart jumped into his throat. For a few moments, he said nothing, just stood and watched her there with the sunset decorating the sky above her head. Her back was to him, but he knew it was her.

He walked toward her, trying not to crunch leaves or rocks. Her head was bent, her hands folded in her lap. Now he stood close enough to touch her, but as much as he wanted to reach out for her, he kept his hands at his side. If he startled her she might run away again. In a quandary, he wondered what to do.

With a soft voice, he said, "Miriam?"

She turned, her red and wet eyes flying open wide.

Chapter 9

The past two weeks had been trying ones for Miriam. She began the first week by asking Leah to get the water each day for her, explaining the extra work she had to do because of her mother's illness kept her from that duty. That way, she could avoid seeing Julius at the spring. She deliberately considered James and his numerous good qualities each time Julius came to mind. Still, the deep ache in her heart persisted. Her steps dragged, her eyes felt puffy and dry, and laughter had been impossible. When Abba asked what troubled her, she said she slept poorly because she worried about her mother. Ima showed no improvement, but she maintained her sense of humor. Still, she seemed more tired than before.

When Loukas came to see Ima again, his usual teasing nature with her mother seemed forced. He took Abba aside to talk to him, and when they returned her father's face looked pale and strained. Miriam wanted to ask him what Loukas said but didn't want to hear the answer.

Abba disappeared into his workshop, and the furious sawing and hammering coming from the shop let Miriam know he should not be disturbed.

Over the next few days, Miriam stayed busy. Ima had not been able to get up for more than a few moments. She tired easily.

Abba seldom spoke to anyone but Ima, and he was so tender with her that Miriam knew something was wrong. Once she asked him if he was all right, and Abba growled that *he* wasn't the one who was sick. Then he left the room.

Leah visited often, bringing the latest news from the marketplace and some fresh bread or fruit. "I saw Mary at the market today. She said Kish went to the Hippodrome to watch the chariot races yesterday. There was a collision, and two horses and one of the charioteers were killed," She down at the edge of Ima's bed. Miriam took a respite from her chores to visit with her mother and her aunt.

"Mary's husband spends his small earnings on those races? No wonder they have so little." Ima raised herself to a sitting position and reclined against the pillows at the head of the bed, scowling at both the pain in so doing and at Kish's extravagance. "And how are Mary's new bruises?"

"Fading. I'm glad to hear she's feeling well again. The cut on her face last week distressed me. It nearly reached her eye. She said she fell." Leah's mouth thinned into a grim line.

"She seems to fall a lot." Ima shook her head. "As if the poor woman could hide her husband's cruelty."

"Yes. Either she is very clumsy, or her husband is less than gentle with her." A frown marred Leah's usually cheerful face. "I doubt she is worthy of such treatment. Mary is so soft-spoken, and she works hard to please him."

"Yes, but she hasn't produced a son for him. We know how Kish feels about that. He blames her, but why does he not just divorce her? Beating her will not produce a child." Ima shifted her position, grimacing.

"Amos tells me he drinks more wine with his meals than most, and his anger increases with each drop he drinks."

"And even without his meals, I think. When they came here for the Feast of Purim, he staggered long before we drank the first cup. And that wasn't the first time. Remember when he worked for Micah? Micah had to send him away because he was so often deep in the wine."

"Poor Mary." Miriam said.

"She never says anything about his treatment of her. One time she says a jar fell on her foot. Another time she tells of tripping, and then she says she slipped when she ran after a chicken." Leah rubbed her chin. "We all know, yet we all pretend we believe her. I know many husbands are stricter with their wives than necessary, but he…well, several of us think he goes too far. Someone should tell Kish to stop. Do you think maybe Micah would?"

"Micah has much on his mind lately. Maybe after I feel well again." Ima's gaze fell upon Miriam. "Poor Micah, he's such a worrier. He spoils me so much I may never work again. In truth, though, I would rather he growled at me once in a while. At least then I would know he is still my husband and not my mother."

Leah laughed. "Deborah, I fear you will even die telling jokes. Why are you never serious?"

"Even our Lord has a sense of humor, Leah. Maybe He would like someone to laugh with, and that's why I was born. Even more than I love to laugh, I love making others laugh. Happy laughter is the most beautiful sound I know, and it is so healing. This pain goes away whenever I laugh."

"I didn't know you were in pain." Miriam jumped to her feet, and her hands flew to her cheeks.

A quick frown passed across Deborah's forehead. "I hadn't told anyone, Daughter, and I didn't mean to tell you now. But my tongue ran ahead of my sense. Please promise me you will not tell anyone else. Your father worries enough without knowing I am more than just uncomfortable. Besides, the hurt will be gone in another day or two." She pushed away the frown with a grin. "Job endured so much more than I do, and look how God rewarded him for his patience. Wouldn't it be wonderful if we became as rich as Job?"

Miriam wrung her hands. Ima had not complained once of her discomfort.

Leah smiled tightly. She touched Miriam's hand, clasping it, and bringing warmth to Miriam's worried heart. "As rich as Job? Well, if anyone deserves it, you would. Now, since we are not rich and have no servants, I need to go and prepare Amos' evening meal." She released Miriam's hand and squeezed Ima's. Then she stood "I pray you will not be in pain long, Deborah."

"Dear Leah, you never could sit still long enough for a proper visit."

"You should rest, Ima," Miriam said. "We are worried about you."

"Indeed, we are," Leah's lips trembled.

"No, no, no. Don't be disturbed. Now go, before your husband grows anxious. You know, you and Amos are well-matched, little sister."

"I know, too serious and too fearful. But we have our share of happiness together, too. We don't spend all our time worrying."

Leah kissed Ima's cheek before leaving.

Miriam fluffed the pillows behind her mother as Leah walked out the door.

Leah had only been gone moments when Hannah entered, stumbling through the open door. Her face was pale and filled with pain and fear. "Miriam, your mother…is she here? My time has come."

Miriam hurried to her, helping her to her feet. "Yes, Hannah, she's here, but she's too ill to help you. I…."

"No…." Hannah made the one-syllable word into five. "What shall I do? I can walk no farther."

"Bring her in here, Miriam," Ima called from the bedchamber.

Miriam guided her friend into the little room. "Ima, you can't be a midwife now. Loukas said you were not to tire yourself, and…."

"I am not going to be the midwife, daughter, you are." She moved forward and slid her feet off the bed. "Here, Hannah, lie down here. I will sit right beside you and you can hold my hands. There now, don't be frightened. Women have been delivering babies for thousands of years. Don't fight the pain. You will find it easier if you push when you feel the pain. Yes, like that. Pull your knees up and push downward."

Miriam looked at her mother. Had she gone mad? Miriam had never witnessed a birth let alone taken part in the process. She took a deep breath and willed her hands to stop their trembling. With her mother's help, she could do this. She must do this. Ima was too weak. She wouldn't be able to hold up. Yet Ima oozed confidence, and Miriam knew she must not act as frightened as she felt.

"Miriam, go ask your father to find Hannah's husband. Do you know where Isaiah is, Hannah?"

"He went to work with his father," Hannah said, between pains now. "They should be on their way back from fishing by now."

Miriam ran from the room and into her father's shop. "Abba! Hannah is having her baby, and she needs Isaiah. Would you go and find him? He and his father should be on their way back from the river."

Abba grasped Miriam's shoulders tight, making her wince. "Your mother…she's not midwifing?"

"No, I am, but she's telling me what to do. Don't worry. I won't let her do too much."

"Good. See to it she does not tire herself. I'll find Isaiah and Zechariah." He hurried out the door, and Miriam ran back to her mother and Hannah. Ima murmured quiet words to Hannah, who looked much calmer. A look of concentration mingled with anticipation had replaced the tight, wide-eyed look that had marred Hannah's face before.

"Miriam, tell us when you can see the baby's head."

"I see something dark. That might be it."

"Push, Hannah, push."

Miriam wiped sweat from her face with her forearm. Ima handed her a cloth, and they both smiled at Hannah and the little miracle in the woman's arms. Miriam had followed her mother's instructions, and a new life had exited the womb.

Male voices sounded, and Miriam lifted the curtain away from the door to her mother's bedchamber and invited Isaiah with a sweep of her hand.

He peered around the corner before stepping inside.

"Come in," Miriam said. "Meet your new child."

Those words brought him inside without a moment's more hesitation. He stood, his eyes wide, and he watched the babe who suckled at her mother's breast.

Miriam moved to stand near her mother.

Wonder filled Hannah's face as she examined tiny toes and fingers. She looked up at Isaiah, who stood unmoving, staring down at his family. His eyes softened as he watched the babe at his wife's breast.

Tenderly, Isaiah sat beside them and stroked the fine black down on the infant's head. "We shall call him Eliab after my grandfather," he whispered.

"I think not." Hannah grinned.

He leaned back. "Oh?"

"Perhaps Martha, after your grandmother, would suit *her* better."

Isaiah laughed. "A girl. Hmm. Maybe Martha would be better. She's beautiful, just like her mother." He leaned over and kissed Hannah. Then he kissed the sleeping child.

"I'll carry you home," he said.

"Nonsense. I can walk. What would the neighbors think? I will let you carry Martha, though."

"They would think you had a husband who cares about his wife. Now, woman, I will take no further argument." He stood. "Miriam, would you carry our little one?" He picked up the baby and handed her to Miriam and then reached for Hannah.

"He's right, Hannah," Ima said. "This time you swallow your pride and allow Isaiah to carry you. Miriam can carry Martha. It would be best that you do not walk much until tomorrow, Hannah. You stay in bed and enjoy your little one this day."

Hannah acted as though she were at ease as the little caravan set out, but the blush on her cheeks set her face aglow. The wide smile on her lips revealed the pride she felt in her husband and new baby.

As Miriam glanced down at the baby in her arms, her heart churned. *So soft, so sweet smelling. Will I have one in a year or two? If I do, it probably will not be sweet smelling. It will probably smell like fish.* Her heart sank at the thought of bearing James' child, and she grimaced.

Chapter 10

Miriam had started to clear away the food from their evening meal when voices sounded from outside.

Abba opened the door. "Ah, James and John, come join us. There is still some stew left, prepared by Miriam herself. Come, James, sample your future wife's cooking."

Miriam winced at her father's words. She wished they would go elsewhere to eat, but they hadn't been to her home often. They spent most of their time with the other man, the prophet who was also named John. When James had tried to talk Miriam into coming with them to listen to John the Baptizer she demurred, saying there was too much to do. She would all too soon be spending more time than she wanted in James' presence.

"We came to tell you John and I will go home tomorrow." James shifted from one foot to the other. "We'll be back before the Passover with my parents, and our betrothal can be official before the wedding. Although I have yet to ask my family about our betrothal, I'm sure they'll approve. You could come with us," he added, a note of yearning in his voice. "I have been hoping for some time for this marriage, and I...uh...I have an addition already built to my father's house. You could see it if you came with us. Two other women are traveling with us, Peter's wife and one more."

Miriam almost smiled as James, the brash, outspoken fisherman, actually stammered and blushed from his thick black eyebrows to his bushy brown beard. He increased the shifting from one foot to the other until John elbowed him and laughed.

Her father didn't look the least surprised at James' discomfiture. "It must take place shortly, while Deborah, I mean, because Deborah would like for the wedding to take place shortly after Passover. Is that too soon?" He looked at Deborah, who nodded confirmation.

Miriam stared at her father, her eyes wide and eyebrows jerking upward. *After Passover? Yes, that's too soon!* But, then, he didn't ask her.

James grinned, his eyes sparkling with his excitement. "No. Tomorrow would not be too soon, except that my parents will need time to come from Galilee. And we will need their approval, too. I'm sure they will agree, but you know my mother. She would be anywhere either of us was to be honored, even if she had to be carried there."

Miriam felt a glimmer of hope. Maybe Salome would not approve of the betrothal, or at least not of a wedding so soon.

"I have a message for you to deliver to your parents regarding this betrothal and marriage, James. Wait here a moment." Abba disappeared into his shop and reentered carrying a piece of papyrus, rolled and sealed.

James took it and almost opened it, but Abba stopped him. "Wait. That is for your parents to open."

James flushed again. "Oh. Of course. Forgive me."

Abba nodded. "Forgiven."

John tugged on James' arm. "James, come. We need to be going now. John ben Zachariah is waiting at the river." He turned his gaze to Miriam's father. "We're going to spend this evening listening to him. After that, we're going back to Capernaum to work with Father until we come back here for the Passover. Micah, if you and your family are coming with us, we will come back and get you first thing in the morning."

"No, Deborah does not feel well. Perhaps Miriam could go if Leah goes with her."

"No, Abba, I need to stay here and help Mother. We need to begin preparations for a possible w-wedding." Miriam tripped over the word, feeling again the now-familiar sense of dread.

James nodded, grinning. Miriam saw the intention in his eyes of stepping closer to her, and she moved to her mother's side, avoiding any possibility of touching. "Good evening to you. Thank you for stopping to tell us."

"Yes. We'll look forward to your return next month," Abba said.

James and John made their good-byes and left, James still grinning.

Married in a month? What was Abba thinking to ask for a wedding so soon? Does he not realize the rumors that will generate about me? And how can we make all the preparations in so short a time? She glared at the floor.

Abba stared at the floor too. He also said nothing. After a few uncomfortable moments of opening and shutting his mouth as though he wanted to explain but could not find the words, he shook his head and turned to his workshop, shutting the door behind him

The next afternoon, Miriam stood in the doorway to her parents' bedroom. Her mother lay asleep in the bed, her breakfast again untouched. Miriam's worry must have shown in her face, because Abba came and put his arm around her in a quick hug.

"I am going to the synagogue. I'll be back soon," he said, bolting out the open doorway. A short time later when he returned, his footsteps heavy and slow, his eyes red and swollen. Concerned, Miriam rushed to him.

"Mirie, come into the shop with me. I need to tell you something." He guided her to his stool and motioned for her to sit.

"Mirie...," he started, a tear trailing down one cheek.

"Micah, are you here?" A man's voice called from outside.

Abba looked uncertainly toward the door.

"Go ahead, Abba. It sounds like Loukas."

Micah opened the front door of the shop, and Loukas entered.

"I'm glad you're here, Loukas. Perhaps you would explain to Miriam what's happening with her mother better than I can. Please excuse me. I cannot endure hearing it again. I will return within the hour." Abba pulled Miriam to his chest, kissed the top of her head, and left.

Miriam turned a frightened gaze on Loukas. "Loukas, does this mean my mother is worse than we first thought?"

Loukas nodded. "I wish that it were not so, but there is nothing more I can do but to try to ease her pain. I have a powder here you can mix with wine to give her," he said, reaching into the pouch he carried.

"Pain? She said yesterday that she has some fleeting pain, but she made light of it. I don't want her to be in pain. She cannot die. I need her. Father needs her. You must be wrong. You said she would be better in a few days. She just needs to rest and eat more. You said...."

"No, she will not improve. I wish I could tell you otherwise. I have seen this disease before, and the end is always the same. Some die sooner than others, but all die. Given the advancing tiredness your mother exhibits, I would say it will be sooner, perhaps only a month or two. I wish it were not so, but I can see no hope for her."

"No...no. You have to be wrong," Miriam cried. "Not my mother. God would not be so cruel. You could talk to other physicians. There must be one who knows a cure. There must be...."

Loukas took her shoulders in his broad hands. "Miriam, stop it. You have to be strong. She cannot see you falling apart. She needs your strength and the strength of your father."

Miriam collapsed onto a stool, shaking. When she was calmer, she looked up into his eyes, "Does she know?"

"No. Or at least I have not told her. It would surprise me, though, if she has not guessed it by now. She is a wise and courageous woman, and I think she pretends to be strong for you. But even the most courageous need the strength of their loved ones when the pain becomes unbearable, which it will before long. There will come a time when you will be praying for her release from the suffering."

Miriam continued to shake her head in disbelief, tears running down her face in cascades.

"I wish I could give you words of comfort, but I would be lying to you. There is no way I know to soften these words that wound you."

Miriam covered her face. She found herself thinking of Julius and wishing she could go to him for comfort, but that would be wrong. *Alone. I need to be alone.*

"I...I have to go find a quiet place to pray. Please, would you tell my father I will be all right? I need to be alone for a time. The evening meal is ready. A fish stew is in the pot on the fireplace. I cannot eat. You could share the meal with my father and mother."

"I need to talk to Deborah. I'll wait for your father. Go, find a quiet place. Pray, Miriam, for strength not just for yourself but also for your father and mother."

Miriam threw him a grateful look and fled. She crossed the city with quick steps, her scarf pulled forward to hide her tearstained face. All she could think of was getting away to somewhere quiet.

She remembered the little grove of trees where she and Julius had talked.

When she arrived at the grove, she looked around to make sure no one was there. Especially Julius. She didn't know how frequently he came here. Probably not often. His duties as a Roman officer must keep him from going for many walks outside the city. She moved to the rock in the center of the grove and sat down, lowering her head and allowing the tears to course unheeded down her cheeks.

She didn't know how long she'd been there when she heard his voice whispering her name. She knew her eyes must be swollen, but she hoped in the dusk he might not be able to tell. She didn't trust her voice, so she said nothing.

"Am I dreaming?" Julius smiled at her and started to sit down beside her then stood again in front of her. "Forgive me for disturbing you. You've been weeping. May I help?"

"No. No one can help. My mother is dying." She bowed her head, tears flowing.

As naturally as if he were a brother or father—or husband—he took her into his arms and held her as sobs shook her body.

"I think I know how you feel," he said. "My mother died only a year ago. Perhaps in this way I can help."

Somehow, his arms around her felt strong, secure, and right. This strength brought calm to her.

Still holding her close with one arm, he tipped her face up and looked into her eyes for a moment. Her heart began beating like a frightened lamb as she raised her eyes to meet his. He lowered his mouth to hers. Miriam felt like melted wax, and she gave herself wholly to her first kiss.

With a ragged breath, he drew back.

"Miriam, beautiful Miriam, you have no idea how long I have dreamed of tasting your lips. They are even sweeter than I dreamed, more intoxicating than the finest wine. I would love to drown in them, in you."

"I dreamed this, too," she whispered, and caressed his face. She touched his lips with one finger. He kissed her again, not quite so gently. This time as he pulled away from it, he groaned low and long.

He pushed her away from him, but not far. "I missed you. I waited every day by the pool but never saw you there. I want to talk to you about something important. I am thinking about becoming a proselyte. I started making inquiries and learning more about your God."

Miriam's eyes widened. "Oh, no." She spun away from him.

"What did I say? Did I offend you?" Julius pulled her back around.

"No, it's not you. It's me."

Julius' brow furrowed. "I don't understand."

"I don't understand myself, so how could you hope to? You see, I am almost betrothed. I...I said I would marry him because...because I cannot m-marry an unbeliever. Now you tell me you are becoming a proselyte, and I did not have to agree to marry him, but now it's too late." Her eyes filled again, and she dashed the tears away with an angry hand.

"You...you care...about me?" Julius apparently didn't hear the rest of her words. "Do you love me?" He grasped her shoulders. "Do you love me?"

"Y-yes, but...."

He crushed her to him, and she thought he would devour her. He kissed her mouth, her eyes, her throat, and her mouth again. With reluctance, she pushed him away.

"It's too late. I am to be married to James." She lowered her head. "I'm not supposed to see you."

He laughed, picked her up in his arms like a child, and swung her around. "She loves me. She loves me. My prayers have been answered."

She started to speak but his lips descended on hers again. The world around her ceased to exist.

She took a deep breath and pushed his face back. "You don't understand. Julius, I am *betrothed*. Or nearly so. I am promised, and the betrothal ceremony will be held as soon as James returns with his parents."

"What problem is that?" He laughed. "It's me that you love. You are not married nor betrothed. Marry me instead. Your parents would understand. Do they not love each other?"

"No they would not understand. It is too late for me. My father promised me to a fisherman called James. Abba won't break a promise. Even though the betrothal ceremony hasn't happened, my father's word has been given."

Julius went still, his jubilance gone. "There's no way to change this, this pseudo-contract?" he asked, his voice hoarse. With obvious reluctance, he set her on her feet.

"Only with great difficulty and embarrassment to my parents and bride and groom alike. The reason for breaking it is assumed to be because the bride committed a-adultery with someone other than her promised one. Or is otherwise sullied." The lump in her throat threatened to choke her, and she felt the heat rise in her face. She backed away from him.

"I cannot believe this is happening. I prayed to your God, and all of my prayers were answered. Except that now you say you love me, but I can't have you. This is cruelty beyond belief." He grasped her and pulled her so close it was hard to breathe. "Would you come away with me, Miriam? We could go to Caesarea, where no one knows either of us."

She broke away from him, retreated a cubit. "I cannot do that to my parents, especially with my mother so ill. They haven't done anything to deserve such behavior from me. My father sought to find a husband who would be good for me, who would try to make me happy. James is a good man." A lump rose in her throat. "If I could marry you, I would follow you anywhere. But I think it must be God's will that I marry James, because I can see no way my father or James would agree to end this promise."

"I would do more than try to make you happy, Miriam. I would love you, protect you from…from anyone who would try to hurt you. You know you won't be content with a man you don't love."

From anyone who would try to hurt her? Oh, no. He did know she was the one he rescued! She twisted, wondering if she should run. But didn't he say he would protect her? Then perhaps he didn't think she had encouraged that beast of a man? Or maybe he didn't know.

He paced to and fro. His fists clenched, and he turned away, kicking a log at his feet. "I don't understand why your God would lead me to hope, and now I find the hope is just a mirage. And I thought to become a proselyte. I'm only glad to discover His true nature before I took that step."

Miriam dared to breathe again. She touched his arm, and he turned. "Julius, don't blame God. Truly, if I had listened to Him, I would not now be promised. It's not God's fault. It's mine."

"Then let's not abandon hope, my love," he said. "If it is your God's will, then perhaps He will still find a way for us. When, uh, how long, until you...until you and the fisherman...I mean, uh...."

"Passover Week," she said.

"When is that?"

"Less than a month."

"That soon?" he groaned. "Will you come here again? I can't bear never seeing you again."

"I cannot. I will come only if a miracle should happen." She laid her forehead against his chest, wishing she could stay there forever.

"Then I will wait here every night, praying for a miracle until I hear you have been...until I know there is no hope. Or until there is."

His eyes widened, and he struck his forehead with an open palm. He looked down into her eyes again. "You just helped me come to a decision. I didn't know if I wanted to be a proselyte because of you, or if it was because I really believed in your God." He brushed a stray strand of hair behind her shoulder. "How could I be angry at a God who doesn't exist? He arranged events for us one after another. I believe not only does He exist, but maybe He is working out a plan for us to be together. Now I know I need to know your Yahweh, whether you and I ever have a chance to become one or not. He is real, and He is powerful. I don't know why I couldn't see this before, but there is no other god to worship. Therefore, I will become His proselyte."

"I'm glad, Julius. He does know what is best for us. I rejoice that you will turn over control of your life to Him."

Julius stepped backward. "I only meant that I would worship Him, not that He would rule me. I don't intend to become a priest. I'm not a stupid man. I know that a man must work for the things he wants. One thing I want; therefore, if there is a way to change this betrothal, I will find it."

She knew neither her father nor James would ever agree to stop what had been set in motion. Still, she vowed she would not cry again. She didn't want to leave Julius thinking she wept all the time.

"Julius, I have to go. My parents will worry because I have been gone so long. But please, will you kiss me one last time?"

They looked into each other's eyes for a long moment, and he lowered his lips to hers, pulling her body to his. The kiss was long and sweet, and her whole heart went into the embrace. When finally they broke apart, both Julius' and Miriam's eyes brimmed with unshed moisture

"How can I let you go? It feels like my heart is being torn from my chest. Miriam, please, stay with me. If you love me, don't leave me."

"My heart stays with you, Beloved, but I must go." She traced his face with both hands, lingering on his hair, his cheeks, his lips. She memorized every line of his face. She dropped her hands, and then her head so he wouldn't see the tears that fell again. In silence and sorrow, she turned and walked down the hill.

Chapter 11

Julius made his way through the narrow streets of Jericho until he found the tall stone and mortar house of Micah. A carpenter shop, evidenced by wooden furniture and loose lumber around it, was attached to the right side of their home. Julius walked through the open door and waited for his eyes to adjust from the bright sunshine to the darker shop. He listened for any indication that someone was in the room, but he heard nothing. Stacks of cut wood, table size and smaller, poles cut in lengths usable for table and chair legs, wooden buckets and crocks containing dowels and nails, and the scent of freshly cut wood filled the room. No one seemed to be around.

Undecided, Julius scratched his head, wondering now what he should do. He knew what he couldn't do, go into the house and bear another tearing separation from Miriam. As he turned to leave, he caught a movement behind a partially finished door on the far side of the shop.

A man sat on a low stool, his broad shoulders slumped. With his elbows propped on a workbench, he pressed his head against his hands. Every line of his body suggested more sorrow than a man should bear. Julius cleared his throat, and the man looked up.

"What may I help you with, young man? Do you need some carpentry done?" He cleared his throat. His voice was rough, as though he had been shouting…or weeping.

Julius squared his shoulders. "No, sir, no carpentry. If you are Micah, I would like to speak with you."

"I am Micah. What is it you wish to talk about?"

"My name is Julius, and I don't know exactly how to say this. Please don't jump to any conclusions. Hear me out before you answer. I love your daughter, Miriam, and I believe she also loves me."

Micah's brows raised high on his forehead. Julius held up a hand to halt the questions he could see forming in Micah's eyes.

"It was nothing she planned to do, sir. You must place the blame on me. I'm the one who spoke to her first. She was not once bold or unseemly. I need to ask you if there is any way Miriam can be freed from her promise to marry this James person."

Micah stared at Julius with his eyes wide. He narrowed his gaze and stood slowly. With a fluid move, he picked up a hammer and smacked the head of it against his workbench. "Freed?" He lifted the hammer and slammed it down again. "What kind of man do you think I am, that my word would be worth nothing?" *Bam.* The hammer hit the wood again. "What kind of father do you think I am, that I would break a promise to a pious…" *Bam* "…honest…" *Bam* "…Jew…" *Bam* "…whom I know and trust"—Micah stopped his banging, pointing the tool at Julius. "…whose parents I also know and trust, and whom I know would take good care of my daughter, and give her instead to a Gentile—and a Roman at that!—whom I do not know at all? And who do you think you are that I would do such a thing for you?" Micah glanced back toward the house. His red face, his fists clenched, and the already narrowed eyes made Julius think he'd rather be shouting then speaking in a low controlled voice his appearance belied.

Julius' face warmed with embarrassment. Still, he had to persist. "Sir, I understand your anger. If I were you, I would also be angry. But if you were me, you would also want to at least try to gain the approval of your beloved's father. Forgive me. Perhaps I am too bold, but I don't know how else to approach you. I understand why you feel as you do. You know nothing about me, and you must think I'm a fool to come in here and make the request that I did. It's true I'm a Roman, but this morning I made arrangements through Loukas the physician to begin the study of your religion. I hope to become a proselyte."

Micah opened his mouth to speak, but again Julius held up his hand. "My father is a good and honest man, well thought of by his compatriots. My mother, dead now for nearly a year, was a kind and loving woman, gentle even to her slaves. She brought orphans in from the cold to feed and clothe and educate, and I often helped her find new ones. There's nothing more I can say in my behalf, and still you do not know enough to entrust your beautiful daughter to my care. I have only one more thing to ask: if the Almighty God should intervene somehow and James would consent to release her from this promise, would you then consider me?"

Micah tossed the hammer to his workbench and snorted. "Since such a thing is as unlikely to happen as darkness at midday, it would be safe to agree. James has longed for Miriam to be his bride ever since she ceased to be a little girl."

A woman who looked familiar chose that moment to enter the shop. "Micah, do you have a moment? Oh, shalom, sir. I didn't know anyone else was here."

"I am not here for long, lady. My business with your husband is finished." Julius shrugged his shoulders, his eyes downcast as he turned to go.

Micah's wife stepped toward him, holding her hand out. "Wait. Aren't you the soldier who carried me to my sister's house?"

Julius glanced up, surprise widening his eyes. "Yes, madam. It is good to see you again. I hope you are...ah...." Julius stumbled over his words. *How can I say I hope she feels improved when Miriam told me she is dying?* "I hope you feel better than you did on that day."

She smiled. "I do. Micah, this is the soldier I told you about, the young man who carried me to Leah's the day I fainted in the marketplace."

The anger dissipated from Micah's face. He extended his hands, palms up, toward Julius. "Now I need to ask your forgiveness. You are a stranger in my house, and I did not offer you even a cup of water. Instead, I insulted and reviled you. Come, I'm sure Miriam would prepare us a cool drink."

"No, I can't, but thank you. I need to return to my men to give the day's assignments. It is considerate of you to offer, and there is nothing to forgive." He hesitated. His gaze moved to the frail woman and back to Micah. "May the one God be with you and your household, sir." With these unfamiliar words on his lips for the first time, he turned to leave.

"Wait. Would you come and break bread with us one evening next week? We would be honored, young man." Micah walked up to Julius and placed his hand on his arm. "Please."

"I am the one who is honored, sir. I am on duty during the days, but perhaps in an evening."

"Evening, then. The Sabbath after Passover." Miriam's mother grasped Micah's arm and leaned against him.

Julius bowed his thanks and left. But how could he face Miriam again? Would she be angry that he accepted this invitation? Could they bear yet another parting, this time with no parting kiss? Worse...would James be there, wedded to her? He would have to find a reason he could not come before then.

Julius walked home bemused. Invited to his beloved's home to break bread with her parents. No touching, no long looks, and definitely no declarations of devotion. What would she do when she found out he would be coming to eat with them? What would she do when she saw him?

He walked into his quarters, his head hung low in thought. What could he do to avoid the scene he knew would take place?

Cyril entered from the kitchen. "That looks like serious thought. What's wrong? A caravan was attacked on the way to Jerusalem?"

"Worse. Miriam's father invited me to their house, right after telling me there was no way he would ever break his promise to marry Miriam to that fisherman."

"What? How did that happen?"

"There was a woman who fainted one day at the market. I carried her to her sister's house. The woman was Miriam's mother." Julius shook his head. "She walked into the shop just as Miriam's father, Micah, prepared to throw me out for asking him to break his promise to the fisherman. You would have thought I'd asked him to destroy the temple. But when Miriam's mother said I was the soldier who rescued her, his whole demeanor changed."

Cyril chuckled. "Only you could inspire fury and gratitude within the space of one breath. When is this meal supposed to occur?"

"The Sabbath after the Passover. I don't know if I dread this event or anticipate it with excitement. It was hard enough saying good-bye to Miriam yesterday evening. To see her again, and yet not be able to touch her.... And if we look at each other, her mother and father will be angry. Miriam said she was to be betrothed and married after Passover. I don't think I could bear seeing her with the fisherman. Somehow, I have to convince them I would make a better son-in-law or find a way to refuse the invitation before then."

"You may as well try to convince them a scorpion means no harm to its prey." Cyril stepped on one of the offending arachnids skittering across the floor. "Most Hebrews consider Romans and scorpions of the same species."

Julius sat down on the bench, his elbow propped on the table, his chin in his hands. "I wish we had never been stationed here. Winning her father over would take a miracle, and seeing her wed another man would kill me. I would rather I'd never seen her or met her than to lose her this way."

Chapter 12

Julius walked the streets of the marketplace, watchful for those Jewish dissenters who would make it difficult for the people of Jericho to conduct their business.

He spied the familiar face of Cyril as he meandered from each merchant choosing the best foods for their meals.

Julius' slave was much more than servant. He was his best friend, and he valued Cyril's devotion. Likewise, he would do anything within his power to make Cyril happy and to forget his slavery.

Julius started to greet Cyril, but his friend stopped suddenly, his attention riveted on something across the way. Julius readied for danger, his hand on the hilt of his sword, as he trailed the path to Cyril's focus.

Julius released his sword, and smiled. He moved closer but out of sight. After all the relentless teasing, Cyril's time had most likely come to get a measure of humility.

With a leg of lamb in hand, Cyril started toward a woman across the street.

"See here, you. You have to pay for that meat," an angry merchant barked.

Cyril turned back to the slight, grizzled shopkeeper and grinned. The shopkeeper hopped from one foot to the other and waved his arms, reminding Julius of a rooster set to do battle. Strange, Cyril did not haggle of the cost of the meat but tossed the coin into a basket of olives and hurried across the street to stand behind Quinta.

Even with her back turned, her blonde hair hidden beneath the brown scarf, and a shapeless outer tunic in a commonplace brown concealing her curves, Julius had no doubt it was her.

"Uh, greetings." Cyril said.

Quinta looked up, her face tinged with pink. "Hello. I remember you. You come to the house of Loukas and Joanna for Purim."

"Yes. I'm Cyril. I'm Julius' slave. I'm looking for meat for his dinner."

Julius winced that his friend so easily announced himself a slave.

"There is a market just across the street with many meats." Quinta pointed toward the hanging meats on the other side of the street.

"Yes, I know. I didn't mean I wanted to know where to find some. I just meant that's why I'm here when you're here. I'm glad to see you came here. Uh…not that I came here to see you.... I...oh, I'm sorry I troubled you."

"Wait. I am sorry, I misunderstand."

At the distress in Quinta's voice, Julius moved slightly for a better vantage point

"I am not speaking Greek well. We speak Aramaic always at Loukas' house. You are Greek, yes?"

Cyril's face had reddened. Up to this point, Julius thought he sounded like a stumbling youth. Was this how he had come across to Miriam? Maybe he wouldn't tease Cyril after all.

"Yes. I think I speak Aramaic worse than you speak Greek, so I'm glad you do speak my language,"

"I am learning the Greek, but I am so slow. I am not Jew. I am from Hispania." Quinta blushed.

"Hispania? You're even farther from home than I am. How did you come to Jericho?"

"My parents very poor, large family, no money to buy food. I am five years old then. They sell me to a nice merchant who travel to many places, come to here. Joanna see me in merchant's tent, she ask him if she can buy me. She say I am too young to lift heavy burdens. She take me home, and I do cooking and cleaning."

"Do you miss Hispania and your parents?"

"Not any more. For a time I cry much. Now I think I cry if I have to leave Joanna and Loukas. They say they set me free, but I do not want to be free from them. They are like mother and father."

"I am close to my master too."

Julius smiled. He thought much of Cyril as well.

"We've been together since we were babes. I was born to slave parents, both of whom worked for Julius' parents. We used to play together as though we were friends or brothers. Even now, it's more as though we have different jobs than different statuses. I don't have any wish to be free of him. Although I would like to be a free man, I guess, because then I would be free to marry."

Julius almost choked, but he managed to hold in the surprise. Marriage? Had his red-faced friend actually mentioned this to a woman?

Quinta's cheeks tinged a lovely rose color. "I think it would be nice to be able to choose, too, because I think Loukas plans someone for me I do not know."

Cyril's face went from red to white. "He has already found someone for you?"

"I do not know. He does not tell me. I ask, but he does not tell."

"Oh, maybe he hasn't found someone yet then." Cyril's relief showed on his face, and Quinta's eyes widened.

If Julius' previous emotions were any indication, Cyril was definitely in love with Loukas' pretty little slave.

"Oh! I should not talk with you, maybe. You should not...you do not know me so well." Quinta turned one way and then the other. Her eyes found Julius, who put a finger to his lips.

Quinta stared down at the dusty road.

"I would like to know you better. But maybe you don't want to know me?" Cyril said.

"Yes, but I do not think we are proper. I do not say this right, maybe? Your master should talk to my master, not you to me."

"But how can I get to know you? Our masters talking will not be us talking. Do you understand what I mean?"

Without lifting her head too high, Quinta once again looked toward Julius. "Maybe our masters will say it is all right for us to talk. Then we talk. And if it is not all right, then we do not talk."

"Even if my master said no, I still would want to talk to you."

Julius smiled. He was sure Cyril's statement was true. Cyril knew he had nothing to fear from him.

"You would disobey your master to see me?" Quinta's hand flew to her cheek.

"I think about you all the time, Quinta. You are so beautiful, and you are good and kind. I want to know you better. Maybe you are the one I want to spend the rest of my life with, but how can I know if I can't see you more? So, yes, I would disobey him to see you. I would disobey Tiberius Caesar to see you."

Julius grinned. He had no doubt that Cyril would do as he had said.

Quinta's face and throat flushed a deeper red. "I must go. Good-bye." She backed up and turned to walk away, but Cyril gently held her arm.

"Wait. I want so much to see you again. Will you be here tomorrow?"

"I do not know. No, not tomorrow. Tomorrow is Sabbath." With another wary glance at Julius, she lowered her voice, and Julius could not hear her reply.

"I'll see you in two days?" With Cyril's answer, Julius could put the pieces together. Hadn't he begged his love for the same snatches of time?

"Maybe, yes, but maybe, no. I pray. You pray too?"

"All right. I'll pray too."

Quinta smiled a very small smile, then turned and almost ran away.

Julius stepped across the road and slapped a hand on Cyril's shoulder. "So, you would disobey me and Tiberius Caesar for one more chance to see Quinta, hmm?

On Sunday, Julius awaited Cyril's return from the marketplace. After several hours, he assumed that either Cyril had met up with Quinta or he was waiting in vain just as Julius did in the grove for Miriam

When the door finally opened, a downcast, Cyril walked in..

"What troubles you, Cyril? Are you ill?" Julius asked, hoping he could hide his amusement.

"No. Would that I were. I think now I understand your moods of the last few weeks. I thought Quinta seemed as interested in me as I was in her. I made arrangements to meet her at the marketplace again today, but she didn't come. Maybe she's concerned because I'm not a proselyte, I think. Either that or maybe Loukas forbade her to see me again."

Julius would not tease his friend now. He nodded. "Yes, the pain of caring for someone who is not free to return your caring. I understand, my friend. Why don't you come with me this evening to see Loukas? He's the one who recommended me to Shelumiel, the Rabbi who teaches me. You might be interested in learning more about their God, too. Loukas is my sponsor. Maybe he'd be willing to be yours, too."

"But I'm not sure that's the avenue I wish to take. I don't want to become a proselyte just to see more of Quinta. I think Loukas and Quinta both would know I was dishonest. Now, that Man you told me about seeing at the river? I could maybe swear allegiance to Him. From your description of what happened, He sounds like someone worth knowing more about. But this God of the Jews? I'm just not sure." Cyril took the basket full of cheese and fruit he brought from the market into the cooking area.

Julius followed him. "Yes, I know what you mean. For whatever reason, that Man at the river got me thinking more about the God of the Jews, even though He said nothing to us. But that Voice I heard saying something about the Man being His 'Beloved Son?' It sounded like the Voice of God to me."

"I confess I'm curious. It can't hurt me to learn more about this God of theirs. I'll go with you to Loukas'." Cyril gave a wry grin. "And I might at least glimpse Quinta there."

Julius envied his friend's opportunity to see the woman who'd stolen his heart.

The sound of footsteps and a knock sent Julius back to the living area, munching on a handful of grapes.

Marcus barged through the door. "The tribune sends you a message, O Noble Julius."

"What does he want, O Lowly Marcus?" Julius plopped another grape into his mouth and chewed, enjoying the sweet burst of flavor.

"He didn't tell me, and he threatened my life if I so much as looked too long at the exterior of this missive." Marcus handed Julius a sealed thick parchment scroll, saluted, and stepped backward through the door.

"That's got to be the shortest stop you've ever made here." Julius broke the seal on the scroll but left it rolled.

"The work of a messenger is never done. I have another scroll for Centurion Sextus." Marcus waved the second scroll and disappeared down the hallway.

Julius stared at the roll, a sick feeling in his stomach.

"Aren't you going to read it?" Cyril asked, wiping his hands on a towel.

"I'm afraid I know what's in it." Julius took the towel from Cyril and wiped the sticky grape juice from his hands.

"And that would be?"

Julius grunted. "I can't talk about it. Rufus forbade it."

"Well, if you can't talk about it, then don't. But you can encourage the knots in your belly, or you can read it and end the suspense. Meanwhile, I have a culina to clean." Cyril snagged the towel and turned back to the cooking area.

What if I have to move to Caesarea now? I'll never know if You will free Miriam from her promise to that fisherman. Adonai, what now?

Julius picked up the scroll and gazed at it as the tight roll loosened in his hand. He opened it and read:

To Centurion Julius Saturnius, greetings. Due to the many attacks recently on the Romans traveling between Jerusalem and Jericho by brigands, no Roman citizen or soldier shall journey henceforth between the two cities without a minimum of one contubernium accompanying that citizen or soldier. Furthermore, you and Centurion Sextus shall each assign one contubernium from your century to patrol the road by day and another two to patrol the road by night.

By the order of Marcius Rufus, Tribune in Jerusalem.

Another sheet fell to the floor. Julius sighed. *This is probably the one I'm dreading.* He groaned aloud. *It won't evaporate if you ignore it, Julius. So read it and get it over with.* He picked it up.

To Centurion Julius Saturnius, greetings. With regard to your transfer to Caesarea, I am informed the senior centurion there will not leave for his assignment in Rome for another six months or more, and therefore you will remain under my command until I receive further word.

Marcius Rufus, Tribune in Jerusalem.

Julius released his held breath, a small smile lifting one corner of his mouth.

That's good news, indeed.

Cyril walked back into the room, wiping wet hands on his tunic. "Shall we go see our friend Loukas?" Julius asked.

"I'm ready," Cyril responded, throwing a cloak over his shoulders. "Did the letter from the tribune relieve your worries or make them worse?"

"Some good news and some news not so good. I can't tell you the good news, but the bad news is that brigands on the road between here and Jerusalem have increased their attacks on Romans. No Roman is to travel without an armed escort, and Sextus and I will need to coordinate patrols along the area. That shouldn't be a problem. The troops have been longing for any activity other than guard duty."

Julius patted his sword. "My own blade has seen no action for some time. Perhaps I should accompany some of the patrols. Although, I'd rather see the capture of these brigands than their deaths. We might learn a bit from them."

"Ah, yes, the receiving end of a scourge does tend to loosen tongues." Cyril shuddered.

"A sorry state of events, but true."

"Maybe you should find some gentler ways to convince them." Cyril pulled his cloak across his mouth and nose and batted his eyelashes.

"Are you volunteering?"

"Not on your life."

"That sounded like a threat." Julius scowled in mock sternness.

"No. Had it been a threat, it would have been accompanied by the point of a sword."

"Maybe I shouldn't be so lenient with you, slave," he teased. "You don't give me near as much respect as you should. Thirty lashes might be just what you need."

Cyril bowed and opened the gate to Loukas' courtyard, waving Julius through. "After you, Noble Master."

"That's more like it." Julius grinned at Cyril as Loukas came out of his house.

"Shalom, friends," Loukas greeted them. "To what do I owe this visit?"

"Shalom, Loukas," Julius replied. "I have another recruit for you. Cyril would also like to learn more about Judaism."

"Ah! What good news."

"Thank you," Cyril responded, looking around.

"If you are looking for a certain young lady of our house, she has gone to the marketplace with my wife," Loukas smiled then turned sober. "You are not considering entering the study of Judaism to please her, are you?"

"Sir, I would be less than honest if I did not say that has a bearing on my decision, but I also have a large curious hole in my head that I would like to fill. Can your God fill it? There is something missing from my life that I don't think even a wonderful woman or a lifelong friend could supply. Something you said when we joined you for the Feast of Purim, that our Greek gods have stone eyes and lips. They don't speak to me, either."

"Exactly," Loukas said. "I think under those conditions, you would be a good candidate to study our religion."

Cyril nodded. "What is my next step?"

"You will have to take your lessons from a rabbi. Probably the one Julius is taking lessons from, Shelumiel. I will recommend you to him, but it will be his decision as to whether he will take you or not."

"Sir, I know this is too soon, but I fear you could promise her to someone else before I have a chance to speak. I am very much drawn to Quinta. Is there a chance you might consider me as a husband for her?"

"My friend," Loukas said, "that depends on more things than I know at this time. First, your acceptance into study by Shelumiel; second, your completion of that study and dedication of yourself to God, making you a proselyte; third, if Quinta is amenable; and fourth, the agreement of your master. If I judge his expression correctly, you have not discussed this with him."

Julius shook his head. "No, but I'm aware of his interest in Quinta."

"I'm sorry, Julius. I didn't mean to hide anything from you. You usually read my mind so easily, I thought you would know. So, do you approve?"

"As the good physician said, that depends."

Chapter 13

James sat with his brother John and their father on the edge of their boat by the Sea of Galilee in Bethsaida. Together they mended their nets, the odor of fish so strong it was almost visible. Two servants brought in the sails from the other side, and James wondered that his father had not asked after the absence of Andrew and Simon, fellow fishermen.

"James, how many times must I tell you to rise earlier? The fish were gone by the time you got here." Zebedee's voice carried across the sand and water as he railed at his sons, berating them for their poor fishing skills. Jesus walked up to edge of the water, followed by Simon and Andrew. Jesus' woven robe billowed out behind Him in the breeze. James looked up, waving away the flies around his face.

Zebedee scowled, but his harsh voice sounded pleasant enough. "Shalom, friends. Did you come for some fish?"

"I came for your sons." Jesus motioned. "James, John, follow me."

James' countenance filled with joy, and he strode forward to greet Jesus. "Master, we couldn't find you in Jericho. How good to see you here."

"Who is this?" The older man growled. "And why does He want you to go with Him?"

"Jesus of Nazareth, Father, and He is the Lamb of God. John the Baptist said so." James shifted under his father's intense stare.

"So what makes this John such an authority?"

"I have need of your sons, Zebedee," Jesus interrupted. "They will be My disciples and carry the Word of God to the world."

Zebedee whirled on Jesus. "Who do You think You are to take my sons from me?"

"I am the Way, the Truth, and the Life." Jesus turned to lead the four fishermen up the slope, leaving Zebedee sputtering behind them.

Over the next few days, Jesus called other men to follow Him, among them Levi, also known at Matthew, a publican who collected taxes in Capernaum. Matthew invited them, along with several of his publican friends and others, to break bread with him in his home.

The outdoor cooking area at Matthew's house was such a flurry of activity that the servants bumped into each other, but they still managed to place the sumptuous meal on the table: fruits, nuts, mutton, quail, fish, two different kinds of bread, and goblets of rich red wine. Forty guests gathered with enthusiasm around the low table set up in a shady area in front of Levi's home, a three-sided courtyard surrounded by blooming roses and lilies and sheltered by massive trees. The guests were a mixture of tax collectors, their spouses and women friends, and Jesus' new disciples. Several passersby sneered and spoke behind their hands as they walked on the street.

Jesus took the bread, broke it, and lifted it above his head.

"Blessed are You, Yahweh our God, King of the universe, who brings forth bread from the earth."

A passing scribe heard Him, and he stared at the group with a look of astonishment on his face. Turning, the scribe hurried toward the synagogue, returning with several of the local Pharisees, the experts in Jewish laws.

One man stepped forward and confronted Jesus. "Why are You here, breaking bread with these tax collectors and sinners, You who claim to be a teacher?"

Jesus put His bread on his plate, finished His bite, and wiped His mouth and hands on a damp towel. "The Son of Man did not come to the ones who are already whole, but to those who are sick. I didn't come for those who are already righteous, but instead to call sinners to repentance."

The three servants cleared the remains of the meal and dishes from the table while guests continued their discussions. James listened in amazement as Jesus told the group of a life in Heaven waiting for them if they would trust in Him. One by one, repentant men and women bowed before Jesus. He commissioned each of the men He had chosen that day to follow Him. His words carried a weight that James had never experienced before, and when all but Jesus' chosen ones left, James stood in awe of the Man who could speak to hearts.

Back in Bethsaida, James paced back and forth on the seashore in a quandary. He was due back for a wedding—his own—in Jericho, but Jesus had commanded him to follow, and James knew in his heart that Jesus hadn't meant for only a few days. His "Follow Me" sounded more like a few months' command, or maybe even a few years. Did that mean giving up the beautiful Miriam? No. She was promised to him. She would wait. They would postpone the wedding. A year. Maybe two. It should make no difference. And yet...James heaved a long and shaky sigh.

Shaking his head and talking to himself, he strode back to his father's house. He could hear Zebedee shouting at John from a block away.

"It makes no sense. You would walk away from a prosperous fishing trade—no, the most prosperous of any fishing businesses in Galilee—to follow a carpenter who left a good living to become a wandering preacher?

"But Father, we had no choice. He called us to follow Him," John said.

"No choice?"

James cringed. His stomach clenched into forty knots when Zebedee yelled at them. He gritted his teeth and opened the door, knowing before he saw it that his father's face would be a ruddy red.

Zebedee rounded on James before he could step over the threshold. "And you, you ungrateful pup, would you betray the maiden promised to you? Just what do you intend to tell Micah? That you're going to follow this penniless prophet as He wanders through the wildernesses of Israel? No respectable man will even consider Miriam if you reject her. You know what people will think."

Salome touched his arm. "Please, Zebedee. Have a care for the neighbors, all of whom can surely hear you." She closed the open door. "And you, my sons, have you thought this through, this whim to follow a Man you know so little about?"

Zebedee lowered his voice to a gritty growl. "James, we will not go with you to Jericho. You can explain yourself to Micah and to his wife, who lies dying and will not see her daughter wed." He waved the small scroll in James' face.

"Dying?"

"Micah says she's sick unto death. You should marry Miriam. *Then* you could go follow your…your 'Lamb of God,' if you must."

"I'm sorry that she is dying, but I cannot change the path the Lord has set before me."

"That's truth." John's voice softened with wonder. "When He said 'Follow Me,' I felt as though this was the call I waited for all my life, as though my purpose had been defined in this Person."

James nodded. "I could no more say no to Jesus than I could to God. The call was indescribably irresistible. I don't know how else to define it."

He held his hands palm up toward Zebedee. "Father, we don't expect you to provide for us. We don't know where we will be going. He said we must leave family and everything we have to follow Him, and that we cannot wait until our father is dead and buried to follow. We won't cancel the betrothal, just delay it. Her father will see the ceremonies, even if her mother does not. We leave Capernaum tomorrow for Jerusalem. I'll tell Micah when we pass through Jericho. We'll say good-bye to you now, because we will spend the night where He is and leave early in the morning."

"Good-bye?" Salome turned the word into a five-syllable protest. "When will you return?"

"We don't know, Mother," John said. "Where He goes, we will follow."

Chapter 14

Miriam knelt on the hard stone floor next to her bed, praying and thinking of her mother. Ima seemed weaker than yesterday. Miriam could see her sinking day by day, although her mother's spirits remained high. Whenever Ima woke, she teased and laughed, probably hoping to raise Miriam's and Micah's spirits. For her sake, both Miriam and her father smiled and teased back, but the joviality was forced.

Sighing, Miriam rose to her feet to begin her day.

She shook her head. Leah had hung around the house the entire week, clinging to Ima, her fear obvious she might not be around when the end came. Leah refused to tease. Instead she burst into tears when Ima attempted to make her smile.

Amos, as intense as usual, was a sea of gloom. Micah took Amos and Leah into his shop where Miriam heard him tell them to go home and not to return until they could smile, however forced that might be.

Miriam prepared her family's breakfast in a fog, and she and her father ate in silence. Her mother refused to eat.

Passover was nearly upon them. Miriam stared at the unfinished wedding dress in her hands. A lump grew in her throat. Would Ima be around to see her only daughter married?

The next garment Miriam would sew would most likely be a shroud for her mother. Perhaps even before she finished the wedding garment. Usually it would be the mother or other kinswomen who sewed this white wedding cloak, but Ima wasn't able. Leah, the only other female relative, was so distraught she'd be no assistance at all.

Leah should help with the shroud, too, but that probably wouldn't come to pass. It all fell upon Miriam to prepare for the Passover, the wedding, and the probable funeral.

Miriam knew she shouldn't feel sorry for herself, but these past few weeks had been a heavy burden. Each night her eyes strayed out the window to the hill where she encountered Julius. She wanted to forget him. Yet in unguarded moments, her heart yearned toward that small clearing and the memory of his lips on hers, his arms around her waist, the feel of his body as he held her. Angrily she brushed the memories aside, and persistently they returned. She needed something else to think about.

Passover week began this day. So much to do. This afternoon, she must buy the lamb. Abba and Amos would take it to Jerusalem for sacrifice tomorrow. She never could bring herself to kill the animals. Her Abba was more understanding than most fathers when it came to killing them. Her heart warmed with gratitude.

She picked up her shopping basket and glanced toward her mother. It was sad her Ima and Abba never had any sons who lived past infancy. Poor little Nathan and Malachi. And Birabrah, the sister she never knew. Born before their time, not one of them lived more than a week.

She walked out the door. "I'm glad You gave me the strength, El Shaddai, to resist the temptation to go away with Julius. That would have been more than my poor Abba could have borne. And Ima. It would have broken their hearts. And maybe James' heart, although I'm sure he could have borne it more easily than Ima and Abba."

Where was James? He was to return to celebrate the Passover with her family, bringing Salome and Zebedee along with him. And John, too, Miriam supposed. When they arrived, they would have a houseful for meals, and their guests would need places to sleep.

Why hadn't she thought of that before? Maybe her father could clear some room in the shop for sleeping pallets.

Miriam hurried back to the shop, looking for her father. She found him kneeling on the floor in front of a chair, coating it with oil.

"Abba, where are we going to put all our guests? James and his family will need places to sleep. Can you clear a place in here? There's not much room in the house."

"What?" Her father started. "A place to sleep. Yes, I could clear a place here. That door will be going out later today, along with this set of chairs for the rabbi. His wife wants to put them in their courtyard. The unfinished bed over there can be moved outside in back of the shop. I'll get Amos to help me."

A knock sounded at the door to the shop, and James entered. He stood in the doorway, blinking his eyes in the dim interior, an odd expression on his face. "Micah, are you here?" he called.

"Shalom. Yes, over here, James," Abba called. "And how is my future son-in-law? Where is the rest of your family?"

Miriam cringed at her father's description but struggled to keep her face expressionless.

"That's what I have come to talk to you about, sir. Oh, hello, Miriam." James wiped sweaty hands on his cloak, flushing a deep red. "I need to speak to your father." James' gaze darted between them.

"Anything you say to me may be said in front of Miriam. I assume this is about her or at least about the wedding."

"Yes sir, it is. I...." He coughed and shifted from side to side. "You see, I have a small problem."

Miriam's heart skipped a beat. What was happening?

"Yes, what is it, James? Did you leave your wits in the Sea of Galilee?" Micah's smile faded, and the lines between his eyes deepened.

James backed toward the door. "I can't marry Miriam quite yet. Perhaps in a year or two." He blurted his news like a ten-year-old confessing to a misdemeanor.

"You *what?*" Abba rose to his feet.

Miriam's eyes flew open wide, and she felt the shadow of a smile playing at the corners of her lips. Sternly, she reminded herself to remain serious.

"I have been called to be a disciple by the Master. By Jesus, that is."

"What do you mean, 'called to be a disciple'? You're giving up fishing with your father? Are you out of your mind, young man?"

"I'm s-sorry sir...and Miriam. Please forgive me, but I have to go with Him. With the Master, I mean. I have to go. Now. Good-bye." James turned and fled through the still-open door.

Abba turned to Miriam, fists on his hips, his eyes flashing fury. Miriam breathed a sigh of relief and hid a smile behind her hand.

"Abba, don't be angry. He'll be back. I'm not in a hurry to marry him. I only agreed because I thought you and Ima wanted it."

"But your mother...she wants to see your wedding, and her strength fails more every day. James didn't bring the bride price nor his parents to join us in the betrothal celebration. You are sixteen years old. Another year or two, and no one will think you are marriageable. 'Another year or two,' he said. That's unacceptable."

Miriam giggled. "I'm sorry Abba, but did you see the look on James' face? It looked as if he'd been caught stealing bread from a Pharisee's table."

Abba's scowl went away as a smile tugged at the edge of his mouth, crinkles at the edge of his eyes, and then he, too, laughed perhaps for the first time since finding out her mother wouldn't be getting better.

Micah recovered first and again looked sober. "Miriam, it occurs to me, there might be another reason you're not unhappy to postpone this marriage. Is there something you haven't told me?"

Her face and ears heated, and she lowered her eyes to stare at her feet. "Yes, Abba. My heart has longed for another man I thought you would not allow and God would not want. I've tried to tell myself that I cannot love him because he is a Roman. But the last time I saw him, he told me he was becoming a proselyte."

"A Roman? And 'the last time you saw him?' Have you been meeting this man?"

"Not by plan, Abba. It seemed like he was just there, wherever I went. The last time was the day Loukas told us that Ima was too ill to recover. Do you remember I went to find a place to be alone? I went up the hill to a quiet clearing in the olive grove. I sat there on a rock, praying, and he came to the clearing, too. We…we talked for quite a while."

"You did no more than talk, Miriam?"

"No. Well, except he…he kissed me." She touched her mouth with her fingers, remembering. "I thought he was kissing me good-bye, but now I wonder…."

"You allowed another man to kiss you, Miriam bat Micah, even though we made a promise to James?" His voice was low. His eyes held her fast for a moment and then he lowered his gaze, staring at the ground and shaking his head.

Shame flamed warmth to Miriam's cheeks. "Yes, Father. I am sorry."

He looked up. "You know our laws."

"Yes, Father."

"What you did was wrong, very wrong. And foolish. You could have been dishonored, if not by this soldier, then by another evil man."

Miriam bowed her head, her mind filled with the vision of the evil soldier pushing her down. Her voice shook. "Yes, Father, I know."

"If you had been seen or worse, been dishonored, it would have brought shame not only on you, but also on our house. If he had not been a good man, you might have been badly hurt."

"I'm sorry, Father." Tears rolled down her hot cheeks. "It grieves me to know you are ashamed of me."

"You have sinned, Daughter," Tears shined in Abba's eyes.

"I have sinned against you and against God. Please forgive me."

The silence stretched between them, and Miriam's shoulders shook.

"I forgive you, Mirie, but we will still need to make a sacrifice for you at the temple."

"Yes, Father." Miriam covered her face with her hands.

"Come." Micah stretched his arms out to her. Miriam took the two short steps to him and cried into his rough tunic.

"Now, dry your eyes, little one, you've work to finish. I'll tell your mother of James' revelation."

"Thank you, Abba." She wiped her eyes. "Abba, he is a good man, the Roman. He rescued...." No! He'd just spoken of dishonor. She couldn't tell her father about that other soldier.

"Rescued?"

"A dog. He rescued a dog. From some boys."

"He rescued a dog. That doesn't mean he might also protect a foolish young woman. Go, then. But only to the marketplace. You must not contact your Roman friend."

Miriam flushed again and hung her head. "Yes, Father. I mean no, Father." She picked up her market basket and hurried out the door.

Micah sighed and walked back into the house. Someday Miriam would understand that chastising the child hurt the parent, too. At least, he hoped she would. His heart weighed heavy in him as he looked around the frame of the door into the bedroom, unwilling to wake Deborah.

His wife opened her eyes and smiled that special smile that she gave only to him. She raised her hand to his as he walked into the small, dark room.

"Hello, Husband. Why are your eyes sad?"

"I had to scold Mirie. It seems she gave her heart to someone other than James."

"Ah, yes, I knew. She told me she developed an affection for someone who wasn't a Jew." She rose on her elbows, and Micah put an extra pillow at her back. She settled on them with a soft moan.

"You knew? Did you also know she met him alone and he kissed her?"

"No. She said she was trying hard to forget him."

"Yes, she mentioned that, too. It explains part of why she's been sad lately. I caught her crying while she sewed her wedding dress. I thought the tears were for you. Perhaps it was the combination." He sat down beside her on the low bed.

"It seems our little girl still hasn't been able to put this Roman out of her mind." Deborah shifted on the pillows.

"Yes. And it seems he hasn't put her out of his heart either. The young centurion you saw in my shop? He's the one. He told me he began taking lessons to become a proselyte."

"Ah, that's why you looked like such a storm cloud when I walked in that day. He had the nerve to ask for your daughter's hand." Her eyebrows wagged.

"He asked if I would set aside the promise between James and Mirie. I told him we would not do that. Then he questioned if we would consider him if the promise was somehow broken between James and Mirie. I said that would never happen. However...."

"However?"

"James came by a few minutes ago. He wants to postpone the marriage for a year or two." A smile teased the edge of his mouth at the memory of James' behavior.

"He *what?*" Deborah struggled to push up from her pillows but sank back, breathing hard.

Micah's mouth lifted in a lopsided smile as he picked up her hand. "The One God works in strange ways, sometimes, my love. I'm beginning to think there's a possibility He might be in favor of a match with the Roman. I want to know more, though, before feeding Mirie's romantic notions. I need to go see our friend Loukas. Until—or if—we wish to change the marriage status, the promise to James stands. If we decide to end this near-betrothal, I'll have to find and talk to James. I won't consider anything else until or if he releases her."

"I agree. Why is it you want to talk to Loukas?"

"Because this Roman says he made his arrangements to become a proselyte through Loukas."

"How did they come to know each other?"

"I don't know. Perhaps Loukas will tell us." He squeezed her hand.

"Yes, my love. So see Loukas. I want to rest for a while, and when you come back, perhaps you will have more information."

Micah leaned down to kiss his wife's pale cheek. "I'll return as soon as I can. I suspect it will be an hour if he is home, but much less if I just leave a message for him. Don't tell Mirie where I've gone."

Miriam hurried to the marketplace, intending to make her purchases. The basket was heavier than she thought it would be for the amount of food they needed for the next five days. She always remembered more once she began shopping.

She struggled under the heavy burden, putting it down only once she reached the shepherd and purchased her lamb. The lamb fought against her leading, almost causing her to drop the food. She had to leave the reluctant lamb behind. Yearlings could be heavy, and she might have to carry it. She sighed. She'd have to take her other purchases home before bringing home a lamb.

Leah was leaving the house when Miriam arrived.

"Hello, Miriam. I stopped to see your mother, but she's asleep. You've been shopping?"

"Yes, but I need to go back and retrieve the lamb. I'll just drop the basket on the table and go. Would you like to come with me?"

"Yes. There are some things we need, too. Amos won't be expecting me back until it's time to prepare the midday meal."

As they passed Hannah's house, she came running out with the baby.

"Wait, Miriam, Leah, are you going to the marketplace? May I come with you?"

"We're not going to the marketplace, but you can come with us. May I carry Martha?"

"I wish you would. After a while, she feels heavy. Especially when I also need to carry a basket of food or a jar of water along with her. Isaiah made this sling for me so I can carry her without using my hands. That helps." Hannah lifted the baby and handed her to Miriam, then arranged the triangular pouch around Miriam's neck and shoulders.

"I need to talk to your mother sometime soon. My own mother is too far away. I have so many questions about babies and motherhood. This is new to me."

"I suppose it would be. I should listen in." Miriam adjusted the sling so Martha, fist in her mouth, could see.

"True. You might have your own little one by this time next year." Hannah threw an arm around Miriam's shoulders and squeezed.

"Probably not. I guess I should tell you. The wedding with James has been postponed."

Leah grasped Miriam's elbow. "Postponed? What do you mean?"

"James stopped to see us and said he wanted to wait a year or two."

"A year or two? That's terrible! Why?"

"It wasn't because he heard about your fascination for that Roman, is it?" A scowl crossed Hannah's brow.

"Maybe she has a fascination for more than one Roman," said Tamar, stepping out from a booth.

"What?" Hannah frowned at Tamar.

Miriam felt her heart freeze. Tamar could be sullen and prone to say hurtful words, but why had she chosen to force her angry disposition on Miriam.

"There are rumors." Tamar's eyes narrowed as she gazed at Miriam. "They're true, aren't they?"

"R-rumors?"

"You went into that old house of Barnabab with one of the soldiers, and you met on the hill with the young centurion. Deny it if you can."

"Miriam?" Leah's eyes rounded.

"No, no, it's not true! Not the way you say." Miriam's gaze flew from one face to the other. "You believe me, don't you?"

"Why should we believe anyone who would consort with the Romans?" Tamar pushed Miriam's shoulder. "You are a disgrace to the Hebrews."

Martha's face pinched into a pout. Hannah stepped between Tamar and Miriam. "Don't you hurt my baby."

"I can't believe you allow this whore to carry your babe."

"Tamar!" Leah pulled the woman back. "You will not speak that way."

"It's true." Tamar glowered at both Hannah and Miriam, and then she stomped away.

The three women stood in stunned silence.

"Miriam, what did she mean?" Leah's eyes pled with Miriam to deny what she'd heard.

Miriam dropped her eyelashes and brushed the tears away. "A soldier tried to...to drag me into Barnabab's house, but a centurion stopped him, arrested him, and took him away. I wasn't, wasn't...He didn't...."

Leah pulled her into her arms. "There, now, Miriam, don't cry. He didn't dishonor you, so you have nothing to worry about."

Hannah patted her on the back. "Hmmph. Tamar listens too much to gossips. But perhaps James did hear about the Roman and that's why."

"No, it wasn't because he heard about J...uh, the Roman. James decided he wanted to follow this Rabbi named Jesus and wouldn't marry me for a few years."

"You don't seem very upset. You should be. What if this rumor gets back to your father? Or James? People will talk."

"Oh, no! What shall I do?"

"Tell your father before anyone else has a chance to. As for James, maybe he left town with the Prophet today."

"Yes, I suppose people will talk. Perhaps they will understand if they see James with the Prophet. James and his brother were supposed to share the Passover with us." Miriam shook her head. "I hope they *don't* show up for Passover. I saw the size of the group following Jesus. It looked like there were at least a dozen men. If they all came, I don't think I could spread the food that far." She pushed a lock of hair under her scarf, then put her hand back under Baby Martha, who was starting to fret. She patted Martha's bottom and murmured a little baby talk to her before returning to the adult conversation.

"Maybe I'd better make some extra bread. That way, with the lamb, lots of bread, and baskets full of bitter herbs, we should be able to fill all their hungry stomachs."

"I wouldn't think that James would have the courage—or stupidity— to show up again at your house so soon," Hannah thrust out her jaw and placed one tight fist on her hip.

"The idea, postponing a wedding to follow a wandering teacher," Leah said. "And don't worry about that wag-tongue Tamar. We'll stand by you, Miriam."

"Please don't feel sorry for me. I'm in no hurry to marry James. And I'll take your advice and tell Abba." She sighed and patted the still-fussing Martha, jiggling her a little.

"I used to think highly of James, too, but no more. Some men seem so nice, but it seems his true self came forth." Hannah sniffed. "Mary's husband is another one. That man treats her like an ox. He orders her around as though she hadn't enough sense to prepare a meal, what to make for their clothing, or how to mend them, even where to put their table." Hannah stomped her foot, and her voice raised in anger.

"She often comes to my house to talk. Kish won't even sleep with her but makes her sleep alone on the floor next to the pallet. Well, except when he wants his husbandly privileges. And then, she tells me he's rough. He often hits her or chokes her. It's no wonder they don't have children. God is probably punishing him. Kish blames her, of course. She just acts like this is all normal."

"That's the thing, Hannah. It is normal. Isaiah treats you so well you forget that a lot of men treat their wives with contempt." Leah touched Hannah's shoulder. "And I really don't think you should be talking about this with others. She told you in confidence, is that not so?"

Hannah blinked and blushed. She hesitated before responding. "You're right, Leah. I hope you two won't repeat any of this, will you? I'll keep my overactive mouth shut from now on. Except maybe with you two, since I already spilled my gall on you. I get so angry because I can't help her. And she won't help herself. She's such a meek little lamb."

"No, we won't repeat anything. I wish we could help her, too. She really doesn't deserve to be treated so badly." Miriam's eyes narrowed. "If I were a man, I'd give him a sample of his own treatment."

"Maybe I get so angry about it because I'm probably pushier to Isaiah than he is to me. He is so good to me, but sometimes I get impatient with him."

"Amos and I are different. He's such a nervous bird, always wants things to be exactly right, so I just let things flow as they might. I'd rather listen than talk, and he talks a lot. He worries that he is doing something to displease God because we don't have children, but I tell him not to be concerned. If we have children, we will be blessed, and if we do not, we are still blessed to have each other."

"Leah, you are so wise. I wish I were as patient as you. Miriam, let me take little Martha back now. She sounds hungry, and you can't feed her. I'll see you at Passover."

"Good-bye, Hannah." Miriam and Leah waved to Hannah and walked on toward the edge of the city to retrieve the lamb she had purchased.

A long line stretched before Micah and Amos when they arrived at the Court of Gentiles. Beyond that, the sacrificial lamb would be taken into the Court of Israel. Still others gathered in different places in the temple, listening to various teachers. Amos left Micah to wander the marketplace outside the temple.

A Man strode into the Court of Gentiles. He marched to the tables of the moneychangers. In a deliberate move, He tipped the tables over and then took a small whip and began to drive the moneychangers, the animals, and the merchants from the temple.

"Here, You. Stop that." One of the myriad of priests, his prayer shawl askew, hurried over to the Man. "What do You think You're doing?"

"You're making My Father's house a house of greedy merchandisers."

"What right have You to be doing this?" another priest asked, scraggly gray brows pinched tight together. "Can You give us a sign that shows us You have this right?"

"You want a sign? This is the sign: Destroy this temple, and in three days I will raise it up." His voice was as angry as the mutterings around Him. The whip He clenched in His hand quivered.

James and John stood among those around the Man, but they didn't seem to notice Micah. Was this the Master James said he wanted to follow? If it was, this Jesus they followed seemed demented. Micah laughed to himself as he thought of the scattering animals and birds and the Man who said He could rebuild the Temple in three days. Micah nearly stepped in a pile of sheep dung, and as he sidestepped, he didn't see Jesus approach.

"I didn't refer to this building made of stone and mortar, Micah."

"What? How do You know my Name? How did You know what I was thinking?" With each question Micah took a step away from Jesus.

"It was written all over your face." The anger had fled Jesus' features. His voice was soft and soothing, His smile engaging, as though He were speaking to a child.

"Who are You?" Micah stopped his backward motion. "You seem to know me. Did James or John tell you who I am?"

"No, my Father told me."

"Oh? Who is Your Father? Do we know Him?"

"Your whole family knows Him." Jesus' eyes twinkled.

"Sir, forgive me, but You speak in riddles, yet you don't answer my questions. You haven't told me Who Your Father is." Micah glanced around. He didn't want to lose his place in this long line, but he wanted to escape this madman.

"You wish to know? Come to Me and bring your family." He turned to go back to His disciples.

"Here at the temple?" Micah asked, but Jesus continued to walk toward His disciples. Micah scratched his head, bemused. He remembered the lamb still next to him, thanks to the rope around his neck. He shook his head, laughed at himself, then turned again and began to mount the steps into the Court of Priests. *What a day, and what a line this is. It could take an eternity to get this lamb sacrificed.*

Chapter 15

Julius had been pleased by the invitation to share the Passover feast with Loukas. He had also invited Cyril and Marcus. Now they sat around the table, and Joanna, Quinta, and three other servants brought the dishes to the table. Four other men sat at the table, servants who took care of Loukas' house, yard, and animals.

"Loukas, thank you for your invitation. Your generosity is inspirational," Julius said, lifting his glass of wine in a toast to their host.

"I agree," Cyril said, lifting his glass also, first to Loukas and then to Joanna and Quinta. "And thank you also to the lovely ladies who prepared the meal, served the food, and grace the table."

Quinta, Joanna, and the other women servants blushed a rosy red, eyes lowered.

"Thank you, sir." Joanna placed the roast lamb in front of her husband.

Loukas lifted a wine glass, blessed it, and passed it around the table.

"Loukas, the last time we shared a feast with you, I asked what the significance of the celebration was, and you were kind enough to explain to us. Could you do the same for us this time? For instance, the bread looks different than flat bread I've seen before. Is there a religious significance to this type of bread?" Julius asked.

Joanna emitted a low cry and turned to Loukas, her eyes filling.

Julius' eyes widened. "Did I say something to distress you? If so, please forgive me."

Loukas held his wife's hand as he turned sad eyes on Julius. "You haven't done anything wrong. It's just that our son, our only child, died two years ago, just after the Passover. He was only ten years old. At this festival, the youngest child asks his parents what this Seder meal is about, as you did. We remember how Enoch asked the questions that year, even though he was weak and dying" Loukas squeezed and released Joanna's hand. He picked up a knife and sliced the meat.

"We celebrate this meal to commemorate the release of the Israelites from slavery from the Egyptians. Moses, a prophet of the Almighty, told Pharaoh he must let the Israelites go, but Pharaoh refused. Moses warned Pharaoh that if he did not, God would send plagues to punish him. Still Pharaoh refused and continued to refuse through nine punishing events." Loukas passed the tray of meat to Julius.

"The final event was the death of the firstborn male of every household and field. The Hebrews killed a lamb for each household, inviting others to join them who did not have a lamb. They saved the blood to spread on the side posts and upper doorpost of each house. When the angel of death saw the blood, he would pass over that household and not take the firstborn. Thus the name Passover."

"Everyone's firstborn?" Cyril's eyes narrowed. "Even the innocents, those who had done no harm, just because they didn't put blood on their doorways?"

Loukas nodded. "The pharaoh was as grieved as the rest of Egypt at the loss of his firstborn, and he told the Israelites to get out of Egypt. God told Moses to tell the Hebrews to hurry as they left, because Pharaoh would once more change his mind. Thus, there was no time to make raised bread. The bitter herbs we eat represent the bitterness of slavery, and they are dipped in this charoset that represents the clay bricks the Hebrew slaves had to make. The parsley represents new life and spring, but it's dipped in salt water to represent the tears of the Hebrew slaves who cried to God for freedom."

"I'm amazed that you remember all of that." Julius' attention had been fixed on Loukas through the entire recital. He accepted the plate of unleavened bread from Loukas and passed the plate on to Cyril.

Loukas laughed. "And that's the short version. The entire story is told at length over and over to the Hebrews while they are growing up and even after adulthood. You'll notice as you study the scriptures how many times the story of the Hebrews escaping Egypt is retold, especially in the Psalms, the songs we sing or chant in our synagogues. You'll hear it so many times that you, too, will be able to recite it from memory before long." Loukas handed Julius the dish of greens.

"I suppose you equate being under Rome the same as being slaves in Egypt, then?" Marcus asked, hesitating before he speared a piece of lamb with his knife.

"I fear many people do, but it isn't the same. The Hebrews are not slaves now, but they still resent being ruled by anyone other than a descendant of David, their favorite king."

Marcus leaned to peer at Julius. "I must ask my friends here, why is this important that you become a Jewish proselyte? When we stepped into the waters…that is, when John the Baptizer pushed me beneath the waters, I felt something stir in my soul like nothing I had ever felt."

Loukas narrowed his eyes at Julius. "What is this?"

Cyril's stare fixed on Julius. "I do not understand."

Julius shook his head. "Neither do I. The God of the Jews seems to be telling me that I must learn the ways of His people, but we were not the only ones baptized by John that day. A Man—"

"Yes, a Man," Marcus interrupted. "John baptized Him, and then a Voice called down, seemingly from heaven. He said that this Man Jesus was His Son, and He was well-pleased with Him."

"John called him the 'Lamb of God.'" Julius looked at the meal before him and thought of Loukas' story. "Could this Man's appearance have any correlation to the Passover? If so, what are we to do with this?"

"I do not know." Loukas shook his head. Then he looked at Marcus. "And you agreed to join us here, why?"

Marcus lowered his head. "Since that day when the Baptizer plunged me beneath the waters, when the Man looked into my eyes and seemed to know me from the very depth of my soul, I have been seeking. But for what, I do not know."

Julius smiled. So Marcus had felt the same unction when Jesus had looked upon him.

"Then we shall talk," Loukas said. "But now, let's finish this fine Passover meal."

In the house of Micah, the Passover waxed solemn rather than joyful.

Miriam focused on her plate. She didn't dare look at her mother who. reclined upon one of the pillows placed around the low table. She winced with each movement and pushed her food around on the plate. Miriam could not eat. If she looked at her mother, she would start crying. And she couldn't look at her father, either. She felt guilty over the truth she kept from them. *Adonai, please help my mother. She never complains, but I can tell she's hurting. I would rather have her die in peace than be tortured this way.* She shuddered at the thought of her mother dying, and again at the story she would have to tell her Abba.

"Are you all right, little one?" Deborah whispered.

Miriam shook her head, and the tears welled in her eyes.

Abba started at the sound of his wife's voice. He glanced down at his untouched food and reached for his knife. At first, Miriam had expected he would act as if this Passover was no different from any other, that Ima was not dying, and that next year, he would not be alone if he still insisted she marry James. Abba seemed dazed for a moment, but Miriam doubted any of the others noticed. The only ones eating were Amos and Isaiah.

"Amos, more lamb?" Abba picked up the platter.

"Yes, yes, indeed. The lamb tastes wonderful, and everything else, too, of course."

Leah glanced at Amos. "You have such a good appetite, my husband. One would think you were eating for two."

Ima chuckled, and for a brief moment Miriam saw a smidgen of her mother when she was healthy. "Isn't it Leah who should be eating for two?" Ima asked.

"Me? Why should I…oh. Do you think that I...?"

"Yes, I do. Am I right?" Ima smiled.

"Well, you could be." Leah blushed. "But *I'm* not sure yet. How could you know?"

"I'm not sure I can put it into words, but there's a difference in you. A softening of the lines of your face, perhaps. A rounding of your body, maybe. If I am right, I'm happy for you, dear sister. After ten years of waiting, it would be a wonderful blessing."

Amos held a piece of lamb suspended between his plate and his mouth as he stared at his wife.

"Did Deborah mean what I think she means?" he asked around a mouthful of bread. He swallowed.

"I think she's saying what you think she's saying, Amos," Abba said.

"My wife is...is...?" He looked wide-eyed at Leah.

"Maybe. I wanted to wait to say anything until I knew for sure." Leah blushed far deeper than Miriam had ever seen before.

"Oh, Leah, that's so wonderful." Miriam leaned over and hugged Leah's shoulders.

"Deborah!" Abba cried.

Miriam jolted at the fear in her father's voice.

Ima had fallen back on her pillow. As the others echoed Abba's alarm, he stood, lifted Ima's thin frame easily in his arms, and carried her to her bed.

Miriam hurried after him. "Abba, what can I do?"

Abba sat beside her mother, stroking her cheek while tears coursed unchecked down his face.

Ima's eyes fluttered open, and a look of dismay crossed her face. She reached a shaking hand up to brush Abba's tears away.

Miriam stood behind them afraid to move.

"Oh, I'm so sorry, my love," Ima said to Abba. "Please don't worry about me, I'm weary and must have fallen asleep. Go back to the table and finish the meal. You and Miriam will have to play host. I'm exhausted. Will you excuse me?"

"Of course. Sleep, my own," Abba said, kissing her forehead.

He stood and led Miriam from the room.

Chapter 16

Julius, stepped into the chariot behind Warrior and Duros. After Marcus and Cyril joined him, Julius tapped the reins on the horses' rumps, and Warrior burst ahead as if he'd been swatted by a lion. Duros whinnied, protesting Warrior's exuberance.

Cyril grabbed for the sides of the chariot.

"Whoa, back a little, Warrior. I know you're eager for some exercise, but we don't need to get there yesterday." Julius pulled back on the reins. Warrior laid his ears back and kicked at the crossbar.

"He's feeling energetic this morning, isn't he?" Marcus laughed, holding on as hard as Cyril. "Maybe you should take him for a run up the hill."

"Might not be a bad idea. You two want to wait here while I work off his vinegar?"

"No, this might be the only excitement we get all week. Let's go!" Cyril grinned and punched one fist into the air while he kept a firm hold on the wall of the chariot with the other.

Julius turned the chariot toward the road to Jerusalem. Warrior threw his head, jingling the harness. Within minutes they sped up the hill, the chariot bouncing over the rocks, Warrior providing the pull and Duros the stability.

Before too long Warrior willingly settled into a trot rather than a run, and Julius pulled the horses to a halt and then in a tight turn to return to Jericho. He took a deep breath of the clean air and smiled at the absence of the odors of the city.

Without warning, a dozen or more rough men armed with swords and spears jumped out from behind bushes and rocks. They brandished their weapons and shouted a warning to stop.

Julius and Marcus drew their swords

"Hold on!" Cyril grabbed the reins and slapped them on their hindquarters. Warrior and Duros laid their ears back and jumped forward. Warrior bit the shoulder of a greasy-haired attacker as the horses charged into the brigands. A one-eyed assailant grabbed at the edge of the chariot, but Marcus swung his sword and neatly severed the man's fingers. Beside him, Julius' sword decapitated another assailant, surprise still evident in the attacker's eyes as his head rolled down the hill. One more man reached for the halter at Warrior's head. The stallion reared and plunged forward, his hoof connecting with the man's shoulder and knocking him under the wheel of the chariot as they passed. A spear narrowly missed Cyril, bouncing off Duros' shoulder. The gelding neighed in pain.

Within seconds, they outdistanced their attackers and their spears, cheering and throwing taunts back at the would-be assassins.

"Pull up just outside the wall, Cyril. I want to check the horses." Julius sheathed his sword, breathing a silent thanks to God. Cyril pulled the still-excited animals to a trot and then to a stop just outside the city walls. Warrior tossed his head and neighed, but complied without a fight.

Julius strode toward the horses' heads, murmured endearments to the animals, and ran his hands over their sweating necks and shoulders, relishing the smell of sweaty horseflesh. A feeling of pride for the two horses filled his chest. Although a scratch etched Duros' shoulder where the spear struck, neither horse appeared otherwise injured. Warrior nuzzled Julius' tunic, hoping for a treat. Julius pulled a tuft of grass and fed it to the stallion. "You deserve more, my valiant boy. Did you enjoy your exercise this morning?"

Warrior threw his head up and down as though in agreement.

Julius laughed. "Yes, I thought so."

"Lucky thing we got away, my friend. Can you imagine explaining to the tribune why we left the city without soldiers accompanying us?" Marcus handed another bunch of grass to Duros.

"I don't even want to imagine. This will be our little secret, right? Not a word to your men or friends." Julius shot a sidelong grin at Cyril. "You either, Cyril."

Julius guided the horses at a walk through the busy streets. Shelumiel stepped out of his doorway as the three men rode up to his house. "Shalom, men. Come in. We have much to discuss." He turned and walked back inside.

Apprehension churned within Julius. He looked at his two friends as they followed Shelumiel into his house. "Are you sure you're ready for this discussion?" He looked at Marcus who, after serious conversations with Loukas and after Loukas' recommendation to Shelumiel, had made the decision to also become a Jewish proselyte.

Marcus gave only the slightest of nods.

"Please, have a seat." Shelumiel waved his hand in the direction of the benches in his courtyard. He pulled a scroll from a pile on a shelf.

"Our reading today is from the writings of Moses, the story of Abram, whom God renamed Abraham. Abraham was ninety-nine years old, and his wife Sarai, whom God renamed Sarah, was ninety, well past the time of child bearing. One day the Lord appeared to Abraham and told him he would have a son, and through that son God would establish an everlasting covenant. As a token of that covenant, every male of Abraham's household was to be circumcised. Abraham took every male in his house and circumcised them."

"Did that include his servants, sir?" Cyril's Adam's apple bobbed.

"Yes. And his son, Ishmael, and after he was born, Isaac, also. It has remained a token of the covenant between all Hebrew men and their God."

Julius swallowed. "Does this mean you believe we're ready for…for…."

"I've been convinced your conversion is honest. Am I mistaken?"

"No, sir." After a heartbeat's hesitation, Julius and his friends answered nearly in unison.

"Loukas agreed to care for you after the ceremony. You won't want to move around much for the first two or three days, and you will have some pain for a few weeks, severe at first, but in a month, you'll be fine. The time to decide is upon you. Is your life with God important enough to you?"

Julius' stomach tightened. "You say it is required for Hebrews. Must proselytes also comply?"

"Yes."

"I have to ask, and I hope you won't think I'm being impertinent. Why does God want men to be circumcised?"

"Am I God? As the prophet Isaiah said, His ways are higher than our ways and thus beyond our understanding. It's a token of our covenant with Him, and it's required in order for you to become a proselyte." Shelumiel's brow creased, and he drew himself up and wove his arms across his chest. "Enough of this. I thought you were ready, but you question the will of God. Perhaps you are not quite prepared to take this step."

"Rabbi, please don't be impatient with us." Julius held up his hands. "We only seek to understand the One God."

"Give this your most serious consideration, you men. It is not a step to be taken on impulse, but if you would be proselytes of our religion, it is required. Your lesson for this day is finished, and do not return until you make your decision."

Shelumiel turned and stalked into another room.

Julius let out a long breath. He stood and walked out the door, and his friends followed him without speaking.

Julius' face warmed. "Not the wisest questions I've ever asked, were they?"

Marcus whistled. "Agreed. Friends, that was close. I thought Shelumiel would oust us for sure. That was one angry rabbi." He stepped out of the chariot in front of their quarters. "I wondered for a while if you'd stepped into a wagonload of stable refuse and pulled us in with you."

"I ponder the same question. Only Julius had the courage to ask. I don't think he was quite as angry as he pretended to be." Cyril grinned as they ascended the stairs.

"What makes you say that, slave?" Marcus gave Cyril a small push as they opened the door to Julius' apartment.

"It fits. He wants Gentiles to become proselytes, or he wouldn't have taken us on. He likes us. When we arrive, his eyes light up. Haven't you noticed? He knows this is a big step for us, and it's a test to see if we're in this for God or just for the fun of it. He doesn't want any halfhearted proselytes."

"No, I don't suppose." Julius nodded.

"He likes us. But that little item about having a circumcision...." Cyril shook his head. "That could put a 'whoa' on the whole procedure, as far as I'm concerned. Maybe that thought doesn't faze you two, since you're such brave soldiers."

"Brave soldiers, hah! The thought breaks me out in a cold sweat on a hot day, but I want to please God. And Miriam and her parents as well. It's a requirement, so I don't see myself making any other choice. Still, I'd rather face a hungry wolf." A shiver ran up Julius' spine.

"Even the thought of the priest with a knife in his hand is enough to send me running for the hills." Marcus grinned. "If I can surmount this obstacle, I don't think any barbarous act will ever frighten me again."

"Agreed. Now, can we find something more pleasant to talk about, like maybe being thrown to the lions?" Julius shook the reins over his team's backs.

Chapter 17

Julius had been able to delay breaking bread with Micah's family for over a month, but he couldn't refuse again without insulting both Micah and Deborah. The last invitation, delivered at the synagogue with a hint that Deborah wanted the meal to happen before she left this earth, Julius had accepted. Now he arrived at Micah's home about an hour before sunset, his body a mass of tension.

Miriam met him at the door, her eyes filled with joyous welcome. He was sure she must be thinking of their last kiss when they thought it would be good-bye, and now, here he was meeting her again in her own home. His heart beat faster than Duros' hooves could race as she led him to Deborah. He bowed toward Deborah's frail form resting on a low bed in an alcove. The smell of roasting meat and onions made his mouth water.

"So this is the centurion you spoke of, Miriam. And he is also my rescuer," Deborah added.

Miriam cast him a wide-eyed glance. If she had not been standing so close to him, he might not have heard the small gasp, which told him she was thinking of another rescue. Of when he rescued her.

"Thank you, sir, for carrying me to my sister's home."

Miriam seemed to relax at her mother's words, but Julius wished he could comfort her, tell her that he would do all in his power to ever keep anyone from trying to hurt her and as long as God gave him the power to do so.

"You're welcome, Lady," he said. "There is nothing to thank me for. I remember thinking of my own mother when you fainted."

"Is she subject to fainting, too?" Deborah asked.

"Yes, she was. My mother died a year ago, but she had been weak and had severe pain in her chest sometimes for a year before that."

A sadness lingered over both women. Deborah looked from him to her daughter and back again. "I'm sorry. You must miss her."

"Yes, Lady, I do. She wrote to me often, but I hadn't seen her for a few years. Still, I knew she was there, and now she is not."

Micah stepped to Julius' side and placed a hand on his shoulder. "I appreciate that you took the time to help. Not that there aren't any Roman soldiers who would have been willing to help but perhaps not many here. God tends to arrange coincidences to bring His will to our attention. Perhaps God is saying something here."

Julius slid a sidelong glance at Miriam and then at Micah and Deborah. "I hope so, sir."

"If you will gather at the table, I'll bring the food," Miriam said, disappearing toward the cooking area. She reappeared moments later. "Our meal is ready," she said, placing a platter of fish and bread to join the cheese, fruit, and wine on the table. Micah carried Deborah to her pillows at the low table.

Deborah cried out, one hand reaching toward her hip. Micah knelt quickly by her side.

"Did I hurt you?" He held her hand and brushed the hair from his wife's face.

Deborah bit her lip and then smiled at her husband. "I don't know what happened. I'm all right now. Don't worry about it."

Clearly, Micah wasn't taking her advice. His shoulders slumped forward, and a frown marred his features as he sat beside his wife. Miriam's face mirrored Micah's so exactly that it would have been amusing under any other circumstances, but Julius couldn't help but notice the alarm written in every line of their bodies and faces.

"Ah, the melon looks delicious," Julius said, hoping to pull the attention away from Deborah, who frowned at her somber family. "As does the bread and fowl. Did you cook all this yourself, Miriam?"

That seemed to break Miriam's concentration on her mother, and she wrinkled her nose at him. "Don't sound so surprised. I've been cooking since the first time Ima allowed me to put my fingers in the dough. After I'd washed the mud off my hands, of course."

Deborah chuckled. "You should have seen the mess in the cooking area when she made her first bread. She liked the cooking, but she didn't have the same fondness for cleaning up the mess."

"And she would have made the Hebrew slaves in Egypt proud over the stout building blocks she'd made," Micah said.

"Abba, how could you say that? You told me it was the best you ever tasted." Miriam grinned and tugged at her father's beard.

"It was. I have never tasted better bricks. Now, if you children will be still, I will ask the One God to bless our meal."

Micah lifted his eyes and hands to ask the blessing and then passed the food to their guest.

Julius took a bite of the flatbread.

"You're right, great bricks. Perhaps a little too soft for building with, though."

Miriam reached for the fruit while laughter rippled around the table. "If I weren't so hungry, I'd throw these at you."

"Don't let them convince you, Miriam," Deborah said, her voice almost too soft to be heard. "You make me proud with your cooking. Everything is delicious."

"I don't know how you would know, Deborah." Micah's worried look came back. "All you do is move food from one side of your plate to the other. You need to eat to build your strength. Try some of this melon. It's fresh and sweet."

"I'll do that," Deborah said, putting a smidgen of melon into her mouth. She chewed the bite until it must have been liquid but spit the remains into a cloth. "Husband, I need to lie down." She leaned her head on Micah's shoulder. "Please forgive me," she said to Julius and Miriam.

"There is nothing to forgive," Julius said. "Is there anything I can do to help? May I carry you to your room?"

"No, I'll do it." Micah's eyes reflected his wife's pain. With care, he lifted her and carried her into the bedroom, laying her on the bed. He murmured something to her, too low for Julius to understand. Then he returned to the table.

The camaraderie of the previous moments was gone, replaced by a palpable silence.

"Is there nothing that can be done?" Julius asked. "I could go get Loukas, if you wish. Perhaps there is something he can do."

"No. He has done all he can. He told us this much last week. All he knew to do is give her a powder that we mix with wine for her. It would take a miracle to save her now, and the most we have with her is another few days. Or hours." Micah's voice wavered, and he stared at his wife lying so still on her bed. He took a deep breath. "I only pray that she does not suffer any more than she already is. She doesn't deserve this. She has done nothing but good all her life." An angry note roughened the edge of his voice.

Miriam looked down at her plate and pushed the meat back and forth with her knife.

They needed their privacy, but Julius proper decorum would not allow him to excuse himself yet. A fearful thought struck him. "Ah, sir, um, Micah, I mean," he said. "Is…isn't it a little dangerous to criticize—even indirectly—your God?"

Micah looked up, eyebrows raised. "No, not at all. Have you read any of the Psalms?"

"No. We have been studying laws, the writings of Moses."

"Perhaps Shelumiel should introduce you to the Psalms. Most were written by King David, a man whom God said was a man after His Own heart. David on many occasions seemed to have arguments or disagreements with the way God appeared to be handling things." Micah stopped. Then he grimaced. "It did sound as if I was accusing God of Deborah's illness, didn't it? I don't know what or who causes illnesses, but the Torah and the Prophets sometimes indicate God uses illness to punish stubborn, rebellious, or sinful people. Since Deborah is none of those things, it seems that God didn't cause this illness or at least that it is not her fault. Sometimes, though, I want someone or something to blame. Perhaps it is my own sin that has caused her illness, and God is punishing me."

"Oh, no, Abba. I can't believe it would be you. You always follow the laws. It's probably me." She buried her face in her hands.

"If it's your fault, Miriam, then it is also mine," Julius said, not wanting Miriam to accept the blame alone. He shifted in his seat. It was all he could do to resist the urge to put his arm around her to comfort her.

"No, no, Mirie, don't blame yourself. Remember, your mother's affliction began before your…your indiscretion. No, her illness is not your fault, nor yours either, Julius," Micah said. "God would not punish your mother for your wrong. Remember that the scriptures say God will no longer visit the sins of the parents on the children. The same would hold true for the sins of the children being visited on the parents. And in any case, she constantly asks for forgiveness for any sins. But we'll go to the temple to offer a sacrifice, just in case."

Miriam sniffled and nodded, raising her head. She rose from her pillow and began taking the remaining food to the cooking area.

Julius stared at his hands on the table. "Sir, maybe you could explain the purpose of sacrifice to your God. Some of the gods I used to worship wanted sacrifices. I think they must like the taste of blood, or maybe the priests did, since the gods were just made of wood or metal. It's something I have a problem understanding: why God would want the sacrifice of an innocent animal."

"It's simple, really," Micah said, gazing into the distance. "Not all sins require a sacrifice of atonement; they require only a repentant heart. That's what God wants most of all. But our laws say serious sin must be punished by death. If not the death of the sinner, then the death of something to take his place. An unblemished animal symbolizes perfection—without sin—and if something free of sin stands in for you, then you don't have to die."

"Do you mean we will live forever if we do these sacrifices and obey all the laws? I've seen some people here who are pretty ancient looking, but I don't think that they are older than people in Rome or other places."

"No." Micah smiled. "This physical life will end, but some of us believe we will still exist if we obey the laws closely enough. There are some Jews, though, a sect called the Sadducees, who believe physical death is final."

Miriam reentered the room and picked up their plates. "Then Ima will surely go to Heaven, Abba, won't she? And she won't have all this pain there."

Micah's face fell, and his voice broke again. "Yes, surely she will be out of this pain there. Perhaps it's wrong of us to want to keep her here. It's just that I would miss her so. God help me. I don't know how to live without her."

Micah sat up straighter. "Mirie, we are not providing a pleasant meal for our guest with this talk. Tell us about…about Hannah's baby."

"Oh, you should see her." Miriam brightened, and she turned to Julius. "My friend Hannah's baby is so sweet and snuggly. Her name is Martha, and she smiles and wiggles and makes baby noises. Yesterday, Hannah said she laughed for the first time when Isaiah held her high above his head and jiggled her. She's such a pretty baby, too, with big dark eyes and thick long lashes. She has pudgy little fingers and fat little feet that beg to be kissed and tickled."

"I haven't seen her since Passover," Micah said. "I suppose she's grown."

"Yes, she feels heavier. She used to be this tiny creature, and it seemed she didn't have a bone or muscle in her little body, she was so pliable. Now her muscles are stronger. Hannah says she rolls over by herself." Miriam laughed. "She watches her hands and seems surprised they belong to her."

Julius hadn't been around many infants, and Miriam's enthusiasm over this one didn't really sink into his thinking, although he smiled and nodded at what he hoped were the right times. He pictured instead Miriam large with his child, and desire for her rose. Warmth rose from his throat to his face, and he hoped neither Micah nor Miriam could guess his thoughts. He couldn't take his eyes off Miriam. *She's so beautiful, and she doesn't even seem to know it. I wish her father would let us marry. I'd spend a lifetime convincing her.*

Miriam's eyes met his. Her cheeks turned rosy. She licked bread crumbs from her lips, and Julius wondered if she felt the same desire for him.

Micah cleared his throat "Ah, Mirie, didn't you make a honey cake for us?"

"Oh, yes. I nearly forgot. I'll get it." She jumped to her feet and trotted into the kitchen.

She reentered the room with a cake and placed it on the table. She sliced it into pieces, one for each of them.

"It looks delicious, Miriam," Julius took the large piece she offered him, brushing her hand with his. She jerked back as though she'd been burned.

Julius took a bite. "Mm." He nodded. The cake was baked to perfection, pinkish in color and sweetened with pomegranates and honey. His gaze rose to hers as he sucked honey from his fingers. He could not turn his eyes away from her. *Most High, please stop me. She's not a woman of the streets. Help me resist the temptation to treat her like one.*

Chapter 18

"Mirie! Mirie!" Micah's panicky voice roused Miriam from the bottom-most layer of sleep. "Get up! I need your help."

Miriam rubbed her eyes, rose from her pallet, and pulled her tunic over her head. "What is it, Abba?" She blinked at the sunrise shining through the window.

"Your mother…she won't wake up."

"Maybe she's more tired than usual." Miriam pulled her warm cloak over her shoulders as she hurried down the stairs.

"No. I tried everything, even slapping her hands. She won't wake. What shall we do?" Her father, usually the calm, competent leader, wrung his hands and pled for help with anxious eyes.

"I'll go get Loukas." She threw a scarf over sleep-tousled hair, a cloak around her shoulders, and ran out the door, heedless of her bare feet.

She rounded the corner of the synagogue and nearly collided with Julius.

"Whoa, Miriam." He caught her arms. "Where are you going in such a hurry?"

"My mother. She won't wake. I need to find Loukas." She broke from his grasp and ran again in the direction of Loukas' home.

"Wait, I'll go with you." He ran after her. When they reached Loukas' house, Quinta answered the door.

"Shalom, Julius." She rubbed her eyes. "There is something wrong?"

"Hello, Quinta. This is Miriam. Her mother is one of Loukas' patients."

"We need to talk to Loukas, please, quickly." Miriam gasped for breath.

"I am so sorry. Loukas and Joanna are not here. They say they go early to the synagogue, to hear a new prophet, I think."

"Thank you, Quinta." Julius waved good-bye as he turned and hurried after Miriam.

Miriam raced back toward the synagogue, battling the strong wind in her face.

She rushed through the gate, looking left and right. Which way would Loukas have gone? Mobs of people extended in both directions. Where did they all come from? She turned to the right and plunged into the crowd, wishing she were tall enough to see over the heads of the people. How would she ever find Loukas? He had to be there somewhere. She turned to ask Julius if he could see Loukas and realized Julius had disappeared, lost in the crowd. *O Adonai, help me. Help me, please.* Miriam hesitated. Should she go back to find Julius or search for Loukas alone? She listened hard, hoping to hear Loukas' voice or Julius calling her name, but the crowd made it impossible to hear anything above the noise. She continued to push through the masses and climbed on a set of steps into the building. *There!* She spotted Loukas and Joanna in front of a Man seated on a low wall. She squeezed past one person after another until she reached Loukas.

She hurried to them as fast as she could and tugged on Loukas' sleeve. "I'm so glad I found you." Miriam had to raise her voice to be heard, even standing next to him. "My mother needs you. Abba couldn't wake her this morning."

The Man hesitated in His speaking and looked straight into Miriam's eyes. Startled at His attention, she fell silent.

Loukas patted her shoulder, and Joanna pulled Miriam close, patting her on the back.

"Wait, child," Joanna said into Miriam's ear. "The Master has nearly finished."

Within moments, Jesus stood. People surged forward. Some supported others suffering from severe disabilities.

Loukas turned to Miriam.

"There is nothing more I can do for your mother, Miriam, but perhaps this Prophet Jesus can. He seems to have a close connection to God. He healed some people who came to Him earlier."

"How can we bring her here? She's not awake and too weak even if she were. I can't carry her, and I don't think Abba can carry her this far."

"We will put a blanket between two poles and carry her. Let's go." He grabbed Joanna with one hand and Miriam with the other. Together they thrust their way through the mass.

Micah met them at the door. Leah and Amos stood behind him. Leah wrung her hands. Tears rolled down her pinched face.

"Abba, we need to take Ima to the synagogue. There is a Prophet Who heals there." Between Loukas and Miriam, they explained their hopes of a miracle from this new Prophet. Following Loukas' instructions, they built a stretcher to carry Deborah.

At the synagogue the sheer number of people exiting the area made it impossible to carry Deborah without being bumped. Leah walked on one side, Miriam and Joanna on the other, trying to thread people away from the makeshift stretcher. When they arrived at the steps where Jesus spoke, He was gone. Micah's face fell, and Miriam's eyes filled with tears.

Loukas turned to a thin bald man with a scraggly beard standing nearby.

"Do you know where the Prophet went?"

"No. He and his friends went that way." He pointed with a sharp chin toward the gate. "I don't know where they were going. Hah! Maybe not far, maybe a long way, but it is soon the Sabbath." He beamed a gap-toothed grin as though he had delivered a great joke. Then, chortling, he turned and left them.

Amos and Micah turned the makeshift stretcher around, and they led the way toward the gate. Every few steps, Loukas would stop someone to ask if they had seen the Prophet. Finally, a man entering the gate said the Prophet and his followers had been asked by one of the Pharisees to join him for the evening meal. Loukas took Amos' place on the stretcher.

"We must have passed Him in the crowd without seeing Him," Miriam said. "Or maybe they took a different street."

"They must have, or we would have seen Him," Amos agreed, wiping his forehead. "Sunset begins the Sabbath, so they will have to settle themselves by then, or surely the wrath of God will fall upon them. What if we don't find Him? How much farther can we go before God's anger is stretched out against us?"

"I don't know what the Almighty would think about that, Amos. It's His job to judge, not mine. The law says we are to honor the Sabbath and keep it holy. The rabbis say we may travel 2,000 cubits outside our city walls and back again. Some more recent rabbis reinterpreted it at 4,000. So, perhaps one could travel all around the interior and even the exterior of this city all evening without dishonoring the Sabbath."

"That would be honoring the letter of the law, but wouldn't it be dishonoring the spirit of the law? I wonder, if we don't find the Prophet by sunset, He might not come to heal her."

"Tell me, Amos, are you seeking to become a Pharisee?" Micah asked.

Amos blushed. "Of course not. But I'm concerned we could be breaking the holy laws. God might punish us by taking Deborah from us this day or perhaps by striking another or all of us with her disease because Miriam wears no scarf. Deborah also has no covering on her head."

Miriam put her hand to her hair and gasped. Micah's eyes widened as he looked at his daughter. His mind must have been elsewhere, too.

Micah's shoulders slumped. "Perhaps we should take Deborah home. One of us can try to find the Prophet and bring Him to our home. If He will. We can't carry her all over the city to find him. I know all this jostling must hurt her." He sighed then turned toward their home, leading the procession back to their house. "No sense in tempting the Pharisees to call for the guards."

Loukas' head twisted right and left as Micah and Amos spoke. His eyebrows angled upward. "It's against the laws to heal on the Sabbath? I've given out potions and set broken legs on whatever day they were needed."

"There are some who would say so. Sometimes obeying all the oral law of the scribes in addition to the Law of Moses isn't practical. Why would one allow a person to die or suffer untreated on the Sabbath?"

Upon arrival at their home, Micah lifted Deborah from the stretcher and placed her on their bed, bending to kiss her cheek.

"Amos can go after the Prophet, right Amos?" Micah said.

"But I...I don't remember all the directions." Amos' brow wrinkled.

"I remember the directions, Husband." Leah tugged at his sleeve. "We'll go together."

"I'll stay here with Deborah." Micah's gaze fastened on his wife. "Mirie, would you fix us some food? We haven't eaten yet this day, and it's midday. Perhaps the Master might also want something."

"We'll eat when we return. Let's *go,* Amos." Leah pulled a reluctant Amos through the door.

"I'll cut some bread and cheese." Miriam's shoulders slumped as she dragged herself into the kitchen. *I wonder what happened to Julius. I lost him in that crowd and never saw him again. Maybe he gave up trying to find me.*

This might be a good time to tell her father about the soldier. The day couldn't get any worse.

Julius and his cohort herded a group of bruised and surly men to the dungeon. *Of all the times for a fight to break out. You'd think at least on a Sabbath, the Jews would be more civil to each other.* One stabbed a publican with a knife because he collected taxes, calling the man a traitor. The man would survive, but his assailant might not.

Julius could only pray that Deborah was all right, but he couldn't leave. He had to finish his duties. If only he hadn't lost Miriam in the crowd when he bent to retrieve the scarf. He would have avoided this matter, and he would have been able to be beside her in this harsh moment that Miriam faced. *Adonai, I cannot protect her from the pain of death. I pray that You will comfort her and Micah.* He clasped the scarf in his hands. *I lost my mother, and I know how she would feel. I do not want Miriam to suffer that pain. Please grant that Deborah will become well.*

Julius brought the scarf to his face and inhaled. The heady scent of his beloved remained on the cloth. If he slept with it at night, he'd dream about her. He tucked the scarf under his breastplate and smiled to himself. On the other hand, he could keep it with him all day, too.

Chapter 19

Leah cast a worried glance in Micah and Deborah's direction as she and Amos left.

The sun was at its zenith. A dog panted in the shade of a tree. A bird perched on a limb, wings out and beak open. Leah wiped the sweat from her forehead. If they didn't find this Jesus soon, it would be only a matter of hours before Deborah would die.

Adonai, please help us find the Healer quickly.

"I hope you remember how to get to this Judah's house. You do know that half the men in Jericho are named Judah, don't you?" Amos scowled, his tone petulant "How do you know where to find the right one?"

"We'll look for the Pharisee named Judah who has a crowd in his home. The man we talked to did give us simple directions. We can find him. We have the Lord to guide us, too."

"I can't help but think maybe He might be reluctant to help us this day. Miriam did not have a covering on her head. Nor did Deborah."

Leah stopped in her tracks. She spun around, hands on her hips. "Amos bar Abram, what kind of God do you think our Lord is, anyway? One who would strike us dead for trying to help someone who is sick? One who is more concerned about the covering on our heads than whether we would go for help for someone we love?"

"Well, maybe *He* wouldn't be so angry with us. Maybe. But what about the Pharisees? Don't they have the ear of God when it comes to matters like these? If they condemn us, surely God would agree with them."

"So you think God obeys the Pharisees rather than the Pharisees obeying Him? Wouldn't that make the Pharisees more God-like than God? Didn't God condemn Satan for that very idea?"

Amos reddened. "Yes, I guess so."

Without anything further, Leah turned and again hurried in the direction of the north wall. Amos followed after her.

When they reached the street next to the wall, Leah turned to the right and stopped in front of a luxurious home. Palm trees swayed gently in the light breeze and acacia trees shaded the spacious brick house. The stench of rotted vegetation and offal, common in the inner city, seemed less noticeable here. Leah stopped, searching about her.

Amos came beside her peering right and left and behind them. "Is this it?" he whispered.

"I believe so. Let's go ask." She strode to the door, but Amos remained in the street, his stance that of a man who would run at a moment's notice.

Leah knocked with more confidence than she felt. A servant opened the door.

She glanced back at Amos, hoping he would speak. When he didn't, she took a deep breath. "We seek the Prophet called Jesus. Is He here?"

"And what is it that you wish? My master is dining with Jesus and his friends and doesn't wish to be disturbed."

He reached for the door to close it, and Leah bolted forward. "It's important. My sister is dying, and I heard that Jesus has the power to heal." Leah raised her voice and tried to sound as haughty as the servant looked, but her tone sounded more like pleading to her ears.

"Come back later. They are eating now. If your sister still lives when they are finished, perhaps Jesus will hear your plea then."

Leah stared at the man, her mouth agape. Then she shook her head. She had to do something or her beloved sister would be gone from her. "I will wait here." She dropped to the ground cross-legged in front of the door. "I will not leave until I see Jesus. If you wish to have passersby seeing a woman sitting in front of your door until they finish eating, then so be it."

The servant's eyes widened. "You cannot do that. You must leave and return in perhaps an hour or two."

"I will not leave." Leah crossed her arms and ignored not only the servant but also the silent signals her husband sent her with his eyes.

The servant curled his lips into an angry snarl and slammed the door as he retreated.

Amos dashed to his wife and whispered, "Come, Leah. We must leave. He'll be sending for the guards, and we'll be thrown in prison." He tugged on her arm. "Let's *go*."

Leah refused to budge or to speak.

The door reopened, and Amos jumped as though he'd been prodded with a staff. The Pharisee stood at the door, his servant hovering behind.

"Leave my property, you scum of a poisoned swamp. Leave now, or I will send for the soldiers. You and your husband—and I only assume this man is your husband—will be imprisoned for a good long time, I will see to it." His eyes narrowed to an icy slit.

Leah glanced at her husband, who threw her a fearful "What-did-I-tell-you?" look.

Leah scooted around to turn her back toward the Pharisee. Amos tugged her arm.

"Wife, we have to go. Now."

Judah turned to his servant. "Inform the guards a trespasser refuses to leave my property."

The servant shot a triumphant glance at Leah and trotted off in the direction of the guards' compound.

Amos tried to lift Leah to her feet, but she kept her legs folded. Then he tried to drag her away. Leah struggled to free herself from him. She could have kicked Amos in frustration, but she had no desire to hurt her husband. Amos seemed determined to hold on without injuring her, and he pled with urgent hisses into her ear.

A Man moved past Judah and knelt at Leah's side. "What is it you want, Daughter?"

Amos gasped, dropped her arms, and jerked backward.

"A-are you the Man called Jesus?" Leah looked up at him. "Yes."

Leah took a deep breath and held her hand to her heart. "My sister, Deborah—she sleeps and won't awaken. She's been sick for months. We've heard You have the power to heal. Please, would You come and heal her? We don't have great riches, but we would give all we have to see her healed."

Amos' eyes flew open wide, and he opened his mouth to speak until Jesus looked at him. Instead he nodded.

"You love her." Jesus' look took in both Amos and Leah.

Leah's eyes filled with tears. "I wish it were me instead of her."

Eyes wide, Amos fell beside his wife. "No, I wouldn't want my wife to trade places with Deborah. But Deborah is a good woman. She's loved by all who know her. Her husband is distraught, her daughter weeps for her, and her sister—my wife—would trade her places without hesitation. We would all be happy to see Deborah back in good health."

"Please, Rabbi, would You heal her?" Leah lifted a teary gaze to the Master.

"I would. Do you believe Me?"

"I do, Lord," Leah said.

Jesus turned to Amos. "And you?"

"I have heard many stories, Sir."

"You won't believe them until you see it yourself, Amos?" Jesus asked, smiling.

"No, that…that's not what I meant, exactly." He didn't seem to notice that Jesus had called him by name, but Leah had heard. She gasped.

"Go. See for yourself, and believe."

"Go where, Lord?" Amos' confusion washed across his face.

"I think we're supposed to go see Deborah," Leah said, hope blooming in her heart. "Thank you, Lord."

Comprehension began to dawn on Amos' face, and he looked at Jesus.

Jesus smiled again and nodded but said nothing.

This time, Amos smiled. Then he held his hands out to Leah, still seated cross-legged on the ground. Leah smiled back and allowed him to pull her to her feet.

"Thank You, Adonai," Amos said as they were leaving.

Chapter 20

Miriam stood outside her parents' bedchamber, her face against the wall, her shoulders shaking with her sobs. Her father had not left Ima's side. He continued to stroke the hair from Ima's face, and Miriam could not bear to watch any longer.

Her mother was slipping away from her. Part of Miriam wanted to let Ima go, to realize that she would be free of pain and at peace, but they still wanted Ima's love and care.

"Micah, my love, why do you weep?"

At her mother's voice, Miriam spun around.

Micah gasped. "You're back! Oh, praise be to God, you are back."

"I'm back? What do you mean?" Ima asked as Miriam dropped to her knees beside Abba.

"I was so afraid you would die. You haven't moved since last night," her father said. "I thought at first you were just sleeping, so I didn't disturb you. But this morning, you wouldn't wake when I called your name, nor when I patted your cheek, nor even when we carried you in search for the Prophet who can heal, you did not awake. For the past hour, you lay so still, and I could not see you breathing. I thought…I thought you had gone from us."

"I feel weak, but I think this is not the day I will die. I'm thirsty. Would you bring me a little milk?"

"Of course. I'll go get some right now. Will you stay awake while I am gone?"

"I will try," she said, a faint smile on her lips.

Micah ran from the room calling for Loukas and Joanna as he went.

Miriam stayed by her mother's side. "Oh, Ima, I'm am so glad you didn't leave us."

"So am I." Deborah said. "I am weak, but I am alive." Her voice was so faint that Miriam had to lean forward to hear her.

"We were so worried about you, Ima."

"I know."

A commotion sounded outside the door.

"Leah and Amos, come in here, to our bedroom." Miriam's father called. "Come see the miracle."

Amos and Leah appeared in the doorway.

"Deborah, you're awake." Leah beamed.

Amos' eyes widened and his mouth formed an "O."

"Yes," Deborah said.

Abba reentered the room, spilling a little of the milk in his hurry. He grinned at the loved ones around Ima's bed and pulled on Miriam's arm to move her aside. He knelt beside the bed and gently lifted his wife's head and shoulders so she could drink the milk. She took a few sips and lay back with a contented sigh.

"That was so good."

"The swallowing didn't hurt?" Loukas asked.

"No."

"The lumps seem smaller." He leaned forward and touched one lump under her chin.

"Good."

Abba kissed her cheek. "Would you like for us to leave you alone so you can rest?"

"No, stay. More milk?"

Micah obliged, and Deborah took a few more swallows.

He turned to Leah and Amos. "Didn't you find the Prophet?"

"Yes, we found Him," Leah said, beaming still. "He…He is the most wonderful Man. So kind. His eyes were filled with compassion. The Pharisee he dined with was a nasty little man, and I had little hope…."

"So Leah sat in front of his door, refusing to leave," Amos broke in. "I was so afraid we would be arrested. The Pharisee…."

Leah waved her hands to silence her husband. "I will not give one more thought to that evil man, but Jesus. He is someone I believe in."

"He asked us if we believed," Amos nodded. "And I think He meant much more than that we believed that He could heal Deborah. When I said I believed Him, I meant that I believed in Him, just not in his words."

"True…and look, my sister lives. How could I not believe in a Prophet who would give my sister back to me.?"

Even in the excitement, Ima's eyes drooped. She rolled her head toward her husband. "I'm a little tired, now."

"Of course. All of you, come back tomorrow morning to break your fast, and we'll continue this story."

"We'll be here," Amos agreed, a catch in his voice.

Miriam bent and kissed her mother and then walked quietly up the stairs into her room. She knelt again on the hard wooden floor beside the pallet that served as her bed. "Adonai, thank You for giving us this time with Ima. I don't know if she is healed. She still seems so weak. This isn't what I think of when I think of healing. I want to see her up and dancing at festivals and being a midwife again. O Adonai, please, complete her healing."

She rose from her kneeling position and got into bed, realizing for the first time that evening how cold she felt. Her feet felt like ice. She wrapped up tight in her lamb's wool blanket, pulled it over her head, and shivered. Gradually, her body warmed, but sleep refused to come. The events of this day exceeded any other day in her memory, and her head whirled. She still needed to tell her parents of her attack, but would it be wise to tell Ima now? It was the fourth watch when she finally slumbered, but even so, her sleep was uneasy. She woke so many times, rolled over, and dozed again. It seemed only a few moments that she slept before Abba called up the stairs to wake her.

Miriam yawned, stretched, and rose from the bed, still ruminating over the previous day's events. Before going to the cooking area to prepare flatbread for the morning meal, she stopped to see her mother. Miriam knelt beside Ima, and she laid her head on her mother's shoulder.

Ima lifted her hand to touch Miriam's mussed hair. "I wish I could comb your pretty hair, beloved Daughter. Perhaps tomorrow I will be stronger. Why are you staring at me so?"

"Ima! Your face...all the swelling is gone around your throat. Your voice sounds better. Clearer. How do you feel?"

"Better than last night. In fact, better than I have felt for a long time. The past weeks seem like such a blur. I'm not even sure what was dream and what was real."

Amos and Leah entered the house, their voices preceding them through the door. Abba came in the back entrance carrying a bowl of milk.

"Good morning, children." Abba's happy voice bounced off the rafters. "Is breakfast ready yet?"

"It will be soon" Miriam stood and called back to him. "I'm headed for the cooking area now, and I'll have it ready in just a few minutes. Patience." Miriam stepped out of the room.

"May I help, Miriam?" Leah spoke with a happy lilt to her voice.

"Yes, would you go to the dugout and bring the lamb leg under the left side of the straw? It shouldn't be hard to find. We'll have some cold pieces of meat with our bread. There should be some butter next to it, too."

"Sounds good to me."

Miriam placed the bread to bake and reentered the main room to place plates and knives on the low table. When all was ready, Abba carried Ima to the table, kneeling and placing her on several pillows. He reclined beside her, offered thanks for the meal, and lifted a cup of milk to her lips. She lifted her hand to help hold the cup. She didn't eat the meat or bread but nibbled on a piece of melon. She laid her head against Abba and watched as the others talked about the previous day's activities.

Leah and Amos still sounded excited about their contact with the Prophet, Jesus. Micah laughed as Amos described trying to drag Leah away from the Pharisee's house.

"I never thought I would have the courage or the audacity to stand up...or rather sit down...to my husband." Leah laughed. "Let alone to a Pharisee. You should have seen the look on his face. Like an evil nightmare. I think he wanted to kill me. If the Prophet hadn't been there, he might have. But then, if the Prophet hadn't been there, neither would I."

"I had a dream yesterday. I think it was a dream, anyway," Ima said.

Miriam jumped at the sound of her mother's voice. "What was it, Ima?"

"I stood in between heaven and earth. Heaven was beautiful beyond anything I have ever seen. The sound of lyres and a myriad other instruments playing, colors beyond my best imaginings, and delightful scents of food and flowers. My mother and father stood in front of a beautiful gate with One Who had a shining face, waving to me, and I wanted so much to go to them. But then I looked behind me—and there stood my husband, my daughter, and my sister, pleading with sad eyes for me to stay. I asked with my heart—because no words were needed—*Which way should I go? To this peaceful place or back to my family in this world of pain?* I knew these precious ones needed me more, at least for now. Someday later, I will join my parents in the beautiful place."

Abba's eyes were moist and his voice broke as he spoke. "Thank you for coming back. You were so far away. I could feel you leaving us, and you were taking my heart with you."

"I'm so very glad to see you awake and feeling better. No words can tell you how glad I am." Leah nodded, her eyes filling with tears, and she lifted her glass of watered wine toward her sister.

Miriam looked at her mother with a tentative hope in her heart. "Do you mean you think you had a choice?"

"It seemed so. But it might have just been a dream."

"A dream, or real, it doesn't matter. I'm forever grateful you are back." Miriam's eyes misted as she reached to hug her mother.

When Julius arrived home he didn't see . He'd gone to the culina to grab some raisins and brought them back to the common area when Cyril entered, his gaze on the floor, his shoulder's slumped forward.

Julius lifted an eyebrow. "What's wrong, my friend? Why so glum?"

"Nothing," Cyril shrugged and tromped into the culina.

Julius followed. "Cyril, you've always been frank with me before, unless someone other than Marcus was around. So spit it out. What's burning you?"

"I told you, nothing. Nothing you can do anything about." He strode past Julius and picked up a cleaver from a workbench.

"Tell me anyway. At least I'll listen. Maybe sharing the burden will make it easier." Julius pulled Cyril around to face him.

"You cannot change the way I was born. I have been a slave all my life, and your 'sharing the burden' will not change that." Cyril sneered the words, and then brushed past Julius to the rump of beef on the table, slashing strips of meat from the bone in angry swipes.

Julius leaned against the wall. "And why is your status so important to you so suddenly?"

Cyril slammed the knife down. "Because I went to see Loukas today to inquire about the prospect of wedding Quinta. It will never be. Loukas and Joanna will be freeing Quinta. They have plans to adopt her, and they will not allow her to enter into slavery again with me."

"Aha!" Julius straightened. "But I *can* change that, Cyril. I wanted to tell you after we...you...were through the course with Shelumiel. I was saving it for a gift of congratulations. I intended to free you then."

Cyril picked up a rag to wipe the table. "Free me? What would that solve? I might be free, but I would have no work to support Quinta, presupposing that Loukas would be daft enough to betroth her to a man with no means to support her." He threw the rag across the room where it disappeared through the open window. A yelp from the courtyard let them know the rag had made contact.

Julius leaned out the window. "Sorry, Marcus. I think that rag was meant for me. Cyril's aim is a little off today."

He turned back to face his friend. "Now, Cyril, listen to me. I like having you around. True, you've been my slave, but you've been more than that. A friend, a brother, all my life. I can afford to pay you a salary. You know that. Or, if you would rather, I can recommend you as a soldier. You might even rise through the ranks and surpass me."

Cyril stood stock-still. His glare weakened. A long pause ensued.

"Why would you do that? I mean, why would you give up good property? Maybe a troublesome piece of property, but I still work." He smiled.

"I think I just said why. I like having you around. And you're a lot easier to have around when you're not like a lion with a sore paw. So, if you are married and still working for me, then I can still enjoy the benefits of having a friend, maybe no longer lionish, by my side. If you are a soldier, unless you surpass me in the hierarchy, I can try to keep you in my contingent. And if you're in my contingent, you're still a friend who would guard my back. At least I hope." He raised an eyebrow and cast a glance at the cleaver.

"I…I think…hmm. What should I say? Other than thank you, I mean. I'm without words. Uh, would you mind if I went back to Loukas' house to tell him this bit of news?"

Julius nodded. "I'd like to go with you. I can reinforce what you tell him and add my approval."

"I guess, uh…yes, let's go." Cyril grinned so hard Julius was sure his jaw must hurt.

Chapter 21

Julius, along with a very happy Cyril, made his way back to Loukas' house. When they arrived, Julius knocked at the door, and Quinta greeted them. She blushed when her eyes met Cyril's. Her eyes were red and swollen.

"Come, I will get Loukas. He is here." Her voice broke, and she turned and ran away.

Loukas walked into the room. "Shalom, my friends. To what do I owe the honor of this visit?"

"Cyril came to talk to you earlier, but he had only half the story," Julius said. "What he didn't know was my intention to free him when he was through with the proselyte training. I want him to either stay on as my servant or to become one of the soldiers under my command, his choice. He says he wants to wed Quinta. Would it be acceptable to you, too, if he were a free man with a steady income?"

Loukas ran a hand along the side of his face, nodding. "That could make a difference. I want Quinta to marry according to her wishes, but as her father, I must also protect her from hardship and the heartaches which can accompany following that wish. Let's just say I would consider it, contingent upon Cyril becoming an official proselyte and free." Loukas' brows drew together. "Still, I will only make a decision that I think will be for her good."

"I am sincere about the desire to become a proselyte, Loukas, and I will do my best to convince you I am worthy of Quinta." Cyril said.

"Perhaps you could ask Shelumiel if he knows how long it will be until you are accepted as a proselyte."

Julius peered about him to make sure no women stood nearby. "He has asked us to consider our dedication and the…um…uncomfortable procedure that comes with it."

"I have decided. If God requires it of me to become a proselyte, I am ready." Cyril beamed.

"Julius, if you, also, have made this decision, we should visit Shelumiel now." Loukas lifted his hand toward the open doorway.

"Second best idea I've heard this day." Cyril laughed as they strode through the opening.

On their way to find Shelumiel, Loukas sobered. "You know, Shelumiel will foremost want to know you two are not going into this for the love of a woman. Our God demands that we have no other gods before Him. If Shelumiel believes the love of a woman is more important to you than your love for God, he will not agree. This is something you have to be absolutely sure of in your heart of hearts."

"I know my own commitment to God is above my commitment to Miriam. I love her with my whole heart, but as I found out when Micah said he would not break his promise, I want God in my life. I needed His help to get through the hurt."

Cyril nodded. "To me it's as though I don't have a choice. I'm convinced there is no god but this God, so where else would I go? There seems to be within me a need for an absolute intelligence who can guide me through the muddles of this life. I know I'm an intelligent man, but I don't know everything. I need someone smarter than I am who will lead me where I should go and help me not go where I shouldn't."

Loukas brushed away a bee from his sleeve. "All of us have those tendencies, I guess. And even though I know that sometimes God wishes me not to go in one direction, it's sometimes more than I can do to resist. Many times, I find myself asking His forgiveness after I've come up short once again."

"You mean He won't remove the temptations?" Julius cocked an eyebrow.

"No, he doesn't, but we can access His help to resist. He doesn't take our evil nature away from us, as much as I'm sure at times He'd like to.

"Come now. Instincts protect us in many cases." Julius put his hand to his scabbard. "You aren't trying to tell us instincts are wrong, are you?"

"No, not always," Loukas said. "But what if we always followed our instincts? In a way, letting instincts be our god? What enters your mind when you see an attractive woman with inviting eyes?"

Julius' face warmed, and he cast a glance at Cyril. His friend's face had also reddened.

"You see? That's instinct. But God wants us to be better than animals, using His strength to resist evil."

The men lapsed silent. They arrived at Shelumiel's residence still quiet. Loukas knocked at Shelumiel's door, and the rabbi answered. He ushered them into his simple dwelling. There were no frills, no elaborate drapes on the walls, but the room was spacious and contained a low table and cushions. A faint smell of incense hung on the air. They sat, and Julius and Cyril cleared their throats almost at the same time.

Julius swiped his hand through his curls. "Rabbi, we came to ask if you think we're ready to become proselytes. We have thought over our last discussion with you, and we feel that we are ready to take that step. Loukas came with us because he is our sponsor, and he's also curious."

"And what precipitates this curiosity from the three of you?" Shelumiel asked. "I hear stories that you wish to be betrothed to a Jewish woman, Julius. I don't like hearing these tales from others. Were you keeping them from me for a reason?" Shelumiel lifted a hand and stared at his wrinkled knuckles as if he didn't care to hear Julius' response.

But on the day when Shelumiel asked about the circumcision, Cyril had believed that Shelumiel truly did wish to see their conversion.

"Did you think that in a village the size of Jericho you could hide your obvious motives?" Shelumiel lifted his gaze and held Julius'.

"No, sir." Julius' response was instantaneous and emphatic. "I mean, I didn't keep anything from you. Although I do care for Miriam, chances are small that her parents will allow her to marry me. She is promised to someone else. In fact, it was finding out about her promise to this other man that made me realize I wanted God in my life whether or not God provided a miracle and allowed us to wed. I have left the matter in God's hands. If He wishes for a betrothal for Miriam and me, He will make a way."

"But you also know that without being a proselyte, Roman, there is no possibility to be her husband. And you want me to believe there was no ulterior motive? Our God does not tolerate deception."

A long silence ensued while Julius struggled with his anger. He remembered Loukas' words about instincts, and he took a deep breath.

"Rabbi, you are right when you say that He is *our* God. I have already decided He is owed my worship. I understand your reluctance to continue with our lessons. If you wish to withdraw, I understand. Perhaps another rabbi will be willing to teach us. Forgive us for taking your time." He bowed his head respectfully and turned to leave.

"Wait, Roman. I did not excuse you. Nor you Greeks, either."

Julius had not known that Cyril or Loukas had also chosen to follow him. He nearly collided with them when he turned.

"I know Loukas' faith to be real, because he came to me with no motive other than to find the One True God. I do not have that assurance with you, although that Loukas came with you today speaks for you. In other words, your faith remains to be proven. With that in mind, I cannot approve your step forward to become proselytes," he said, as their faces fell. "At least not yet. But I'm willing to be convinced."

"Rabbi, you taught us for the past couple of months. We came to you in good faith that you would teach us to know better the God we came to believe is real. I have to admit it was the hope of being able to meet Miriam that first introduced me to Him, but that's not what keeps me wanting to know more. The more I learn about Him, the God Who cares about even the smallest man, the more I want to learn. Even saying this, I'm not sure anything I can say will make you believe in us." The bitterness Julius felt seeped through his voice and filled his face and rigid posture.

Cyril shrugged. "I thought you wanted to teach us more about God. I came to you wondering if God is real. Julius certainly believes so. Through you and through Loukas and Julius, I began to be convinced. We bared our thoughts to you and trusted you and your words. Now you tell us you think we played you false. Perhaps it is the other way. Perhaps it is you who played us false." He lifted his shoulders again and turned to Julius. "Shall we go, master? I do not care if he has dismissed us or not."

"Wait. Julius, Cyril, hear me out." Loukas turned a pleading countenance on Julius and Cyril who had stepped toward the door. In unison, Julius turned with Cyril.

Loukas clasped a hand on the rabbi's shoulder. "Shelumiel, maybe you are not convinced of the truth of their desire to know God, but I am. I have spent more hours in their company than you, and it could be I know them better. They broke bread with me twice, during the Feasts of Purim and Passover. I watched their eyes go from curious on Julius and disbelieving on Cyril to both of them avidly and joyously learning all they could. Is there a wrong reason for wanting to get to know Him as long as it is an honest desire? If people decide near death that they want Him in what is left of their lives, should they be refused? Some do not believe until they see a miracle; is it wrong for them to be convinced by such an act? Some might find themselves fearing for a loved one's life or health and turn to Him; would God then turn his back? I think not. Would you not, if they were unbelieving, want to persuade them our God is real?"

Shelumiel nodded. "You state convincing arguments. I will give these some thought."

"Does that mean we are accepted as proselytes?" Julius' tone was still flat, but a note of hope began to sing in a corner of his heart.

"Be sure this is your honest desire."

"It is, Rabbi." Julius' muscles relaxed a little.

Cyril's arms folded across his chest. "I'm not so sure. I want to continue studying, but I'd like to study under a rabbi who believes in me and in whom I can believe. God, I believe in. Julius, I believe in. Loukas, I believe in. You? Now, I'm not so sure."

Shelumiel's eyes widened. *"You* don't believe in *me?"*

"Maybe you should tell us why we should continue studying with you." Cyril's eyes began to twinkle.

A corner of Shelumiel's mouth twitched. "I understand. Come back tomorrow. I'll let you know my decision, and you may let me know yours."

Chapter 22

Julius strode away from Shelumiel's door, following his two friends.

"That turned out better than it might have." Loukas grinned and cleared his throat. "Would you like to hear some good news?

"From the look on your face, it must be *very* good news. What is it?" Julius asked.

"Deborah was very near death, in a deep sleep that she would probably not awaken from. But now she is feeling much better. In fact, I'd call it a miracle."

Julius stopped and grabbed Loukas' shoulders. "What? How did it happen?"

"You remember that Prophet, Jesus?"

"How could I forget Him? Did He go to their house?" Julius thought back to the scene at the river.

"No, but He did heal her. Deborah's sister and her husband found Him and asked for Deborah's healing. He told them to 'Go and believe,' and when they got back home, she was awake and drinking milk."

"Blessed be the Name of the Lord," Julius murmured in awe. If the One God could heal Deborah, maybe He could also provide a way for Miriam and him.

Cyril touched Loukas' elbow. "I'm glad God heard their prayers and healed her. It reminds me, a few months ago, you told us you believed in God because of an answer to prayer. Tell us about it?"

"There was a time when Joanna was very ill, like Deborah has been. She grew weaker and weaker until she could do nothing but recline on our bed. Nothing in my training provided the knowledge I needed to treat her." Loukas rubbed his forehead. "I left her in the care of the servants and went as fast as my horse could carry me to Antioch to consult with physicians there about the illness. They recommended several things from bloodletting to burying a freshly killed squirrel during the full moon, but none seemed to know how to cure this disease. I searched for one of the Greek temples in town to seek help from the gods and came across a Jewish synagogue first. I figured one god was as good as another and this was closer, so that's where I went." Loukas wiped he sweat from his forehead and waved a fly away.

Julius swatted at the same fly. "You didn't have to shoo it this direction, did you?"

"I didn't, but I guess he liked your smell better than mine." Loukas laughed at his own joke. "Anyway, a rabbi met me at the door and said I could not enter because I was a Gentile, but he would go with me to a quiet place, a nearby wooded area. There he listened while I poured out my worries for my wife. Sometimes he'd get a faraway look in his eyes. Soon he held up his hand to stop me and said, 'God says you should turn to Him and be exceeding glad, for He has heard your heart.' I asked if that meant Joanna would be restored to health. He just shook his head and said, 'I don't know.'

"I left for home. When I arrived, Joanna not only felt much better, but she flitted about telling the servant what to fix for dinner and to make enough for me because I would be home that day. When I asked her about it, she said our Adonai healed her. And more, it seems she'd been sneaking over to the synagogue behind my back. She'd been a proselyte for a year. I never knew."

He laughed and shook his head. "All the time I had been knocking on the doors of false gods, seeking help for her while she prayed to the One God for me. I decided to become a proselyte, too."

"That's a story for the ages." Julius clapped Loukas on the back. "Thank you for telling us."

Cyril smiled and nodded. "Yes. By the way, thank you for stepping into the conversation with Shelumiel. If it hadn't been for you, we might have been booted out with no hope of return. And if Shelumiel refused to accept us, I think no other Rabbi would teach us either. Your words of belief in us touched my heart."

"You would do the same for me if my sandals were on your feet."

"We owe you more than you can know and more than we can pay," Julius said. "You have only to ask if you ever have a need."

"Remember what you owe, and one day you will find a person who needs a favor. If you pass on the favor I have given you, you'll repay your debt to me and make our world a more pleasant place."

"I'll watch for every chance to convince you, especially as an outside chance still exists you might become my father-in-law."

"Wait, Cyril. Not only are you not yet a proselyte, you are not free, and I haven't agreed to anything. You count your colts before their dams are even pregnant."

"I am but a humble slave, o noble Loukas, and thus am used to subsisting on hopes and dreams." Cyril grinned.

"Slave you may be, but I've yet to see humility from you, and I've known you a long time." Julius stretched out his arms to show how long.

"Speaking of being humble, master of mine, have you asked the tribune if you may marry a local girl, supposing her promise ever gets cracked? Seems to me, that's a requirement, isn't it? His answer might keep you humble for some years to come."

"Yes it is, and yes it could. I'll go tomorrow. After we've seen Shelumiel and if he has decided to proceed."

"This is where I part from you for the evening," Loukas said as they approached an intersection. "I need to talk to Micah and Deborah before I go home. Deborah's healing still fascinates me."

"We could come with you." Julius raised an eyebrow. "Just for protection, you understand."

"Oh, yes, I do understand. Go home."

"Very well, we'll go home but only for a time. I've been invited to break bread with them again this evening. Or rather we have. Cyril will come with me."

Loukas stopped and turned to his friends. "You're getting to be a regular visitor there. Does this mean Micah is softening his position toward you?"

Julius scratched his head and smiled ruefully. "Not that I can tell. That man truly believes a promise must be kept."

Miriam woke and stretched, smiling to herself. Julius had come again for supper the evening before, this time bringing Cyril. They talked about their meeting with Shelumiel that morning, and Miriam felt sure this was the day they would be approved by Shelumiel. She held a small hope that her father would then drop the promise to James and agree to a betrothal with Julius. *This is the day that the Lord has made, and I will rejoice in it. O Lord, Master of the Universe, thank You for the words of Loukas yesterday that softened Shelumiel's heart, and please go with Julius and Cyril today. Open Shelumiel's eyes to see the sincerity in their hearts and the love they bear for You. Fill their mouths with wisdom as they answer his questions. And Adonai, if it is not too hard for You and if You agree, would you think about opening the way for Julius and me to marry?*

Miriam smiled. Her parents had warmed to Julius. They almost treated him as one of the family, and her mother teased him until his ears turned as red as his cloak. She softly sang a psalm as she hurried to the kitchen to prepare breakfast. She stopped short. Her mouth dropped open. Ima stood at the work table kneading the bread.

"Good morning, Daughter. Your voice is full of sunshine today."

"Good morning, Ima. I didn't expect to see you in here. Does this mean I'm free of breakfast chores?"

"Don't get your hopes too high. My little time of rest is over, and I'm happy to be back in the kitchen, but that doesn't mean you are free from any responsibilities. You may go get some eggs for us and set the table."

"Eggs? The chickens quit laying a month ago. They agreed it's too hot to work."

"Humph.. Lazy chickens. Cut their pay." Ima gave the bread dough an extra punch.

"Right—one locust instead of two for them today. But how do we convince the locusts to stay out of sight?" Miriam grasped her chin with one hand, her elbow with the other, a mock frown of thoughtfulness creasing her brow.

"That's your job. And my mouth hungered for eggs this morning. I guess we'll have figs and bread." Ima placed the loaves on the metal shelf on top of the fireplace.

"Given your improved appetite, perhaps I should bring in a leg of lamb, or maybe two." Miriam grinned.

"Good idea. I need to give your Abba something other than a skin full of bones to hold at night. There are entirely too many bones and not enough fat covering them. But if I keep this up, soon he'll be complaining I take too much room."

"Like Leah?" Miriam's eyes twinkled.

"I don't think that will happen. Only three more months until Leah has a little one in her arms, though. Then poor Amos might have to sleep on the floor."

"Not that it would hurt him. She spoils him. I wonder if he won't make her take the baby to the temple to give to the priests like Hannah did Samuel. Amos won't like having to divide Leah's attention between the baby and himself."

"Oh, I don't know. He's telling everyone who will listen that he's about to have a fine son. But I wonder what will happen if 'he' is a fine daughter, instead."

Miriam laughed. "That could be a brutal shock to his plans."

"He has plans? I never noticed." Ima chuckled, too.

"What are my girls giggling about?" Abba yawned and scratched his head. "How do you expect me to catch up on my lost sleep?"

"Good morning, Abba. We speculate on Amos' state of mind if their baby has the audacity to be born a girl instead of a boy."

"Hmm, that could be a problem." He joined in their laughter.

Chapter 23

Julius woke, his heart filled with anxiety and anticipation. Cyril walked into the room as Julius put his feet on the floor.

"Today is the day, isn't it?" Cyril brought Julius' tunic to him.

"You could say that." Julius heard his voice shake as he pulled the tunic over his head.

"I'm not sure if I'm looking forward to this or dreading it." Cyril walked back through the door to the kitchen.

"Let's get it over with. Breakfast, a brisk march, and then...." Julius tied his sandals and followed Cyril.

"Yes. And then either feast or famine."

"As God wills. He's a lot wiser than I am. I'm happy to leave my future in His hands, whichever way it goes."

"I wish I could say I am willing. Accepting, maybe. Perhaps even accepting with reluctance."

"Yes, that could describe me, too."

Julius had just sat down to eat when, with a knock on the door, Marcus walked in.

"Ah, I'm just in time, I see."

"Marcus the Mooch. I might have known. This is not the day you will starve, though. I bought a little extra yesterday." Cyril went after another plate. "Sit. We're going to see Shelumiel, Marcus, after we have eaten. Will you be joining us?"

"There's still a possibility he won't keep up the lessons because of rumors, mostly true, about my attraction for a certain Jewish woman," Julius said. "I am sorry that we may have hurt your possibilities as well, even though Loukas did speak up for us yesterday. Today we learn our fate, because if Shelumiel won't teach us, probably no other rabbi in Jerusalem will, either. And if we don't become proselytes, Miriam's father and Quinta's soon-to-be father won't allow them to be betrothed to us, nor will we be allowed to participate in any of the Sabbath activities or festivals. We would lose both ways."

"On to cheerier subjects. I've arranged an appointment with Rufus for tomorrow for the two of us, Julius. And it was a trick, too. He's busy. The senate wants reports on about everything under the sun in the Jerusalem area."

"For what purpose?" Cyril's left eyebrow did the dance it did whenever he was curious. He set a dish in front of Marcus, who promptly loaded it with bread and melon.

"For what purpose does the senate want the reports, or for what purpose do we want an appointment?" Marcus spoke around a mouthful of melon.

"I couldn't care less whether the senate wants a report on how many latrines have been built." Cyril scowled at Marcus and started to pull his plate away from him.

"Wait, wait! Don't take my food, I'll tell you anything you want to know, vicious slave." Marcus grabbed for the plate, but Cyril held it just out of reach.

"Then confess. Why did you make an appointment with the tribune?

"How else shall we get approval to become proselytes and be circumcised?" Marcus cringed, warding off an imaginary attack on his groin area. "Imagine that, seeking approval for torture."

Julius laughed. "It does sound strange. But necessary. Thanks, Marcus."

"Hmm," Marcus said. "That means you are in my debt. I guess that pays for my breakfast."

"Well, I don't know. Those eggs cost a king's pay, and the melon was the best they had," Cyril said.

"Which king, Cyril? King of the locusts? King of the mosquitos?"

"Does it matter? Let it just be said they were expensive. Maybe this breakfast is worth more than your purse, Marcus. Perhaps we should hold you for ransom, not that anyone would pay much for you."

"I'll have you know my mother considered me quite valuable. However, my father has yet to confirm that."

"If you two would quit yattering, we could get done with this breakfast and go find out our fate." Julius scowled with mock fierceness, finishing his last bite.

"I'm finished, o most wonderful of masters." Cyril bowed low.

"Yes sir, o noble centurion." Marcus made a show of shoveling the remaining food into his mouth.

"What are we waiting for? Let's go." Julius rose and made his way to the door, followed by Cyril and Marcus. When they reach Loukas' house, Meskhanet, another of his servants, admitted them, holding a graceful finger to deep red lips to caution silence. Julius chuckled when Marcus' gaze followed the pretty Egyptian. He chuckled to himself remembering Marcus' fascination with the Egyptian dancing ladies and wondered if she also danced. She led them to the courtyard where they found Loukas talking to five other men, the rest of the household gathered around them.

"Quinta is my slave, and her six years of service are completed. I release her." They heard him saying. Loukas brought Quinta forward, and the other men nodded.

"She is free, then, to pursue her life in whatever manner she wishes," one of them said. "Go in freedom, young woman."

"Quinta, you are free to go. Or, if you wish, you may stay in our household as our daughter. Joanna and I desire to adopt you, if you are willing, in the presence of these officers of the synagogue."

"Are your parents here to approve this adoption, Quinta?" the officer asked with formality.

"No. My parents were poor. They sell me to have food to eat. Their home is many days from here, and I do not know where they are since then. They sell me to a kind merchant ten years ago. Master Loukas and Joanna buy me from him and treat me like their own family six years ago."

"Is it your wish to remain in this household as their daughter?"

"Yes, I wish very much."

"Then, as officers of the synagogue, we witness and authorize this adoption." They nodded agreement and in turn signed a scroll of papyrus on the table. "As the daughter of this household and as the only child, you will inherit this man's home and his wealth, unless they have a son or until you marry. Then your inheritance will go to the first-born son or to the man you marry. Is this agreed?"

"We do," Joanna, Loukas, and Quinta nodded.

"Let it be known that this young woman, Quinta, is now as though begotten by you, and is entitled to be treated in all ways as a daughter of the family."

"Let it be known," Loukas said, eyes shining.

The men bowed to Loukas and exited the house, leaving teary-eyed Joanna and Quinta hugging each other and Loukas smiling damp-eyed at his wife and new daughter. The rest of the group applauded.

"Well, Quinta, now it's official. You are a free woman and the daughter of Loukas the Physician and Joanna. How do you feel?" Julius asked.

"I feel so good I could fly." Quinta said, hugging herself, and then flinging her arms wide, as though she would take off in flight.

Amid the laughter, she twirled and danced, laughing with them.

"I suppose you three are on your way to see Shelumiel," Loukas said, turning to his guests. "Want me to accompany you?"

"We hoped you would come with us," Cyril said, "just in case Shelumiel is still lathered up about anything more this morning."

"I wouldn't miss his pronouncement for all the gold in Galilee." Loukas brushed a hand over his short beard as he followed the three men toward the gate.

"I think it's safe to say we're all eager to find out. Shall we be on our way, then?" Julius exited the door, followed by Cyril, Marcus, and Loukas.

"Wait," Julius grabbed Loukas' arm to prevent him from knocking on Shelumiel's door.

"Is something wrong?" Loukas asked.

Julius leaned against the wall, dizzy and uncertain. "When we step through that door, Shelumiel's words could alter my hopes and dreams for my entire future. Cyril's, too. I find I would rather face a troop of enemy soldiers alone, armed only with a piece of broken pottery. Couldn't we postpone this a day or two?"

"Julius, think logically. What do you think Shelumiel would conclude if you would not face him today?"

"You could tell him I'm sick."

"You want me to lie?" Loukas' eyes narrowed.

"No. I *am* sick. My stomach feels the urge to rid itself of everything I've eaten for the past week. It wouldn't be a lie." Julius grasped both Loukas' arms and looked pleadingly into his eyes.

"We're going in there, Julius. Get hold of yourself, man." Loukas gazed sternly into Julius' eyes.

The door opened, and Shelumiel stood in the opening. He scowled and waved the men into the house.

"You were raising such a commotion out there that my neighbors would be irritated. Must you shout?" Shelumiel asked, glaring.

"My friend here fears the great Shelumiel," Loukas said. "Because if you refuse to teach him any more of the Jewish faith and laws, word will spread and no one else will teach him, either. He also fears that if you reject him, you will also reject his friends Cyril and Marcus."

"Yes, I gathered that. I'm not young, but my ears haven't stopped hearing yet."

Julius hung his head in shame, his body alternating between cold and hot. "I'm sorry, Rabbi. I don't remember being this frightened before, though I've been more than once in deadly circumstances."

"What frightens you, Centurion?"

"You spoke aright yesterday. I love a Jewish maiden, and I want more than I can say to marry her. Her father wouldn't allow that to happen if I don't become a proselyte, but he probably won't approve it anyway. Worse than that, though, is the fear that if you refuse to continue your lessons with me, is that maybe God Himself might also reject me, and that would be a loss more than I could bear. I've become accustomed to feeling His presence with me."

Shelumiel's eyebrows arched. "I think you overestimate my influence on God's decisions. I am His servant; He is not mine. And if my decision were that I did not want to continue your lessons, I would not spread that news throughout the synagogue. However, that is not my decision. As I'm sure you have, I've talked to my God and asked for His wisdom. I feel His wishes are that you should all continue your lessons with me."

Julius burst into tears. His head in his hands, he leaned into the wall and sobbed. Cyril's touch on his arm brought Julius' head up. Marcus placed his hands on his friends' shoulders. Loukas and Shelumiel looked at each other and nodded.

"I'm sorry. I don't know why I did that." Julius fought to control his emotions.

"Perhaps because your next step is to be circumcised," Shelumiel said, his tone dry.

Julius, Marcus, and Cyril winced and groaned in involuntary harmony.

"Marcus and I will need to get the approval of the tribune," Julius said. "But please don't take that as reluctance. It wouldn't do to be sent off to battle the next day."

"Of course." Shelumiel inclined his head. "Come back to see me when you have clearance. Meanwhile, Cyril, are you ready?"

Cyril's Adams apple bobbed. "Yes, sir, whenever you are. Or whoever performs this surgery."

"Tomorrow, then. I'll be the one to perform the ceremony. Plan on very little activity for the next few days."

"Rabbi, I am a slave. My activity or inactivity depends on my master."

Julius smiled at him. "You can have a few days off. Maybe Marcus would even be so kind as to provide his chariot for you to ride back to our quarters. I don't think you will feel much like walking."

"Allow me to provide the ride and take him to my home." Loukas touched Julius' arm. "I have a small wagon. It will be easier for me to take care of him…and you two, too…at my home. That way, you can spend the day persuading Tribune Rufus that you can still be good soldiers even though you are proselytes of the Jewish God."

"That could be a neat trick. The reason we are here is to keep the Jews in line. I think he might not look with great pleasure on us joining the Jewish religion." Marcus' brow furrowed. "How do we convince him?"

"Leave it up to God. I think He wants to bring you into His fold, and if this is within His purpose, He will smooth the road before you. Have faith in His abilities," Shelumiel said. "If this isn't the road He would choose for you, I'm sure He'll make the right road known to you.

"I didn't think of that. I'm wondering, if it isn't an imposition, that is, sir, if you would ask God for us about this?" Marcus hesitated. "I don't even know how or what to ask."

"It's always best to speak with frank openness to God. Although He already knows our thoughts, He still wants us to talk to Him about them. Remember our talks about the writer of many of the Psalms. David in particular spoke to God with great bluntness. David was a soldier, even as you are, and it would be good if each of you on his own spoke to God about your own concerns. I will also speak to Him, but I want you to do this in your own closet. I think…I hope…you will speak more openly with Him if you are alone."

"Yes, Rabbi. I think I speak for all of us. We will do as you say." Julius raised a questioning eyebrow at Marcus and Cyril, and a nod from them confirmed it. Shelumiel nodded in turn, this time in approval.

Julius motioned Cyril, and Marcus from the house, leaving Loukas behind with Shelumiel. The two men talked, their heads together, their expressions serious.

"Would you mind if I did not prepare a meal for you until later?" Cyril broke their companionable silence.

"Actually, I believe I'll fast until we meet with Rufus."

"Fast? Why?" Marcus asked.

"Last week, Shelumiel talked about God's chosen fast. The Prophet Isaiah spoke about it in his writings. Since the rest of my life pivots on the outcome of this talk with Rufus, I'd like to go into the discussion with every piece of armor available."

"Hmm. Could be a good idea. Can you tell me anything more about it? What does it say?"

"God expressed displeasure over the reason some people had for fasting. They fasted because it made them seem holier to the people. And for the people to know, the person fasting had to tell everyone about it. God said they already had their reward. But if the reason to fast was in order to provide for someone who didn't have anything to eat or clothes to wear, or if for some other good and noble purpose, such as to lift burdens, free the oppressed, or break the bonds of slavery, that was the fast He would choose for us. If this isn't a burden to be lifted, I don't know what is. And speaking of breaking the bonds of slavery, Cyril, I'll draw up your emancipation papers when we get back to our quarters."

"You're freeing Cyril? What will he do then?" Marcus turned to Cyril. "Did you know about this? Do you have plans?"

"Yes, I knew. Julius intended to save my freedom for a gift on the day I was accepted as a proselyte, but I forced his hand yesterday morning. I will remain his servant. I don't know what I would do otherwise, because I've never done anything else."

"I don't know. Not many slaves or even free men are as well educated as you. You sat in on Julius' schooling. You could easily get a job tutoring some rich man's offspring."

"Let's not encourage him to go find someone else to work for. I might want him to tutor my own offspring. If I ever have any offspring." Julius' eyebrow raised and he grasped Cyril's shoulder.

"Actually, I plan to be rich someday, and I could hire him myself." Marcus grinned and slapped his hand down on Cyril's other shoulder.

"Considering your past history, that could be in the distant future. He's safer under my employ."

"Don't I have any say in this?" Cyril cast a glance at both his friends. "Who offers the best wages? I will need a good wage to support my own growing family."

"Growing family?" Marcus cleared his throat. "Is there something you've been hiding from us?"

"Only that I want to ask for Quinta's betrothal to me tomorrow, provided that I am able to say anything other than 'ow.' I don't know how long a betrothal is supposed to last, but I hope not long. Maybe a month. Just long enough to heal from my little wound."

Julius rubbed his hand over his chin. "I've heard most betrothals last about a year, sometimes more or sometimes less, depending on circumstances. I know when Micah promised Miriam to James they were only supposed to be betrothed a few days before the ceremony, but that was because Deborah was so sick."

"Is she still betrothed to him? What happened? Or is this a sensitive subject?" Marcus glanced at Julius.

Julius frowned. "She's still promised. The betrothal never took place. I don't know what Micah plans. I can only hope he will withdraw the promise."

"Why would he withdraw it?" Marcus glanced sideways at Julius.

"James started following that Prophet, Jesus. Somehow, I can see why James would be so inclined, can't you?"

"What do you mean by following Him?" Marcus asked.

Julius shrugged and grinned. "As His disciple. Something about the Man. His gaze reaches inside you, as if He has known you even before your birth. I'm not sure exactly what those who follow Him do, but it has postponed her betrothal to James. I think Miriam's father isn't happy with her potential spouse."

"You don't look unhappy. Does this mean you might have a chance with her?" Marcus waggled his eyebrows.

"Let's just say I feel more hopeful than I used to."

"You look more hopeful. In fact, you look like a man in lo-o-o-ove."

"Your turn is coming, Marcus, your turn is coming. Remember how besotted Cyril became so fast? The same thing could happen to you."

"Not me. I'm destined to be alone. I have no desire for a wife."

The other two men looked at each other.

"That's what we thought just a few short months ago, old friend." Julius laughed.

Chapter 24

Julius awakened early that morning. His first thought was of Cyril and the endurance he would need. He lifted his hands and spoke to the One God. "Adonai, please grant Cyril courage this day. I know this is what Your scriptures require and You never intended for this day to be without pain, but please give him a healthy dose of your peace and let the sense of You be present with him. And, Lord, please guide Marcus and me, too, as we go to Rufus with our requests. Only You can smooth the way for us to become proselytes. Thank You, Jehovah Jirah. You alone are holy."

Julius rose from his knees and strode into their tiny kitchen where Cyril usually waited for him with his breakfast ready to place on the table. Cyril must have already left for his appointment with Shelumiel.

This day Julius would fend for himself. He stopped and smiled to himself. His stomach growled. Fasting was more difficult than he had thought.

A knock sounded and Marcus entered. "Ho, Julius the Just."

"Ho, Marcus the Mighty. Apparently the thought of becoming a proselyte improved you. I thought I would have to enter your quarters and drag you out by the heels as you still slept."

"You see? I still have a few surprises for you."

"True. Are you ready? Have you thought of all the arguments you will need?"

"No, I haven't. I don't have the first idea what I'm going to say. I'll just have to wait and see what falls out of my mouth when we get there."

"That's my good friend Marcus. Never prepared, but always glib. I'm not worried that you won't find something to say. I only worry your mouth will speak before your mind knows what's going on."

"Me? How about you? Have you memorized a speech, then?"

"Well, no, not exactly." Julius rubbed his cheek. He'd need to shave himself this day.

"Not exactly?"

"Let's just say I'm as prepared as you are." They both laughed and punched each other on the shoulders as they exited. They hitched Warrior and Duros to the chariot, and fell in behind the morning road patrol to Jerusalem.

When they reached their destination, both men hesitated for an instant. Drawing deep breaths, they entered.

"We have come to see the tribune, Decanus."

The decanus pounded his chest in salute and turned to enter the tribune's chamber.

A moment later, he returned. "The tribune has little time to spare, and he says you must make your audience brief."

"We will try to do just that." They followed the decanus into the hall, and Julius breathed one last prayer as they saluted their commander.

"Hail, Tribune Rufus."

"Pax, Julius and Marcus. What is the purpose of this visit?"

"Sir, the two of us find the religion here to our tastes, and we wish to become proselytes. I also ask permission to wed a Jewish maiden."

Rufus frowned at the parchment scroll in front of him, wrote a few words, and glanced up.

"You both want to join their religion, and you, Julius, wish to marry." He returned his gaze to the parchments littering his table. "Why should I care?" He grabbed a blank parchment, signed his name at the bottom, and rolled it. "Fill out the rest of it, and see that it gets back to me." He handed the scroll to Julius.

"Ah, sir, joining their religion requires a minor surgery, a, uh, circumcision. We could be unable to perform our duties for a week." Julius felt the sweat running down his forehead and the back of his neck and fought the urge to wipe it away.

"A week. Fine, just find someone to assume your duties first. Now go, I'm busy." His impatient tone and furrowed brow brooked no hesitation.

"Yes, sir." Julius and Marcus saluted again, spun on their heels and left.

When they were out of earshot, Marcus shook his head. "That was incredible. Can you believe it? We didn't have to state our cases or argue or plead or even pledge our first child."

They stepped into the chariot, and Julius waved the patrol to fall in behind.

"I won't question the ways of God. Who could doubt He was in charge in there? I know we're allowed to worship wherever we want, but I'm surprised Rufus didn't blink at the week off. Or at approving me, a soldier, to marry anyone, let alone a Jew. Let's go back to my quarters to finish this order, and we'll have to find one centurion and one decanus to fill in for us. Not a lot of choices as far as centurions go, but there are a few decani around."

"Yes, a few. You could write in a huge raise in our pay." Marcus shook his head. "A blank order. Whoever heard of that? We ought to add a few items. A bottle of wine every week and..."

"Let's not press the tribune. I'm not fond of the idea of being imprisoned. It would throw a crimp in my marriage hopes."

"It amazes me you remain hopeful that the carpenter and the fisherman will release Miriam." One eyebrow lifted as he cast a sideways gaze at Julius.

"That needs yet another miracle."

"I think you're letting your dreams overshadow your logic."

When they reached Jericho's gate, Julius ordered the patrol to continue their traverse of the road. They took the chariot back into the compound, handing the horses off to a stableman to care for.

"Not to change the subject, but I wonder how Cyril feels now. Maybe we should go see him." Marcus jerked his head in the direction of Loukas' house.

"Let's get these papers done and to the quartermaster before we go."

Marcus made a wry face and nodded. "I suppose we should."

By the time they finished everything on their list, the sun had set. They postponed the visit to Loukas' home until the morning, but Julius mounted Warrior and galloped toward Micah's home.

He dismounted in front of their house. Whispering a quick prayer, he knocked at the door. Deborah answered, and her welcoming smile warmed his heart.

"Shalom, Julius. Come in. Your face is a study. I can't tell if you are worried or excited."

Micah strode into the room from his shop. "Shalom. Please tell us that your tribune gave his approval."

"God provided a miracle today. The tribune's workload made him agree to everything. He let us fill out all the details. Everything but his signature, which he signed to a blank document." Julius grinned. "I'm still scratching my head."

"I thought he might approve. When I prayed, it seemed so. Soon, then, you will be an official Jewish proselyte." Micah grasped Julius' shoulders with both hands and pulled him into a back-pounding hug.

Julius returned the hug and pulled back. "Uh, I guess Miriam isn't here?"

"No. She and her friend Hannah took some food to their friend Mary. Mary was injured. In a fall, I think she told them." A quick scowl darkened Deborah's face.

"I wanted to tell her, uh all of you, that is, the news that Shelumiel accepted me as a proselyte. I will be, I mean, he will, uh...." Julius stammered, unsure how to acceptably say in front of Deborah that he would be circumcised.

"So we heard." Micah's eyes twinkled. "Please accept our congratulations."

"You heard?"

"Yes. Shelumiel sent word to me." He winked at Julius.

Julius' eyebrows shot upward. "That was nice of him."

"We thought so."

Julius shifted from one foot to the other and drew in a deep breath. "Is it too soon to ask...to ask if you...if you would approve of marriage between your daughter and me?"

Micah's smile disappeared. "Yes, it is. I told you, Miriam is promised."

Julius' spirits fell. "I hoped, maybe, since James hadn't been pursuing the marriage, or at least I thought...."

"We do not look on promises lightly." Micah's stern look stopped anything further from Julius.

Miriam walked in the door and pulled her scarf off. She saw Julius and put it back on again. "Oh, shalom, Julius."

"Shalom, Miriam." He bowed his head.

Deborah pulled Miriam to her side. "You're back quickly, Daughter. Was Mary not at home?"

"Yes, but Kish was drunk and belligerent. We said we were sorry she fell, and he started cursing and threatening to throw us out. So we left. We didn't even get to leave the food."

Micah growled. "If he touches you...."

Julius gazed at Miriam, scowled, and clenched his fists. "Sir, you could be in trouble with the Roman authorities if you carried out what you're thinking, but if I were the one who teaches this Kish a lesson, it would not be frowned on by anyone." He would keep her from harm, if only they would let him. And if anyone hurt her again....

Miriam's eyes and small smile thanked Julius, but she said nothing.

Micah cast an approving glance on Julius. "Let us hope it won't be necessary for either of us to take on that chore."

Julius placed the helmet back on his head. "I'm sorry I can't stay. There are things I need to get done tonight, not the least of which is some time in conversation with God." He bowed to Miriam and her parents and left.

Chapter 25

Julius rode at a trot to Shelumiel's home and tied his horse to a tree. Shelumiel opened the door.

"Shalom, Julius. You're riding a horse this time? I thought you always walked."

"I needed to go to Micah's house, then yours, and then home. It was too far to go in what's left of the evening, and Warrior here needs the exercise." He patted the horse's neck. "I wanted to let you know Marcus and I are cleared to participate in the circumcision ceremony. Can you do it tomorrow?"

"Yes, I was expecting you tomorrow morning."

"You knew?"

"I know our God."

Julius grinned. "I should have known He would tell you first."

Shelumiel gave Julius one of his rare smiles. "I'll see you in the morning about the third hour of the day."

Julius leapt with ease onto Warrior's back.

"You might not want to ride a horse tomorrow, Julius."

"My father didn't raise any idiots, Rabbi." Julius waved. "Warrior might need to pull a chariot tomorrow."

"I think Loukas intends to bring his wagon again tomorrow. It appears he plans to have a house filled with patients for a few days. You are indeed blessed to have a friend such as Loukas."

"I agree. If it were not for him, these circumcisions would not be happening. Until tomorrow, then, and may God's peace rest on your house, Rabbi."

"Shalom to you, too, proselyte."

Morning light leaked through the wooden slats on the shutters and woke Julius. He threw them open and breathed deeply of the morning air. "Good morning, Lord," he whispered. "I can see why the Psalmist said, 'This is the day that the Lord has made, and I will rejoice and be glad in it.' I know that this day will bring pain, but the pain is worth being a part of Your followers. I am grateful that You called me to You."

Julius felt the Lord's smile on him, and his feeling of gratitude was almost more than his heart could hold. Smiling, he went out the door to find Marcus.

After they ate breakfast at the barracks, the two men made their way toward Loukas' house. Marcus seemed so serious that Julius wondered if his friend regretted his decision to join the Jewish religion.

"Why so glum, my friend?" he asked.

"Not exactly glum, Julius. This is such a big step for me. Although I have to admit I'm dreading the knife, it's more than that. I don't understand why God requires it. I have no doubt that He must have a good reason, but it's beyond me. I've been hanging around Cyril too much. Isn't it said that Greeks are always questioning, questioning, questioning?"

"Yes, although I'm afraid that maybe Cyril missed his calling there. Or maybe because it's drilled into a slave from the beginning not to ask why, like soldiers. I don't know why, either. Maybe Shelumiel knows."

"Do you think he would consider it sacrilege if we asked?"

"He didn't take kindly to our questions, did he?"

"I don't want him to postpone this event or to think that we are wavering. Maybe we should wait until afterward."

"Good thought. Spoken like an honorable coward." Julius laughed at his usually cavalier friend.

"An honorable coward. One who is terrified but goes into battle anyway?" Marcus' sneer came with a slight chuckle.

As they approached Loukas' home, they saw Quinta, a large basket on her arm.

"Sometimes I wish Cyril either were not my friend or that he hadn't set his heart on Quinta. That is one beautiful young woman." Marcus' eyes widened with admiration.

"It wouldn't be a good idea for you to set your cap for her. I fear even Cyril could become aggressive if you tried."

"I know. There are few things more important than friends, but I think he considers Quinta one of those things. Not that she's a 'thing'."

"Definitely not a 'thing'."

"Shalom, Quinta." Julius raised his hand in greeting. "How is Cyril this morning?"

"He is well, I think. Lou..ah, my father will not let me see him yet. But my...mother tells me Cyril is eating today. He did not yesterday." She smiled as she stumbled over the new endearments for her parents. She turned and led them back into the house, calling, "Mother," with a proud voice.

Joanna hurried into the room, wiping her hands on a clean scrap of material looped over the belt at her waist.

"Shalom." she said. "Did you come to see Cyril or Loukas?"

"Shalom, lady. We came to see both. Cyril first." Marcus made a respectful bow to her.

Joanna led the way to the room where Cyril lay. "It'll be easy to see them. They're both in here. Would you break your fast with us?"

"We ate with the soldiers this morning, but thank you," Julius said as they followed her into the dining area.

"Speak for yourself, man. I could still put a little more into the stomach." Marcus rubbed his midsection.

"Shalom, Marcus and Julius. You might not want to eat, Marcus. Some lose their breakfast after an operation such as this." Loukas stood from his place at the table.

"I never thought about that. Joanna, may I change my answer to no, but thank you for the offer?"

"All right, but please allow my poor starved husband to eat before you take him away."

She left them and hurried toward the kitchen.

"Poor starved husband, indeed." Loukas patted his stomach. "Even though I fasted yesterday, I don't think I'll pass away today. And speaking of not fasting, is the news good from your tribune?"

"Yes. He granted us the time to heal from the circumcision, provided that we find our own replacements while we are off. It seems he was pressured to finish some reports. He gave me his signature on a blank parchment scroll and told me to fill it in."

"I wanted to fill in a good deal more than the two items, but Julius, dutiful centurion that he is, wouldn't even add a case of wine to the list." Marcus tipped an imaginary glass to his mouth.

"Such a lost opportunity." Loukas shook his head and led the way to the room where Cyril lay.

"How do you feel this morning, Cyril?" Julius sat on the bed beside him.

"Better than yesterday. I think maybe this afternoon I'll get up and around some."

"No, I think not," Loukas said. "Tomorrow, maybe. Today, you'd break the scabs. They're too fresh to take much friction."

"I don't remember the last time I lay in bed so long. I suppose I must have in my early childhood, but slaves are not allowed time off as a rule."

"When did I ever deny you time to get well? Uh, I mean, I would have if you had ever been sick. And anyway, you're no longer a slave, so you can lie abed as long as you'd like. Not too long, though, because I would have to cut your wages."

"I think I will be up before you will be."

"That's true. We're going to Shelumiel's now. I suppose we'll be joining you here later this morning." Marcus chewed on his lip.

"God go with you, my friends. When you come back, we can commiserate." Cyril offered them a mock salute, and before they could get out of the door, he asked to talk to Loukas in private.

While Julius loitered with Marcus outside, a loud shout of victory rang through Loukas' home followed by an equally loud moan.

Julius slapped Marcus on the back. "I believe our friend, Cyril, has just learned that sweet victories sometimes come with pain. I have prayed and will continue to pray that I have the same experience."

Chapter 26

Miriam bent over her friend, Mary, as Mary lay in Ima's bed. Miriam brushed the hair from her bruised and swollen face. "Mary, I'm here. Can you hear me?" A tear slid down Miriam's cheek and fell upon her unconscious friend's arm.

Ima knelt down with a bowl of water, and she and Leah gently wiped the blood from Mary's forehead and arms. Miriam's father paced, his muttering no doubt prayers for God to send a thousand curses on Mary's husband, Kish. In the corner, Amos stood like a man shaken by the knowledge that such evil could be done.

A knock on the door brought Miriam to her feet. She rushed past her father and pulled the door open. "Oh, Loukas, you arrived just in time. Please, can you help Mary? Hannah found her this morning on the street outside her home. Amos carried her here."

Loukas bent beside Ima and Leah. He turned Mary's face and examined the bruises before he spoke. "Miriam would you please help me? The rest of you, please leave the room."

He pulled the curtain across and sat down beside Mary. With gentle hands, he removed her cloak and lifted the tunic.

He said nothing, but he gazed in dismay at Mary's thin frame, bruised so badly it appeared she'd been marched on by an entire regiment. "She has a shallow cut here." Loukas pointed to her forehead. "That's the reason for a lot of the blood, but it is this...." He lifted Mary's head carefully. "This deep dent is evidence of a broken skull." Loukas slowly lowered Mary's head to the bed. "Do you see here? She has drops of blood seeping from her ears. Her arm is bent where it shouldn't be. The deep blue bruising on the skin around her ribs is an indication that several may be broken."

Mary breathed in shallow gasps. Loukas placed a finger over the pulse at her neck. With his free hand, he placed a finger to his lips asking for quiet.

Miriam nodded as tears spilled down her face.

After a moment, Loukas rose and shook his head, holding the curtain open for Miriam to exit.

Ima stepped forward, and Leah stood beside Amos, her fingers clasped together and raised to support her chin. "Will…will she be able to survive this…this terrible…." She turned into Amos' arms.

Loukas shook his head. "There's nothing we can do for her. She's close to death. Is she married?"

"Yes," Abba growled through clenched teeth. "Perhaps Amos and I should go get him." He jerked his head toward the door.

"If he is to see his wife while she is alive, yes."

"I'll get her mother." Leah ran toward the door.

"Tell them to hasten."

Miriam slipped back through the curtain. She bent to her knees and held Mary's hand. "I'm so sorry…so sorry, Mary," she whispered. She sat there in silence, watching Mary's labored breathing. She thought of the man who had beaten his wife so that she would soon die, and she remembered the cruel soldier who'd meant to do her harm. She recalled Julius and how he'd rescued her that day. She knew he would love and protect her. If her father would just allow it.

She bent her head and cried. She was thinking of Julius while her friend would soon depart this world. Mary had lived every day with a beast like the soldier who had tried to harm Miriam, and Kish probably would not pay for what he'd done. At least he wouldn't pay enough.

Loukas reentered the room. He placed a hand on Miriam's shoulder and shook his head. Miriam looked at the still form and sobbed.

"Where is my daughter?" Mary's mother, Zellah, cried with a raspy breath.

"In here, Zellah," Ima led Zellah into the bed chamber.

Miriam stood and wiped her eyes as Zellah fell beside Mary.

"I'm sorry, little mother." Loukas bent beside Zellah. "She is gone."

"No, she can't be. I just saw her yesterday." Zellah's voice rose to a keening note, and she knelt next to her daughter. Zellah rocked, holding her hands to her head.

Leah came into the room. She dropped to her knees and placed her hand on Zellah's shoulder.

Zellah wailed softly, rocking to and fro.

Miriam's glowering father shoved Kish through the door. Amos followed close behind.

"We found the man drunk on his bed. Look at his knuckles. Look at this blood on his cloak and sandals. There can be no doubt he's the one who killed her." Amos spat at Kish.

Kish shook his head as if rising from a deep night's sleep.

"You abomination. You killed my daughter. You killed my daughter!" Zellah screeched and launched herself at Kish, fingernails clawing for his face.

Ima stepped in front of her, and Leah took her arms.

"No, Zellah. If you do what I'm sure you want to do to Kish, we won't be able to show the Sanhedrin what he did to Mary," Ima spoke softly but firmly to the distraught woman.

Zellah struggled for a moment before calm and reason began to return to her eyes. Once more she began to weep, burying her face in her hands. Miriam slipped an arm around Zellah and allowed her to cry against her.

Kish, who'd backed up when Zellah jumped toward him, blanched.

"The Sanhedrin?" he slurred. "I haven't done anything wrong."

"You beat your wife, my sister, to death." Amos took a half step closer, fists clenched.

"My wife?" Kish asked. "My wife would not get up and fix my meal. I had a right to thrash her."

"You didn't just 'thrash' her. You killed her." Loukas gritted his teeth. "Look at her." He pushed Kish toward the bed where Mary lay.

Kish crashed to the floor. He rose to his knees and peered intently at his wife. "She's dead? No, she wasn't dead last night. She was on the floor, and she wouldn't get up. So I fixed my own food and let her lie there. Lazy woman." He raised his voice. "Wake up, you lazy woman. Show them you're not dead." He raised his fist to strike.

Abba scowled and jerked Kish around to face him. "How did she get outside, Kish?"

"I threw her out. She wouldn't fix my food."

"Now she's beyond your ability to hurt her further. Let's take him to the Sanhedrin." Abba nodded to Amos. Abba grasped one arm and Amos the other, and they muscled him through the door.

Kish made ineffectual, inebriated efforts to pull away, but neither man loosed his grip.

"I'll get pipers and wailing women." Ima stepped toward the door.

"No, that's my job. She's my daughter." Zellah turned and gazed at Mary's still form.

"Yes, usually it would be, but the men need your testimony, Zellah." Ima pulled her toward the door and said softly, "Go with them, Zellah. We'll take care of Mary."

Zellah hesitated. She nodded and took one last look at her daughter before she stumbled outside, tears running down her face.

"I'll go with you, Zellah. I also have something to tell the Sanhedrin." Leah put an arm around Zellah's shoulders.

Ima ran her hand through her hair. "I can make arrangements for the pipers and wailers. Miriam, go find her burial clothes. Spices, too." The woman ran from the house.

"Zellah, wait!" Ima caught up with the group. Miriam was amazed at the strength of her mother as she found it hard to keep up with her. "Do you know where the tomb is?"

"I don't know where Kish's family buries theirs, but I'd like to put her in ours. I don't want her buried beside her murderer." Shoulders slumped, she turned to follow the men.

Zellah's son Azariah charged around the corner, nearly colliding with her. "Mother! What happened, Mother? Bartemus said that...."

"Mary is dead. Kish killed her, beat her to death."

Miriam stepped back, her head bowed. She knew from her conversations with Mary, that she was very close to Azariah.

"He killed Mary? But why?"

"He was drunk. Kish...." Zellah spat on the ground. "Kish said she wouldn't get up and feed him, so he beat her. She is gone from us."

"Where is he? It's my right to throw the first stone."

"You forget, she was his wife." Loukas stepped close to Azariah and grasped his arm.

Azariah jerked free and looked around. "I don't care. I'll kill him. Where is he?"

"Amos and Micah took him to the Sanhedrin for judgment. You would not help your sister or your mother if you took vengeance into your own hands, Azariah." Loukas moved in front of him as he turned. "Let wisdom fill your heart, not revenge. Remember that vengeance belongs to the Lord. He will exact the punishment."

Azariah reached up with both hands to push Loukas out of his way.

Zellah took hold of his arm. "Wait, Son. Let's see what the judges have to say. Let's go listen, and we'll tell the judges what we know too."

Azariah curled his hands into tight fists, but he held them at his side. The flames diminished in his eyes as with visible effort he brought himself under control. He nodded his head with one stiff movement, and they left for the gate.

Ima drew a deep breath. "Miriam, we have a job ahead of us. Let's go. I will get the pipers and the wailing women. You will get Mary's burial clothes."

"Let me help, Deborah." Joanna said. "We are acquainted with both wailing women and pipers. I often go to help Loukas when there is a death."

Thank you, Joanna. You've been so quiet I forgot you were here. I'm not sure why you came over here this morning, but I'm sure you weren't expecting anything like this."

"No, we weren't, but we can talk about other subjects when this crisis is past. Soon after, I hope."

Miriam walked the dusty street in a bit of a haze as it occurred to her that her mother, for whom she had only recently thought she would be sewing a burial shroud, was healthy and hurrying to help with the burial of a woman much younger than herself.

Her tears began anew. Mary should not have had to suffer and die at the hands of her husband.

Hannah stepped forward and laid her hand on Miriam's arm. "I can help, too. Neighbors around Mary's house have seen me there before. I will help look for Mary's burial clothes."

Miriam sat at the table with her family and friends, wondering if the day would ever end. She pushed the food around on her plate. In this day filled with pain, how could she eat? She would miss Mary, her friend since childhood. Miriam flinched as she thought of how Mary died, crushed by one who should have been her protector.

Was this what happened when a marriage existed without love? If her father did not break the betrothal and allow Miriam to marry Julius, would this happen to her? James would be angry when he found out she didn't love him. Especially if he knew she loved someone else. If he found out about…Miriam shook her head and pulled her attention back to their guests.

Loukas and Joanna smiled at each other.

"It's nice to have some good news to share on this day that's been filled with so much sadness. Cyril and our little Quinta were to be betrothed tomorrow evening, although now it appears we will postpone it a week." Loukas dropped his gaze to his feet and frowned, but then he looked back up and smiled. "You're all invited, of course."

"I'm so happy for them." Miriam forced a smile onto her face, hoping it didn't look as false as it felt. She picked up and ate the food but tasted nothing. How long could she keep smiling?

Loukas stood. "I hope you will excuse us. Joanna and I must return to care for our patients."

"I'd almost forgotten about your patients. How are they?" Abba stood and wiped his hands on a damp towel.

"Progressing. They'll be back to work in a week. I thank you for our meal. We will repay when Quinta and Cyril are betrothed. Come, wife. It's time we go home."

They're betrothed and happy. I will never be happy again. Miriam jumped to her feet and turned her back, running for the stair. "Excuse me, I need to change my tunic." She darted for the stairs to her room, hoping the tears wouldn't start before she got out of sight. *I wish it were possible...no! Stop thinking that way. Abba keeps his promises all too well. There's no sense dwelling on it.*

Chapter 27

A week later, Miriam was resting in her room when she heard a knock at their door.

"Come in, Tamar. Miriam is in her room. I'll get her," Ima said.

Miriam bit her lip. Tamar's visit could not bode well. Miriam descended the stairs, bracing herself.

"It's you or Micah I came to see. But you might not want to hear me," Tamar said.

"What is it?"

Miriam stopped on the stairs and peered toward the doorway. Neither Ima nor Tamar could see her. Ima was seated on a bench, and Tamar stood wringing her hands. Her face was tight, and her eyes narrowed.

"I'm tired of the whole village thinking that your daughter is such a paragon of virtue. She is not."

Ima straightened in her chair. "Perhaps you should explain, Tamar."

"I saw her. Several months ago. A Roman soldier took her into the house of old Barnabab. Then a…a friend told me she went out of the city gate with another Roman. You should tell her to stay away from the Romans. They're all evil."

"All? Why do you say they are all evil?"

"Everybody knows it. They…they rape the women, and then the women's husbands will no longer touch them." Tamar's gaze darted over her shoulders, right and left.

Miriam leaned out of view for a moment and then took up her post.

"And now Miriam consorts with them. For all we know, she leads other women to them to rape. For all we know, she, too, is evil."

"Tamar, come here. Sit by me." Deborah patted the chair next to her.

"I…I cannot."

"Of course you can. Come." Miriam's mother held out her hand to Tamar. Slowly, she moved toward Ima, still glancing behind her.

When Tamar sat on the edge of the chair, Ima touched her hand. Miriam knew that touch, one to reassure Tamar that she had nothing to fear.

Miriam bit her lips and tears fell. Tamar was telling Ima what Miriam should have confessed long ago.

"Now, how is it you know of women being raped, little one? Did this terrible thing happen to you too?"

Tamar jumped to her feet and pulled her hand free. "No!" Her eyes widened, and a flush mounted her cheeks.

Ima patted the chair again. "It was not your fault. You did not ask him to rape you, did you?"

"H-how did you know?" Tamar slumped to the chair and covered her face. "Who told you?"

"You did, child. Your body and your face told me. Do you want to talk about it?"

If Ima could see the truth in Tamar, if Tamar had been raped, could Ima have known just by looking at Miriam that she had been attacked?

Miriam bowed her head. Attacked and taken inside the house, yes. But Julius had rescued her before…before the man could do such an unspeakable act.

"If you could see it…it must be that everyone knows. I will not be able to hold my head up in this village ever again."

"No, that is not true. Perhaps only God knows. But how did your husband find out?"

"I-I told him. I thought he would kill the man, but no, instead he reviled me. He says I must have enticed the soldier. Otherwise he would not have, have…."

Miriam descended the stairs. "Hello, Tamar. I thought I heard your voice."

Tamar cried out. "Evil woman! How long have you been listening?" She raised her fist.

Ima grasped Tamar's hand "Perhaps you should tell Miriam what you told me."

"Yes, I shall. You, Miriam, you have been consorting with our enemies."

Miriam shook her head. "What? Our enemies do not receive any of my time." Tamar might believe all Romans evil, but Tamar did not know Julius and his goodness. She did not see the love behind his smile, or the laughter in his voice. She had never had someone like Julius to comfort her.

"I saw you with that soldier. He took you into the house of Barnabab, I saw it."

"If you saw it, why did you not help? That beast tried to rape me." Miriam's voice raised in pitch to a near scream.

"Tried?" Deborah asked. "What is she talking about, Daughter. What happened?"

Miriam's shoulders shook. "I was afraid to tell you, Ima."

"Afraid?"

"I thought you might think I...I lured him in some way. I wanted to tell you. I almost did, several times but could not."

"Tamar had the same problem. Was it the same soldier, Tamar?"

Tamar was quiet for a long moment. Her tight features softened, and her gaze upon Miriam filled with repentance and not hate. "I think so, but they all look so much alike. I'm sorry, Miriam. I was afraid too. I ran away." Tamar slumped again.

"Then you didn't see the centurion arrest him. I was fortunate. He did not..did not rape me. He tried, but the centurion stopped him before he...he...." Miriam began to cry.

Ima stood and slipped one arm around Miriam and placed one hand on Tamar's shoulder. "The two of you experienced something no woman should ever have to, but I'm afraid too many women do. You should talk with each other. It will help. And Tamar? I will ask Micah to go talk to your husband. He's a wise man. He will know the words to say."

Tamar bowed her head and fell silent for a few moments. She raised her red, swollen eyes to Ima. "Thank you, Deborah. You, too, are wise." She stood to her feet and walked out the door.

Ima turned to Miriam. "Ah, Daughter, I wish you had told me. And now tell me, was it Julius who saved you?"

"I think so, even though all I saw was his back. But his back looks different from the other centurion here. Julius is taller."

"It would surprise me if it were not Julius. It seems his nature to rescue."

"Yes, it does. I'm sorry I didn't tell you earlier." Miriam hugged her mother for a long while before she slowly ascended the steps to her room.

Chapter 28

Miriam took a deep breath of the freshly cleaned air as she passed the window. The first rain of autumn had fallen the night before, leaving that delicious scent of moisture on thirsty earth and providing a cool breeze. She paused by the opening and rejoiced that God had once again pushed the hot summer into the past. It felt good to be able to rejoice, even though her sorrow still weighed so heavy on her heart.

She smiled again as she stepped from the stair onto the floor. Ima and Abba were hugging. "Good morning, Abba and Ima."

Ima turned and held out a hand to Miriam. "Good morning, Daughter. Are you ready to break your fast?"

Miriam moved in with a quick hug for both of them. "I *am* hungry. Is it ready?"

"It is. You could help me bring it to the table," Ima said.

Abba patted his stomach. "Soon, I hope. I need sustenance before I walk up that road to Jerusalem."

"Why are you going to Jerusalem, Abba?"

"There is someone I need to talk to. Now, would you bring some breakfast before I faint from hunger?"

Micah walked up the winding road to Jerusalem murmuring to the donkey alongside him. "What do you think, Bobo? Will this plan work? I want Mirie to be happy. You and I both know she won't be happy with James."

The donkey swished his tail at a fly and snorted.

"Huh. You think you know so much. *You* come up with a better plan." Micah chuckled. "I hope those men hiding behind those rocks over there think I'm a demoniac and leave me alone. Shall we give them more reason to believe that, my hairy friend?"

Micah roared with laughter and clapped the donkey on his neck. "That's a fine joke, Mother. Tell me another one. Shall we have some cheese?" He picked up a rock from the road and held it to the donkey's mouth.

Shadows flitted from one rock to another.

"So, Mother, what will we discuss today? I think we should talk about this nice rain we're having." He held out one hand and drizzled dirt on it from his other hand uplifted in the burning sunshine. He patted Bobo's neck, giving him an extra push backward. The startled donkey sat back on his rump, braying a protest.

"Why, yes, Mother, I'll have some wine. Thank you." He pulled the water skin from his waist and took a healthy swig. "You want some?" He lifted the donkey's head and poured water into his mouth. Bobo backed up, obviously thinking his master had slipped over the edge. Bobo pulled back against his rope, but Micah sat down in the shade of a rock, wrapping the rope around his waist. *Hmm. Back off a little, Micah. Bobo acts more convinced than the brigands.* He bowed his head, leaned against the rock, and wiped his forehead. He peered out from between his fingers and saw nothing.

"Well, Adonai, are we safe now?" Micah stood, one hand shading his eyes as he stared hard across the road where he'd seen the men. "Have You saved my donkey and me this day? I thank You, Most High God."

A stout, bushy-bearded man stepped out from behind the rock. "And perhaps some thanks to Barabbas, old man. Your act didn't convince me, but you did lighten my mood this day."

Micah whirled, pulling a knife from his girdle. "I may be old, but I can still do you some damage, boy," he growled.

Barabbas laughed. "Relax, old man. I don't rob my countrymen, not that it looks like you have anything worth stealing. What do you have in these bags?" He rummaged in Micah's belongings while three others stepped from behind some trees and rocks across the road and two came from behind Barabbas. "Water and dried fish. Not worth bothering, anyway."

Micah lowered his knife. "Barabbas? Seems I've heard of you."

"You will hear much more if we are successful. We rid this land of the traitors and Romans, not honest Jews. Go on your way, elder.

No one here will hurt you. But watch out for the Romans. They are rough and evil men."

"Some are, some aren't. Just like the Jews. Some good, some not." Micah's eyes squinted hard at Barabbas.

"We're not evil; we fight evil. The only ones we kill are Romans and traitorous Jews."

"So you say. Are you the almighty judge, then, to say who should die and who should not?" Micah's grip tightened on the knife.

"And who are you, old man, to judge us? We spared your life once. Go now before we change our minds." Barabbas pulled his own knife, and his sharp black eyes narrowed.

Micah gritted his teeth and started to retort, but the thought of his wife and daughter waiting for him at home stopped him. Scowling, he picked up Bobo's rope. "A word of warning for you, Barabbas. One day your actions will cause your downfall. The One God does not abide murderers. Think on this before you act." Micah turned and led the donkey up the hill toward Jerusalem.

He made camp outside the gates of Jerusalem that night, and the next morning he entered the walls to search for James. It took numerous questions to countless passersby before Micah located anyone who knew where the Prophet Jesus and His disciples could be found. The news didn't help. Jesus and His followers left Jerusalem ten days previous, going north toward Sychar. Micah scratched his beard. *Now what, Adonai? My wonderful plan to talk James out of marrying Miriam is traveling north, and now James might not return until next Passover. I have two choices: follow and see if I can find him, or go back and face my daughter's sad countenance.* He sighed, patting the donkey. "We'll have to go home first. I'll need more food and water. Well, let's go, Bobo. And Adonai, it would be nice if we didn't run into that band of brigands on the way home."

The next morning, Micah smiled as he woke up, reaching his arm around his sleeping wife, nuzzling her bare back and tickling her with his beard.

"Mph. That's a mean way to wake me up, Micah ben Elias." Deborah turned over, yawned, and stretched, thumping Micah's chest with her open hand.

"It's time for you to get up and get my breakfast, woman. I have a big hunger."

"Hmm," Deborah said. "I thought we took care of that hunger last night."

Micah chuckled and pulled her to him. "Yes, and I'm hungry for you again, but I have some traveling to do and need a good meal under my ribs."

"Traveling?" Deborah lifted an eyebrow.

"I didn't accomplish my mission yesterday, wife, and unless we want to watch Mirie cry for a year, I have to find James. Now, out of bed with you before I change my mind, lazy woman."

Deborah giggled. She threw the blanket back and rose, pulling on her tunic. "I'll fix some breakfast while you milk the goat."

Cheese, bread, and watered wine greeted Micah when he came back in the house with the fresh milk, and he sat down, ravenous. Deborah handed him a pack wrapped in wool.

"See that you come back to me whole and soon, Micah. You're going into a wilderness thick with all kinds of thieves and murderers who'd as soon steal coins and food from a dead man as a live one."

Miriam came down the stairs and stopped in mid-yawn at her mother's words. "Who's dead, Ima?"

"No one, Daughter. I'm only cautioning your father to be careful as he travels through Judea."

"Where are you going this time, Abba, on a buying trip?" She walked up to her father and hugged him.

Micah eyed his wife. "Uh, more of a bargaining trip. I should be back in a week or two. Looking for some, um, something different to build upon." He patted her back.

Miriam moved to her mother's side. "Ima and I can take care of things while you're gone. She's feeling so much better she doesn't even need me anymore."

"Ah, but I do need you. This house will shine before your father returns, Little One."

Miriam groaned. "There are times, Ima, when I wish I'd been born a boy."

Micah stopped in Ephraim, asking anyone who would give him their time if they'd seen the Prophet and His followers. It wasn't long until he found one who'd seen Him, a Pharisee who wasn't pleased with the Prophet, but either he was disinclined to offer help or didn't know where they'd gone. Just knowing that they'd been there was enough to send Micah looking for the local synagogue and rabbi.

"Shalom, Rabbi." Micah bowed his head toward the bent old man squinting up at him, wiry gray hair protruding around his head in tufts.

"Shalom." The rabbi's voice quavered.

"I come seeking friends and hope you might be able to tell me where they've gone."

"Eh?"

"Some friends. I've come seeking friends."

"Yes?"

"Have you seen the Prophet Jesus and his friends?"

"Eh?" The old man cupped his hand behind his ear.

"Jesus. The Prophet Jesus. Have you seen him, or do you know where he went?" Micah raised his voice until he thought everyone within five miles could hear him.

"Yes?"

"Yes, what?"

"Eh? What is it, young man? Speak up. I don't have all day to listen to your mumblings."

"Jesus. Have. You. Seen. Jesus of Nazareth?" Micah bellowed.

"What isn't easy? Life isn't supposed to be easy, young man. An easy life leads to destruction."

A younger man hurried out of the synagogue. "I'm sorry, sir, Rabbi Eliah can't hear much. Here's a tablet. Do you know how to write?"

"Yes," Micah said, taking the wax-coated tablet from him. He scribbled his question and handed it to the Rabbi.

"Ah, Jesus. Why didn't you say so?" Rabbi Eliah warbled. "He left here a while back. On His way to Jerusalem, I think, or maybe from Jerusalem. Hard to say for sure, though, because He mumbled, too."

Micah bowed his head to the old rabbi, and smiled at the younger man, "And you, sir, did Jesus tell you where He would go?"

"No, I wasn't here, but some others said he was going west to Bethel." His eyes twinkled. "Next time you have a need to know something from Rabbi Eliah, ask for me, Zichri. I'll help you the best I can. God go with you. I hope you find Him. He is worth listening to."

"I'll remember, Zichri. I thank both of you. God be with you, too." Micah tugged on the donkey's halter. "Come on, Bobo. We have a long way to go this day."

By the time Micah had been on the road a week and stopped in several villages, his steps were slower and his shoulders slumped. In the latest village, Sebaste, no one had seen anything of Jesus and His followers.

"I don't know, Bobo. The trail grows colder instead of warmer. What do we do now? And why do I keep asking you? Will you turn into Balaam's donkey and begin talking to me? I surely do wish Adonai would somehow point us in the right direction. At the rate we're going, it would have been handier to wait for James to come back for the next Passover."

Bobo shook his head and flicked his ears to get rid of a pesky fly, jerking his nose to the right.

"What? Go to the right, you say? It's as good as the left, and you have as good a chance of being right as wrong." Micah took the right fork in the road ahead and hadn't gone more than a half mile when he saw a group of men coming toward him.

"Hmm, Bobo. You might be related to Balaam's donkey after all. I think that's James. And Jesus. And all of the rest of them."

"Micah, what are you doing here?" James extended his arms to Micah, palms up.

Micah clasped James' arms and pulled him into the greeting kiss. "Shalom."

"It is good to see you, Father-in-Law."

"That's what I came to see you about, James." Micah dropped his arms and backed up.

"What do you mean?"

"I came all this way to find you. I want you to release us from the marriage promise."

James' jaw dropped. "Release her? Why?"

If I say she loves another, he will accuse her of adultery. What do I say, Adonai? Micah hesitated, staring at his feet. *Ah, yes. Thank you, Adonai.* "You said you want to follow this Man, Jesus, and you don't know how long that will be. How long do you expect her to wait? Until she can no longer bear a child? You aren't betrothed, so I ask this out of courtesy. I could say it's over, and it would be over. In fact, it could be said you broke your promise. You were to bring your parents at Passover for a betrothal ceremony."

"But Micah, I waited for her for two years to grow up. Could she not wait a few years for me? Father was angry with me when I decided to follow Jesus, and he would not come for a betrothal ceremony then." A small scowl and a flush crossed James' face. "You know how Father is. He'll get over that soon, though."

"And meanwhile, I should turn away the matchmaker and every suitor who shows up, thinking maybe someday you would decide to face up to your responsibilities?" Micah crossed his arms and frowned, hoping he looked fierce.

James' small scowl cut deeper into his brow, but his retort was chopped short by Jesus, Who laid His hand on James' arm.

"What troubles you, James? Do you want to go home for a betrothal and marriage?"

James shook his head, the scowl erased as though it had never been when he looked at Jesus. "No, Master, at least not yet. Or maybe just for the betrothal."

"Do you not remember? Moses told men who had taken a wife to spend a year at home with her. If a wife is what you want, you must not accompany Me. We have hardships no new wife should have to bear. We sleep on the hard ground, we depend on the generosity of townspeople to provide food, and one day even this life will seem a luxury. You must make a choice. Take a wife, or follow Me."

James looked down at his feet for only a moment. "If I must make a choice, Master, the choice is to follow You." He turned to Micah. "I release you from the promise, Micah."

Micah noted James' eyes seemed more than a little moist. "I commend you, James. You made a difficult choice, but you made it with wisdom and compassion. May God go with you."

James nodded and drifted off toward where his brother sat on a rock.

Micah bowed to Jesus. "Thank You, Lord. Not just for this, but also for my wife. You might not remember, but my sister-in-law and her husband sought You out and asked You to heal her."

Jesus smiled, His eyes full of compassion. He nodded. "I remember. You and your family's faith in God, together with your love for Deborah, accomplished wonders. My Father heard your heart's cry."

Tears stung Micah's eyes. "You are truly God's Prophet, Lord."

"Truly I tell you, Micah, that and more." Jesus spoke to his ears only. Micah didn't think anyone else heard. Even James had moved away to talk to John, probably telling him why Micah had come.

As Jesus' words sank in, Micah's mouth dropped. He dropped to his knees and pressed his forehead into the dust of the road.

"Lord, I'm a sinful man."

Jesus reached down and raised Micah to his feet.

Hot tears washed Micah's cheeks. "What can I do to become worthy of You?"

"Believe in Me."

"I do, Lord, and I will, always."

"Go home now, Micah. Your family waits for you."

"I'll tell them about You, Lord." Micah backed away, bowing repeatedly. Jesus turned back to His disciples.

As he made his way home, Micah sang the old psalms of David, but as though he heard them for the first time. "Sing praises to God, sing praises: Sing praises unto our King, sing praises. For God is the King of all the earth: sing ye praises with understanding."

His feet felt feather-light, and his deep voice soared like a gull on the breeze. Even the old donkey seemed to enjoy the trip. The two days it took to journey home again were short and filled with awe at what he'd discovered.

He walked in the door and called out, "I'm home. Anyone here?" Silence greeted him. "Deborah? Miriam?"

Chapter 29

Miriam caught sight of Julius marching his men to their guard posts and felt her heart stretch out toward him. She stood in the shadow of the synagogue, wishing she could go to him, speak to him. Wishing, but knowing she couldn't, stirred up an ache that spread from her toes to the roots of her hair. Her eyes threatened to spill with tears. Pressure built in her chest, and she turned away and ran for home. She found her way more by instinct rather than by sight, stumbling into the house, sobs ripping from her throat as she shut the door behind herself.

"Mirie, what's wrong? Is your mother...?" Her father grasped her shoulders, his frightened stare demanding answers.

Miriam gasped. "Abba! Where did you come from?" His sudden appearance startled the tears away.

"Where is your mother?" Abba shook her shoulders, his eyes wide.

"Ima's all right, Abba. I cried because I'm feeling sorry for myself." She sniffed and dried her eyes with her scarf. "She's at Leah's."

Abba breathed a sigh, and his face relaxed. He pulled her into his embrace. "Ah. And just why is it you are feeling so sorry for yourself, as if I didn't know. Do you want to talk about it?" He tilted her chin, but she couldn't make her eyes meet his.

"Same reason, Abba. I thought I was resigned to marrying James, but every time I see Julius, I feel as though my heart is being torn in pieces." Miriam hung her head. "I'm sorry, Abba, I know I disappoint you in this. I will honor the promise."

"What if I told you James has released us?"

Miriam covered her mouth with her hands. A long pause ensued while her eyes searched his. She backed up a step. "Please, Abba, don't tease me."

"I'm not teasing." Her father smiled and his eyes shone.

"Do you mean that...are you saying that...I mean, James didn't...did he?"

"It seems he has made his choice to follow the Messiah."

Miriam gasped, and thoughts of James and Julius fled before this new excitement. "The Messiah? You found the Messiah? Is it Jesus that James already follows or John the Baptizer or who? Where did you find Him? Is He here?"

Abba laughed. "One question at a time, Mirie. Yes, I found the Messiah. Or maybe He found me. Jesus, the one James is following, is the Messiah. We met on the road. He and His disciples were headed north. Bobo and I were walking south."

"How do you know He's the Messiah? Did He tell you?" Miriam shook with excitement.

"Not exactly. I don't remember exactly what He did or said, but I said to Him that He was truly a prophet of God, and He said something back, like 'I'm more than a prophet.' I can't remember His exact words, but it's like the heavens opened with a huge finger pointing at Him. I could feel the presence of...of holiness."

"Oh, Abba, how I wish I could have been there. What else did He say?"

Abba hugged her. "He told James to choose between following Him and marrying you. James chose Him."

Miriam's intake of air stuck in her lungs for a moment, then she exhaled with a soft cry. She tore loose from her father's arms, eyes wide. "I'm free? I mean, we're free? May I...we...tell Julius? Now?"

"Not right now. We should wait for your mother, don't you think? I'll go and invite him to come break bread with us in a day or two. Meanwhile, you will practice being patient. These negotiations are not for a daughter to discuss."

"Oh, Abba, it will be so hard to wait."

"But wait you will. No arguments, Mirie. I have my reasons, and you have to trust me."

Micah walked to the Roman officers' quarters after breakfast. He walked toward a guard in front of the building. "Shalom, sir."

"What is it you want, Jew?" The broad-shouldered, thick-browed soldier swaggered up to Micah and pushed him.

"I would like to speak to Centurion Julius." Micah brushed imaginary dirt from his chest where the guard touched him.

"The centurion is busy. Come back another day, Jew."

"How do you know? I don't believe you, young man. Go, fetch the centurion."

"You heard me. Be off with you." The guard pushed him again, this time with greater force. Micah staggered backward and fell.

"What do you think you're doing, soldier?" An icy voice and firm pull from behind stopped a kick aimed at Micah's head.

The soldier whirled, pulling his sword, and blanched when he apparently recognized a superior. He snapped a quick salute and stood at attention. "This Jew tried to start a ruckus, Decanus."

"Try that again, soldier, and you'll be cleaning latrines for a month. I saw and heard what you did." The man stepped over to Micah and held out his hand to help him up.

"Yes, sir. I mean, no, sir, Decanus." The guard glared at Marcus' back, a sneer on his lips.

Micah's rescuer turned back around. "Brutus, back to your duties. Don't let me hear of you roughing up civilians again."

"As you wish, Decanus." Brutus marched away with stiff back and angry stride.

"They should never have released that man from prison," the Decanus muttered.

Micah's eyes narrowed. "If I were you, Decanus, I would wear all my armor when that man is around."

The soldier laughed. "He's his own worst enemy. The man's temper and roughness has gotten him into more stocks than dogs have fleas. He likes to pick on those who can't or won't fight back."

"I saw the look in his eyes when you turned your back on him, and his hand fingered his sword. I thought you should know."

"Thank you. Now, did you come to the officer's quarters for a reason? May I help you?"

"I hope so. I'm looking for Julius. He's a friend of my family."

"Ah, you must be Micah. I'm Julius' friend Marcus. He talks about Mir...ah, your family often."

Micah grinned. "I'm sure it's Miriam whose name is most often on his lips."

Marcus laughed. "'Often' accurately describes it. 'Every other word' might be even more accurate. Julius is patrolling today, but I should see him this evening. What should I tell him?"

"That I wish to speak to him. Maybe you could send word to the house of Micah when he returns?"

"My guess is that he won't bother sending a messenger. He'll come himself. Probably at a run or galloping his horse through the streets."

"Ordinarily, that would be acceptable, but not this time. I want to speak with him away from my home."

"Hm. Well, he can always send me. Where do you live?"

Micah gave Marcus turn-by-turn directions, then made his way home.

"I wonder why Micah didn't want me to come to his house. This doesn't sound good." Julius paced the floor in his apartment.

"It might not be anything bad. He didn't seem upset with the idea that you spoke often of Miriam."

Julius stopped. "What? What did you do, tell him I talk about her all the time?"

"It slipped out. But the point remains, he didn't act angry or upset. At least not at you. You remember Brutus, that soldier who was in trouble last week for single-handedly starting a riot between the men in the barracks?"

"I'd like to forget him, but yes, he comes to mind. What's he been up to this time?"

"He pushed Micah down and was about to kick him in the head. As it happened, I saw the whole incident and stopped Brutus. He wasn't happy with me, but he complied."

"He might find himself transferred to one of the fighting battalions." Julius walked to the window and looked out. "He's out there now, walking his line dutifully. Your words must have made some impact on him."

Marcus joined him at the window. "Some, but I don't hold out a lot of hope for his abject repentance."

"So, how am I supposed to meet Micah?"

"I told him you would send a messenger—probably me—to his house to let him know you were back."

"Consider yourself sent."

Marcus saluted smartly and marched toward the door. "Aye, sir."

Julius waited at the west gate the next morning for Micah, sweat rolling down the back of his neck. Could this heat last much longer? Surely October should begin cooler weather.

Micah arrived wiping his forehead. "Shalom, Julius."

"Shalom, Micah. How was your journey?"

"How was it you knew I went anywhere?"

"I saw Miriam at the well. Don't worry. We only spoke for a moment, and she was well chaperoned. Did you find the bargain you sought?"

"Let's sit in the shade. It's hot enough to fry my feet here." Micah led the way to the gate, under the branches of a huge tree. Several large rocks and logs had been placed there in a circle for elders to sit and listen to the complaints and pronouncements of the citizens. Some seats were occupied. Micah chose one close to the others. The elders stopped their conversations and turned curious faces turned toward him and the Roman. Micah waved Julius to a rock at the edge of the circle.

Julius sat. What was Miriam's father doing?

"Shalom, Elders." Micah bowed his head respectfully to the men present.

"Shalom, Micah, son of Elias. Did you ask the Most High for this heat?" One of the men, wizened and weathered, nodded his bald head, and his long, full beard twitched into what might have been a smile.

"No, Simon. I thought you had." Micah's smile showed through his close-trimmed beard.

"Elders, I come before you in a quandary. Months ago, James, the son of Zebedee, came to me and asked for the hand of my daughter, Miriam. I gave my consent and asked that he bring his parents back for the betrothal ceremony. When he returned, however, he did not bring his parents. He said his father was angry and wouldn't come. When I asked why Zebedee was angry, James said it was because he, James, wanted to follow the Prophet Jesus. He said he wanted to delay the betrothal and marriage for a time."

"Unusual. How long a time?" The elders leaned forward almost as one.

Forever, Julius hoped.

"He did not say, Reuben. This Roman centurion has also asked for Miriam's hand and...."

Julius sat straighter, his attention riveted upon Micah.

"A Roman? You know we are forbidden to give our sons and daughters in marriage to Gentiles."

Julius lowered his head. Would he get this close only to be denied?

"Yes, this I know. This man is perhaps different. He is a proselyte, circumcised some time ago by Shelumiel."

The elders murmured amongst themselves, and hope surged within Julius once more.

"Yet a promise was made and must be kept." A round-faced, gray-haired elder tugged at the curled corner of his beard.

"Yes, unless the promise is made null, Enoch." Reuben nodded.

"Which it has. I met with James. He released us from the promise." Micah fanned himself with a large leaf.

"He did?" Julius started, but Micah raised his hand to silence him.

"Hmm." Enoch scratched his beard. "Hmm."

"If a betrothal to a proselyte were approved, would the children of the marriage be raised in the Jewish religion?" Reuben straightened and looked hard at Julius.

"Of course," Julius nodded. "There is no god but the One God. My children will be raised to worship only Him."

"Will you take your sons to Jerusalem for the Passover?"

"Whenever I am able, Elders."

"Will you protect your new brethren against attacks even from Rome?"

"That depends on the circumstances, Elders. Would you agree that sometimes I must protect Rome against Hebrew brigands on the Jericho road?"

The elders drew their heads together and whispered amongst themselves.

Reuben turned back to Julius. "We agree that there are times that could be necessary. We ask that you never take up arms against Palestine."

"My earnest hope is that I never have to make that decision, Elders, but no, I would not want to go to war with those who are now my brothers."

"Go now, Roman. You, too, Micah. Come back tomorrow at this hour, and we will give you our decision."

Julius stood alongside Micah, bowed to the elders, and turned. As they walked back to the marketplace, Julius felt a smile tug at the corners of his mouth. "So, Micah, I find myself in your debt. Was that the whole purpose of your journey? If so, I'm honored more than I can say."

Micah chuckled. "I thought you might be pleased. You might like to know, Miriam is also happy. I feel sure the elders will agree."

"And if they don't?"

"If they don't? That would indeed be an unhappy ending, wouldn't it? We will of course abide by their decision."

Chapter 30

Julius strode home whistling a lively military tune. When he entered his quarters, Cyril stood sweeping the day's dirt out. Julius grabbed the broom and danced it around, grinning as though his face would split.

"Let me guess," Cyril said. "You saw your pretty little Jewess, and she agreed to run away with you rather than marry the fisherman?"

"Even better." Julius tossed the broom into the air and caught it behind his back. "Her old agreement is out the window, and her father all but welcomed me into the family."

"Oh, really?" Cyril said, taking the broom back.

"Really. I'm serious. Micah met me today and took me to the gate where the Jewish elders sit, and he made the case for me to be betrothed to Miriam. Micah's promise to Fisherman James is off, agreed to by James himself. Micah invited me to their house tomorrow for the evening meal."

Cyril nodded. "Congratulations. So when do you announce this betrothal?"

"I hope tomorrow. It depends on the elders at the gate, though. That's still an anxious spot in the back of my brain. Micah wants them to approve her betrothal to a Gentile. They have their qualms, even though I'm a proselyte. I wonder why Loukas didn't ask them before you were betrothed?"

"Maybe because Quinta wasn't already promised to a real Jew. Maybe because she is also a proselyte."

"That makes sense. Where's my meal, slave?"

"You forget; I'm no longer a slave."

"True. Then where's my meal, servant?"

"Where's my pay, employer?"

"Oh, no, I forgot again. I'm a rotten boss, Cyril. Here." Julius handed him two denarii. "You'd think I'd remember, since we do this every day."

"You'd think. I shouldn't complain, knowing that you pay me more than most servants. But remember, I'm saving for a wedding." Cyril grinned and added the coin to others in a cloth bag. "I pierced the first ten you paid me for Quinta to wear like a crown around her head. The bride price, you know. Do you have some for Miriam? Micah's not going to be satisfied with silver coins for her, you being a centurion."

Julius struck his forehead with the flat of his hand. "I didn't think of that. Five aurei, pierced. And gifts like bracelets, necklaces, earrings. How am I going to get these gifts by tomorrow?"

"Try the marketplace." Cyril placed two dishes of stew on the table. "If you want, I could help."

"I do want. I've got more on my plate than I can handle. Micah and I meet with the elders again tomorrow before the sixth hour, and I've got patrols to organize and dispatch. I should accompany the earliest patrol, but I've got to be back for the meeting with the elders. They threw me a couple of sharp questions yesterday. I don't want to fail this test."

"Don't worry. I'll get the gifts and pierce the aurei and bring them to you before then. Where will you be?"

"I'm not sure. I'll have to meet you here. I can still hardly believe it. I want to shout from the window that Miriam will be my wife. The most beautiful, voluptuous, and tantalizing woman in Judea will be my wife, and there's not a thing this world can do to stop me." Finished with his meal, Julius stood up and stretched, grinning again, and leaned out the window.

He straightened as a sudden thought hit him, and he turned to Cyril. "Did you have gifts for Quinta?"

"No, just the coins for her headband. Loukas realizes I'm not as rich as you, you know."

"Take this and get gifts for Quinta as well as gifts for Miriam. Consider it my gift to Quinta." Julius took out his coin bag and shook out several gold aurei.

"I can't allow you to give my bride gifts, Julius." Cyril turned his back and placed the food he'd carried from the kitchen onto the table.

Cyril's stiffened spine told Julius his friend meant what he said.

"Then consider it past wages. In truth, you've earned more than this."

"No."

"A loan?"

Cyril turned back to Julius, scowling. Opened his mouth, shut it, and then paused. "All right. A loan. But only one aureus. I don't want to start our married life in debt, not even to you."

Julius clapped Cyril on the shoulder. "You drive a hard bargain, man."

Marcus knocked at the opened door and walked in. "My timing is getting better. Got enough for a hungry decanus, Cyril?"

"If your hunger is for stew, we have plenty. Maybe even a piece of bread."

"We should start charging for your cooking, Cyril. We could give the camp cooks some competition." Julius moved over to allow Marcus room on the couch. "By the way, Decanus, you might want to slow down some. Your chariot nearly clipped one of the priests today."

Chapter 31

Julius stood at the gate and pulled his helmet off. He wiped his forehead and pulled a cloth from his girdle to run it across his dripping hair. He wished Micah would arrive. At the sixth hour, the elders were there, murmuring among themselves, casting glances at him while he stood roasting in the hot sun, but no one waved him to a seat. He wondered how badly he would hurt his cause by asking if he could join them in the shade. Would they consider him brash, demanding, authoritative? Would they think him friendly if he smiled? On the other hand, they might think he was baring his teeth, instead. Where in this world was Micah? *Adonai, are you listening? I could use Your help.*

To Julius' unbridled relief, Micah came around the corner of a nearby building, tugging a reluctant donkey behind him. His face reddened with the effort. Deborah held onto a strap around the donkey's girth with one hand and held a veil in place with the other, an amused twinkle in her eyes.

"My apologies for being late, Elders," Micah puffed. "I decided at the last minute to bring my wife. She often exhibits great wisdom. And she has been ill, so we needed this stubborn donkey to give her a ride."

Deborah dismounted the donkey and gave it a pat on his sweaty neck. Micah tied him to the tree, not that he was likely to go anywhere. The beast had found a patch of grass in the shade and showed no interest in moving from the green stuff.

Micah took Deborah's arm and led her to a shady boulder, pointing Julius to another rock in the shade with his chin. He took a corner of his tunic and wiped his face before joining the others.

Enoch, Reuben, and Simon weren't alone at the gate this time. Another elder, a tall scowling Jew wearing the bells of a Pharisee, sat alone in stiff disapproval in the center of the widest bench. Julius and Micah exchanged glances.

"Judah, it is good to see you. I hope you have been well." Micah bowed his head respectfully, first at Judah, then at the others. "Shalom, my friends. This must be the last of the hot days this season."

"Indeed. Shalom to you, too, Micah and...Julius, was it?" Simon nodded at them, and Reuben and Enoch followed his lead. Judah maintained a stony silence.

"Have you come to a decision, Elders?" Micah asked the three, not looking at Judah.

Julius held his breath for the next few seconds, watching the elders glancing at each other and then at the Pharisee.

Simon cleared his throat. "Ah, we thought we had, but Judah here says we are in error. It was the opinion of the elders that the marriage between this proselyte and Miriam could take place, especially after we questioned him. But Judah has a different opinion."

Judah folded his arms across his chest. "The purity of their children would be in question. We cannot allow Jews to mix blood with Gentiles. It is against the law and the prophets."

Deborah cleared her throat. "Honored elders, may this old woman speak?"

All but Judah nodded.

"Judah, you are the Son of Zeruriah, right? I have heard him say he is descended from Boaz. Is this not so?"

Judah shifted on his bench. One eyebrow twitched. His cheeks reddened. His scowl deepened. "That was an exception. Ruth took care of Naomi and became a follower of the One God through her."

"In other words, Ruth became a proselyte." Deborah said, eyes lowered, voice soft, almost as though she were talking to herself. She stared at the ground. "Her mother-in-law guided her. It is my thought perhaps this Roman would have a mother-in-law to guide him, also. Ruth became a proselyte even though no Rabbi gave her lessons. This Roman has had the teaching of the Rabbi Shelumiel and has been circumcised. If he married into this family, he would have father-in-law, mother-in-law, and wife to make sure he obeyed the laws of God."

Micah grunted. "This is truth."

Judah said nothing, but a glare and clenched jaw made his thoughts clear.

Enoch's eyes smiled, but his voice sounded stern. "Then it is settled. This Roman proselyte, Julius, may marry the daughter of Micah."

Julius, along with Micah, and Deborah, bowed their heads to the elders, rose. Micah retrieved the reluctant donkey from the grass.

When they were out of earshot, Julius turned to Deborah. "Thank you, lady. You are my savior."

"No, Julius, only God is your Savior." Deborah smiled at him from the donkey's back. "I'm only a listener."

"A listener?"

"I just listened in my mind for His prompting and then spoke."

"It was a miracle they were willing to hearken to a mere woman, wife. Except I don't think the elders much wanted to follow the Pharisee's lead. He's spent the last couple of years trying to convince everyone only he has God's ear, since he's so very righteous." Micah bent down to pick up a thatch of grass and held it in front of the donkey's nose. "Come, Bobo. We want to get home for dinner today."

Deborah patted the donkey's neck as he increased his plodding to a faster walk. "You will stay to break bread with us, Julius, of course."

Julius shook his head. "Thank you, but not now, lady. I have duty yet this day, until the evening."

Light worry lines ran across her face. "How late do you work tomorrow?"

"Tomorrow I am free at about the same time—at the beginning of the first watch. I could bring the betrothal gifts to your house this evening, though. Is that what's required to make our betrothal official?"

"We'd like to invite our friends to the event, Julius. Then tomorrow, when you are free, the wine will flow and the ceremony will begin." Micah lifted his hands and moved his feet in a stomping dance, inspiring Bobo to jerk backward, ears laid horizontal, teeth bared.

Deborah slid off the donkey's back with a laugh. "Don't worry, Bobo. He won't make you dance with him." She walked into their house calling for Miriam.

"Here, Ima." Miriam walked around the corner of the house, and her expression filled with joy when her eyes met Julius'.

I love the way her face brightens when she sees me, and I love knowing it's only for me that she looks that way. His mouth split in a wide grin. "Hello, beloved." *At last I can say that.*

A quick cry escaped her lips. "They agreed?" She turned to her mother. "They agreed!"

Deborah laughed. "Yes, they agreed. And tomorrow…tomorrow we shall have a ceremony."

Micah hummed and danced as he dragged Bobo toward the small corral in back of the house. Bobo laid his ears to his neck again, dragging against the lead rope and braying his irritation at the mad man who led him.

"What does this ceremony involve? What do I need to do to get ready?" Julius asked.

"You will need to bring the bride price and gifts for Miriam. You and Micah must agree on what the price will be." Deborah slid her arm around Miriam and squeezed her shoulders.

"I left Cyril with an assignment or two in regard to gifts and bride prices. I should go home and see if all is ready."

"What? You sent Cyril after gifts before the approval of the elders? Such confidence." Deborah's eyes twinkled.

Miriam blushed crimson. "Ima...."

"I hope they are adequate for such a treasure, lady."

"Julius, when will you stop calling me that? You make me feel older than Methuselah. 'Mother' will do from now on."

Julius decided it was his turn to tease. "Perhaps I should call you 'Ima,' instead."

"And you could call my father 'Abba.' I like that, don't you, Ima?" Miriam twirled.

Deborah laughed. "That could be an experience. I'd like to be there the first time you call him Abba, Julius."

"What time should I be here tomorrow, my future mother?"

"Let's say sundown. That should be enough time for us to tell those we want to invite. A betrothal isn't quite like a wedding, with the whole village there." She held out a hand to Micah, who approached from the back of the house.

He touched her hand and then clapped Julius on the shoulders. "Sundown tomorrow. Be there, or I'll give Miriam to the first passing stranger."

"Nothing could keep me away." Julius bowed to both Miriam and Deborah and saluted Micah. "I'll see you tomorrow."

Chapter 32

Miriam stretched, smiled, and threw her blanket back. *This is the day, Adonai, and how beautiful you have made it. I know a morning's red sky speaks a warning, but this one is splendid beyond description. Red, crimson, orange, amber, even purple. I don't think I've ever seen one prettier, Adonai. Thank You. I can scarcely wait for the evening. I'll string the coins he brings for the bride price like a crown across my forehead from this day forth. After this evening, the world will know that my heart belongs to a Centurion who guards Jericho. From this evening forth, I will be betrothed to Julius.* Miriam rose from her bed and donned her old tunic, still smiling to herself. She'd have time to change into a better one later in the day. There was much to do. She'd help Ima prepare the house. They'd go to the marketplace for food and wine, and she would bathe. It would not do for her to smell of sweat and smoke for her betrothal. She chuckled as she descended the stairs and hummed a psalm, sniffing appreciatively at the smell of baking bread.

"Behold, our happy daughter has returned. I thought we would never see her again." Abba beamed from the kitchen.

"It's so good to hear you singing again. I feared you had forgotten how." Ima pulled Miriam to her, holding her for a moment before pointing her toward the table. "Would you set the plates on the table so we may break our fast? I'm as hungry as a dog in the street."

"And I'm even hungrier." Abba patted his stomach.

"You must have my appetite. I have no hunger at all." Miriam sat by the table but pushed her plate away. "All I want is a little milk."

"You should eat something. You'll need your strength to get everything done that needs doing before the sun sets." Abba pushed the plate of bread toward Miriam.

"It smells good, Abba, but I don't want anything."

"There will be time enough for eating later, and we won't throw out the bread. Don't worry, Micah, one day our daughter will again feel hungry." Ima smiled.

Miriam pulled the new tunic over her head and wondered if the sun was stuck in the sky. *This has to be the longest day of my life.* She trotted down the stairs and found her mother slicing cheese in the kitchen.

"Ima, how does this tunic look?" She twirled in front of her mother. "Is it too long in back?"

Ima wiped her hands on a cloth tied to her waist as she walked around her daughter.

"There is only one problem with it as near as I can tell, Daughter."

"Oh, it *is* too long, isn't it? I'll have to take out the hem and do it over." Miriam glanced down.

"No, the hem is good. The color is beautiful. The blue makes your eyes brighter."

"Then what's wrong with it?"

"You don't look like my little girl any more. You look like a young woman."

Miriam looked at her mother's moist eyes, and her own began to sting.

"Oh, Ima! Am I really? A woman, that is? Sometimes I feel like I am, but sometimes I still want to go out and play with my friends." Miriam sat on a stool and put her cheeks in her hands. "At this moment, I don't know if I want to laugh or cry, and I feel like running away at the same time that I want to run to him."

"Yes, that sounds like a young woman. A young woman who is about to promise herself to a man she knows only a little of. Tomorrow you'll wear the headband of a woman betrothed. Today you may still be my little one. Go, wash your face, and then lie down and put a wet cloth on your eyes. They're a little red." Ima hugged Miriam, turned her, and gave her a small push toward the stairway. "People will be arriving, and you want to look your best."

When Miriam again descended the stairs, Loukas and Joanna had arrived with Quinta. Miriam stretched out her arms to Quinta, and Quinta squeezed her tight. When they broke apart, Miriam touched the coins decorating Quinta's forehead.

"They make you look so…well, so betrothed." Miriam giggled.

"In a few hours, your face will look so betrothed too." Quinta blushed. "My Cyril comes with your Julius today."

"When will they be here? He sounded so eager yesterday, I thought maybe he would be the first to arrive." Miriam grinned. "Do you think it would be unseemly to stand in the road and watch for him?"

"Yes, it would. You will stand here and greet the guests." Abba scowled with mock fierceness.

"Yes, Father, it will be as you wish." Miriam bowed her head as Leah and Amos walked through the door. "Greetings, welcome guests."

Isaiah and Hannah followed Leah and then Shelumiel, and before long, several neighbors joined them in the living area. Ima brought wine and Miriam did not miss the worried glance her mother cast toward her father. Abba raised his eyebrows in response just as the door burst open.

Chapter 33

Julius looked around him with wide-eyed wonder. Except for the wind, this had to be the most perfect day. He'd taken in a beautiful sunrise and only a drizzle or two had fallen. He inhaled the clean, moist air. Enough rain to cool the air, finally after all the heat they had.

Julius pulled Miriam's scarf from beneath his armor, rolled it into a ball, and tossed it into the air, laughing out loud for the joy of living. He lifted his voice in song, not caring if everyone in Jericho heard. "Behold, you are fair, my love; behold, you are fair. You have dove's eyes behind your veil…."

A gust of wind caught the scarf, tossed it high, and blew it behind him into the street. Julius whirled, running to catch it before the racing chariot could….

The chariot bore down on him quicker than he had thought it could. He tried to dodge.

"Whoa!" Marcus' bellow lifted in the air.

Too late!

The horses screamed as they slammed into him. Julius' bare arms and legs scraped the rocks in the road. He tumbled under the horse's hooves, helpless. A hoof thrashed toward his head.

Warm liquid moved across Julius' face as though through a great fog, distant yet surrounding him. He didn't want to wake up. He wanted to sleep until the hurt was gone. Where was his mother? She would make him feel better.

"Julius. *Julius*! Do you hear me? Julius!"

The fog held Marcus' voice at a distance too. He wanted his friend to go away. His head hurt too much to play today.

"I'm so sorry, Julius. I tried to stop the horses, but they were going too fast. Wake up, please, Julius, wake up. Don't die on me, my friend. Please don't die!"

He moaned. Why would Marcus think he would die? It wasn't time to die, just time to sleep. And his mother had warned him not to get dirty. Aunt Lucilla was visiting today.

"What happened?"

Now Cyril had come. Couldn't they just leave him alone?

"I stopped at a merchant's stall to buy a gift, and now...what's this? Is that Julius? Is he dead?"

"Cyril, I didn't mean to hit him. He came out of nowhere, and I couldn't stop the horses. Please, Cyril, believe me! I was hurrying to his betrothal, and all of a sudden there he was, in front of me."

Julius didn't like their game. Betrothal? Oh, how his head hurt.

"I believe you, Marcus. Now, let go so I can go find Loukas."

"We have to help him. Look at all the blood! He could be dying." Marcus—at least he thought it was Marcus—lifted Julius. When had Marcus become stronger than him? And where did he think they were going?

"Wait, Cyril. I need your help to get him back to his quarters. Get in the chariot, and hold him there."

Julius just wished they'd be quiet. His head hurt, and Mama said to play quietly.

"Do any of you know Loukas the Physician?" Marcus bellowed.

Not so loud. Mama said to be quiet.

"I do."

Are there other friends here?

"Here. Run to his house, and if he isn't there, you might find him at the house of Micah the Carpenter. Tell him to come to the house of Julius. Now, repeat that back to me."

"Go first to Loukas the Physician's house. If he is not there, look for him at the house of Micah the Carpenter. Send Loukas to the house of Julius.

"Good. Now, run as though your feet had wings."

Julius heard nothing else.

In Cyril's anxiety, he burst through Micah's door without knocking. In a moment, Cyril was again at a run, this time followed by Loukas. By the time they arrived at Julius' quarters, both were out of breath. Loukas strode to Julius' side as Marcus told him about the accident. As soon as he finished, Loukas patted Julius' shoulder.

"Julius, can you hear me? Open your eyes." Loukas' voice sounded insistent.

"When I speak, I can see his eyes move, but they don't open. I think he can hear me." Loukas leaned down closer. "Julius. Open your eyes now."

Julius squeezed his eyes shut tighter as Loukas tried to lift one lid.

"You try, Marcus. He might respond to your voice better than mine."

"Not me. I've tried. He might be mad at me for running over him. You try, Cyril."

"Julius, open your eyes. Please, Master. We want to know how badly you're hurt." Cyril stroked his arm, hoping against hope.

Julius opened one eye in a tight squint.

"Go away," he whined in Latin. "My head hurts. I want to sleep."

"Does anything else hurt?" Loukas leaned over Julius, a cloth in his hand.

"Yes." Julius covered his eyes and rolled over with his back to them. "Go away. I want my mama."

Cyril lifted worried eyes to Loukas. "What do you think?"

Loukas walked to the other side of Julius' bed. He bent down and gazed at Julius' forehead.

Cyril, who had followed Loukas, gasped at the indentation there.

With gentle fingers and a clean cloth, Loukas wiped the blood and dirt away. A bone fragment protruded through a cut. Julius jerked back from his touch, but Loukas persisted.

"I can see that the bone above his eyes head is broken. Those bone fragments will have to be removed or they will kill him. I'll need a sharp knife, and I'll need you to hold him. Marcus, I will need at least two more strong men. Maybe three. Cyril, I'm also going to need a needle and some thread."

Marcus ran out the door in a heartbeat, and a moment later Cyril heard him in the courtyard recruiting men to help. Four men walked back through the door with Marcus.

Loukas stationed the men at Julius' legs, arms, head, and gave Cyril orders to lie across Julius' torso. When he cut at the edge of the wound, Julius screamed and struggled, but the five men held him as still as they could while Loukas laid the flap of skin back from his forehead and removed each splintered bone fragment. When he finished sewing the skin back in place, Loukas wiped the sweat from his eyes. Julius lay quiet, probably unconscious.

"At least the fragments were small. We need to keep his head still for a few days and prevent him from touching it. Marcus, we need ropes or chains to hold his hands."

Loukas gazed at the gathered pale-faced and glassy-eyed men. "He will probably rest for a time. It could be a few days before we can tell how badly he's hurt. Sometimes people behave differently for a time after having a head injury. Sometimes they never recover. If he is worse, I will let you know quickly. Meanwhile, it will do no good to stand around his bedside worrying."

Cyril nodded.

Marcus looked for a moment like he might protest, then shook his head. "Call me if you need anything or want to leave or rest. My room is at the other end of the hall. Caius, Antonius, and Lysius, you are dismissed. I thank you for your help."

"And I will be in the cooking area, through that door." Cyril pointed toward the room. "I'll bring you something to eat."

Cyril left the room but stepped back to look inside. Loukas pulled a bench from the table and set it beside the bed. He shook his head and heaved a sigh.

Cyril understood. They were in for a very long night.

Three days had passed since the day that was to have been her betrothal to Julius. Miriam paced the floor in her room, praying aloud. "Adonai, I'm so worried about Julius. He's been hurt, and I can't go see him. Please be there with him, and give Loukas guidance in treating him. Julius is precious to me. Have mercy on him, and if You will, please provide a way for me to see him. Thank you, O Great Jehovah Jirah." She sat down at the edge of her bed for a few moments longer and then lay down, hoping for sleep, hoping for sleep, but sleep was fragmented by horrifying dreams.

After a long night, Miriam descended the stairs to find her parents, Leah, and Amos around the table. She walked to the table and sank to the cushions without speaking.

They all started at an insistent knock on the door. Miriam jumped up and ran to the door. She threw it open only to see a dog in the shade of the house scratching himself, bumping the door post with each scratch. She sighed and closed the door, close to tears. She leaned back against the door. "I don't understand why Loukas or Cyril haven't come or sent word yet. They must know we are worried."

Ima looked up from her sewing. "I understand your worry, Miriam, but we haven't any choice but to be patient. Loukas said he would let us know how Julius is, and he is a man of his word."

Abba stood and went to Miriam. He pulled her into his arms and tucked her head under his chin. He rocked her to and fro, patting her back.

For a few moments, she said nothing, comforted by her father's love. At last she stepped back. "Abba, last night I asked God to show us how I could go see him. This morning I had an idea. Julius' slave, Cyril, said no women were allowed in the officer's quarters other than women who cleaned the quarters or…or prostitutes. I would not care to go as the latter, but if Leah would agree, we two could go as cleaning women. If you approve, Abba."

Leah sat up straight, eyes brightening. "We should go there while it is still early in the day. Cleaning women always arrive early."

Abba held up his hand. "I do *not* approve, Daughter. The men who live there are rough Roman soldiers. They are not all trustworthy, and they will not care if you are cleaning women or a woman of the streets. In addition, you know the Law forbids Jewish people to enter a Gentile's home."

"And I also do not approve of Leah's participation in this endeavor." Amos moved to his brother-in-law's side, sliding a chastising glance at Leah.

"Wait, husband. Hear her out." Ima reached for Micah's hand. "Think. If it were I who lay injured, would you go?"

"You know I would."

"Then help Miriam see the one she loves. She won't rest until she has seen him or at least knows how he fares."

"Please, Abba." Miriam's eyes filled.

"Humph. What can I do when you both stand against me? Very well, we will go. But only you and I, Mirie. And we will not enter his quarters but instead send word inside for one of them to come out to talk to us."

Miriam nodded, eyes on her feet. *Adonai, please, I need to see him, not just talk to someone who has seen him.*

"Shall we go now?" her father asked.

"Yes, now would be good. I'll fetch a scarf." She tugged a scarf from a hook and pulled it over her hair.

"We'll be back soon." Abba opened the door and held it for his daughter.

Chapter 34

Cyril entered Julius' room for day three of their bedside vigil.

Loukas, who had not left Julius' side, woke with a start. He rubbed at his neck and winced when he stretched out his arm.

"Did he wake up any last night?" Cyril asked.

"No. He was restless, and he moaned a few times, but he didn't open his eyes."

Marcus knocked and then entered the doorway, eliciting a scowl from the prone centurion on the bed.

"Julius, are you awake?" Loukas laid his hand on Julius' shoulder.

Julius tugged at the ropes restraining his arms. He had just enough latitude in the ropes to roll on either side, and he flounced away from them.

The other three men looked at each other in surprise.

"Julius, can you hear me?" Marcus bent close to Julius' ear.

"Would you like for me to bring you anything? Are you hungry?" Cyril asked.

Julius scowled again.

Loukas tipped his head toward the door. When they were outside the room, Loukas frowned. "I'm a little confused by Julius' behavior. Have you seen him act like this before?" He cast his gaze from one to the other.

"No. I've never seen him act like this. At least not since childhood." Marcus glanced back toward the bedroom, a worried scowl on his brow. "Julius, Cyril, and I grew up together. We've known each other since we were babes. Julius sometimes acted like an imp when we were young, but he grew out of it fast when his father took a hand in his education. Actually, in *our* education, beginning when we turned twelve."

"Marcus is right. Julius was a little pampered by his mother. But I haven't seen this type of behavior from him in the last fifteen years.

He's awake, but he turns his back on us and curls into a tight circle like a petulant child."

"That's what I thought. There are times when a head injury can cause odd behavior." Loukas' frown deepened.

"What can we do?"

"This injury could take a long time to heal. Perhaps months, perhaps years, perhaps the rest of his life, if he lives through this. You should contact his superiors and his family. He probably will not be able to continue military duty for some time, if ever."

Marcus stared at his feet for a few moments, and then he looked up, determination in his eyes. "I'll handle the military end of it, Cyril, if you will send word to his father. Loukas, I'm assuming the tribune will want you to continue his care until he is transported to Rome. Someone may have already informed him there's been an accident, but I'll give him the official report. I'll go see him today. Now, in fact."

"I sent a letter to his father yesterday," Cyril said. "I'm not sure where he is now, but once Julius said he had been sent to Germania. I sent the epistle to Rome, though, because they would know where it should go."

Loukas nodded. "Marcus, when you get back from seeing the tribune, I assume you'll have an answer. I'd like to take Julius to my home. My wife and Quinta can assist me, and I can sleep in a bed when not caring for him." He rubbed his neck and tilted his head to the right and left.

"I'll have a wagon brought around for you," Marcus said, striding toward the stairway that led to the outside door.

"I'll help you get him to the wagon. If he is actually awake, he should be able to walk. His legs aren't injured, are they?" Cyril's worried scowl matched Marcus'.

"Bruised and cut, but no breaks. However, judging from the attitude exhibited a few minutes ago, it might not be easy to talk him into walking anywhere. It could take force, and he could get hurt worse that way. Or it might mean we carry him. And I suspect he's no featherweight."

"If he's gone back to his childhood days, sweets often worked." Cyril looked toward the kitchen.

"Sweets. Where are we going to get sweets?"

"He always had a sweet tooth." Cyril almost smiled. "I keep dried grapes for him in our quarters, and I have some honey cakes, too."

"Let's try it." Loukas sighed. "If it doesn't work, we'll recruit help again.

Cyril and Loukas reentered the room. "Julius, wake up. Let's go for a ride," Loukas said. "We have some sweets for you."

Julius lay unresponsive.

Loukas tapped his shoulder, but there was still no response. "He may have slipped into a coma, or maybe just a deep sleep."

Cyril gathered up blankets and handed them to Loukas. He reached for Julius, placing hands and arms under his shoulders and knees. Loukas moved Julius' head to Cyril's shoulder, and they made their way to the yard where one of the soldiers had a wagon loaded with straw ready for them. Loukas spread the blankets on the straw. As gently as he could, given Julius' weight, Cyril placed his master on the blankets. Loukas covered him and sat next to him. Cyril walked to the horses' heads.

Cyril glanced at Julius and then to Loukas. "Do you think he's asleep, or is it something deeper than that?" He grasped the reins and led the two horses in a slow walk.

"I don't know at this point, Cyril. I hope he's just asleep."

Miriam looked up at the approaching wagon. "Abba, there's Loukas...and Cyril and Marcus." She picked up her cloak and ran. She peered into the wagon, and a low cry escaped her lips. "Oh, Loukas, is he...?"

"No, Miriam, he isn't dead. He might be asleep or in a coma, I don't know right now. We're moving him to my house. Come, join us." Miriam clambered into the back of the wagon.

Her father climbed in behind her.

Miriam sat by Julius' head, and Abba sat on his other side.

Loukas set the wagon in motion. "I'm sorry we didn't come to talk to you. There was nothing I could tell you yet. After that first night, he hasn't opened his eyes or spoken, although it appeared sometimes he might be awake. I decided to move him to my house where it will be easier for me to take care of him until his superiors decide what should happen from here. His recovery could take a long time. Months or even years. Cyril will notify his father. Julius told me his mother died last year."

"Yes, he told me too." Miriam's eyes threatened to spill, but she held the tears in check.

When they arrived at Loukas' home, Joanna and Quinta came out to meet them.

This time, Loukas, Cyril, and Micah formed a living cradle with their arms to carry Julius into the house. They placed him in a bedchamber on an elbow-height bed. He stirred slightly as if moving into a more comfortable position.

"Julius, are you awake?" Loukas patted him on the shoulder.

A tight scowl and a tightening of the shut eyes was the only reply.

"Miriam, speak to him. Maybe you can reach him," Loukas urged.

"Julius, please open your eyes, please? I need to know that you will be all right."

To her surprise, Julius opened one eye just a slit, then both eyes, blinking, trying to focus. "You aren't my mama. Who are you?"

She turned to Cyril. "What did he say? I don't understand the Roman language."

"I don't think he recognizes you. He's asking for his mother." Cyril frowned.

Miriam gave a low cry and turned away. "Adonai, where is my love?"

"Do you know who you are?" Loukas asked him in Latin.

"Of course I know. I am Julius Saturnius. Everybody knows that."

"How old are you?"

"I'm eight. Where is my Mama? Mama will make my head stop hurting."

"Your Mama isn't here, and you have had an accident. Your head hurts because a horse kicked you."

"Can you make it feel better, like Mama?" He gazed at Miriam.

It sounded so odd, hearing a child's lilt from a man with a baritone voice. Miriam wept, tears rolling unheeded down her cheeks. What should she do?

"Do you recognize me?" Cyril asked.

Julius scowled in concentration. "You look like Cyril, only bigger."

"I *am* Cyril."

"But you're grown up. What happened?"

"We grew up, Julius. You did too."

Julius wrinkled his brow. He lowered his gaze to his arms and body, lifting one foot and then the other with surprise written on his face.

Loukas stopped them. "He needs to rest now, Cyril. There will be more time to discuss things tomorrow. Lie back, Julius. I'm going to clean your wound, then we're going to leave you alone. You need to sleep."

"But I don't want to be alone. I want my Mama."

"I'll stay with him, Loukas." Miriam grasped Julius' hand. He looked up at her, and his eyes drifted shut.

"I'd like to speak with you a moment, Miriam. Come out into the next room with me," Loukas whispered, leading Miriam by the arm.

Miriam joined him outside of the bed chamber.

"Miriam, there is something you need to know." He reached for her hand. You are aware one of the horses kicked Julius in the head. Sometimes a severe blow like this can cause a person to lose the memory of the previous hours, days, years, or even their entire memory. That piece of his life might come back, or it might not. It appears as if Julius has lost about fifteen years. If his memory or part of it does come back, it could be years before he is himself. Or maybe never. Sometimes people are so changed that it is as though they were a different person altogether. They can become childish or cruel."

Miriam cringed. "Do you mean that he might never remember me or that he loved me?"

"That's exactly what I mean. I'm sorry to be so blunt, but I don't want to build your hopes up only to see them crushed."

She stared in silence at the floor. After a few moments, she looked up at Loukas and pulled her shoulders back. "I'll still stay with him. He's afraid to be alone."

Loukas grasped her shoulders. "Miriam, you need to look at this logically. The man you loved might not return to you. He might never remember you. As he is, he could not be a husband to you. As he might become, he could be far worse…immobile or brutal. It would be better if you returned to the house of your father. If he returns to himself, we will tell you. Better yet, he could speak for himself. But I must warn you, child, I do not believe this will happen. Based on my experience and the history of injuries like this, I think he will never be back to the way he was before. Go home, child. You are young, and you think now you will never recover from this hurt or stop wanting him to be your husband. But you will, and one day you will love again."

Miriam paused and looked down. Her mother's health restored, James' release of her promise…even the love she shared with her Roman centurion. These were all miracles. She would not stop believing in them. If it took the Lord years to restore Julius to her, Miriam would wait. She raised her gaze to Loukas' eyes. "Please, I need to be with him."

Loukas hesitated. "It's only partially your choice, Miriam. Your father must make the final decision. Let's talk to him and see what he thinks. " He opened the door and asked Abba to join them. Once her father stepped out of Julius' hearing, Loukas repeated his diagnosis.

"Miriam wants to stay here with Julius. I told her that was not possible unless her father agreed. What do you say, Micah?"

"I knew she would want to stay," Micah said. "You or I would do the same thing for our loved ones. Let her hope while she may. Despair may follow, but only the One God knows that, and even so, God will be with her."

Marcus joined them. "I've seen injuries like this before resulting from battles. I haven't seen any whole recoveries, Miriam. He might not ever know you. You would be better off to go home and forget him, go on with your life."

Miriam shook her head, not trusting her voice. She would not leave Julius.

"If something changes, we would send for you, Miriam." Cyril's soft tenor voice caught, and tears filled his eyes. "For your own good, it would be better if you went home."

"I know you all mean well, but you cannot send me away. I love him, and somewhere in his damaged head he loves me, too. I believe in the strength of our love. I also believe in the God Who will hold us up through times of trouble. If my love is so weak that I let the first bump in the road throw me, then it is not love. I will stay." She held her chin high and looked all the men squarely in their eyes.

The men looked at each other and then at Miriam.

"I'll stay." Cyril lifted his shoulders. "I know that's my duty, but he is also my friend."

Chapter 35

Two days later as Miriam waited at Julius' bedside, a knock sounded at the outer door.

A mumbled conversation caught Miriam's ear, but she would not leave Julius' side. She looked to Loukas, who shook his head.

Cyril entered with Marcus and Tribune Rufus. When Julius refused to even look at him, the tribune pulled Loukas aside.

"Is he going to stay like this?" Rufus' eyes narrowed.

"I don't know. This is how he's acted since his injury, but it's only been a couple of weeks." Loukas picked up a jar and offered to pour the tribune a glass of wine.

Rufus shook his head. "I'm going to have to replace him."

"Right now? If he begins coming to himself, having no rank or position could set him back."

Miriam held her breath. They could not take away what Julius had worked so hard to obtain. They couldn't give his job to someone else, someone who might not offer protection to women like her. Someone who might do the same as that other Roman.

"Maybe not today, but it can't wait much longer." The tribune cast a weary glance at Julius.

"A week, then. Can you wait a week? By then, there could be some indication that he will recover. Or that he won't."

"A week, perhaps two. Julius was a good centurion. He deserves a week, but I need two centurions here. Sextus has been stretched to his limit. Send word to me, physician."

Loukas nodded. "I will."

Two weeks later, a clamor outside Loukas' house woke Miriam. She sat up and realized she'd fallen asleep, her head in her arms, leaning against Julius' empty bed. Julius sat on the floor beside Cyril as Julius played with a wooden toy shepherd and sheep.

A man with a rumbling voice demanded something in Latin, then rough Aramaic. "My name is Gaius. Where's my son?"

Quinta's voice responded. "Is your son Julius?"

Miriam stood and straightened her tunic.

"Yes, my son is Julius", the man said. "I received word he's been hurt."

"Come with me, please. He's in here."

Miriam spared a glance at Cyril who winced. "Gaius is gruff, but he is fair," Cyril whispered to her.

A large-framed man entered the room as Cyril pushed to his feet.

Julius looked frightened for a moment, and then his brows furrowed in what Miriam had come to understand was puzzlement. The hoof-shaped scar on Julius' head surrounded a red and misshapen forehead, and his expressions were a little lop-sided.

"Hello. Are you my father?" Julius asked. "You don't look as big as my father, and you're old."

Gaius' eyebrows drew together in a deep crease similar to his son's. "Yes, Julius, I'm your father. What are you doing?"

"I'm pretending these sheep are soldiers. Loukas doesn't have any soldiers, Father. Could you buy some for me?" Julius stood to his feet and staggered, but Cyril braced him. Julius squinted. "Are you sure you're my father?"

"Son, you're an adult. Why are you playing with toys?" Gaius wiped his hand across his face. His gaze settled upon Miriam but only for a moment before he looked back to his son.

"That's what Marcus said, but I don't understand. Mama told me I was eight years old on my last birthday. Have you come to take me home?"

"Mama?" Tears sprang to Gaius' eyes.

Julius' eyes filled, too. "Didn't you bring her? My head hurts." He put both hands to his head. "I want Mama."

"No." Tears made runnels through the dust on Gaius' face. He moved forward one unsteady step at a time until he folded Julius into a brief hug, but he turned abruptly away. "I have to go. I'll be back tomorrow."

"All right. Bye, Father."

Gaius held up his hand and marched toward the door.

"Sir?" Quinta called to him.

"Yes. What is it?" Gaius spoke without turning.

"Would you like to talk to his physician? He is talking to another patient now, but he will be done soon."

"Yes. I'll wait outside."

His voice sounded strained, and Miriam's heart broke for both father and son.

Gaius stood outside staring at the ground when a man stepped through the doorway.

"Shalom. My daughter Quinta wasn't sure you speak Greek, although it is my guess you can. You must be Julius' father. The resemblance is appreciable. I'm Loukas, Julius' friend and physician."

Gaius nodded. He opened his mouth to speak, cleared his throat, and began again. "Greetings, Physician. Yes, I'm his father, and yes, I speak Greek. They told me Julius was hurt, but they didn't tell me he was destroyed, at least as a man. He's a child in a man's body."

"Yes. It's too soon to know if this symptom will be permanent, but it doesn't appear hopeful now."

"I'll take him to Rome. There are numerous physicians there who have extensive experience with battlefield injuries."

"That might be a good idea," Loukas said.

Gaius' eyebrows rose. "You don't object?"

"No. Being around you might jog memories that will help him. He thinks he's eight years old. He told me some months back that his mother died a year ago, but now he thinks his mother is still alive, and he keeps looking for her."

Gaius cleared his throat again, blinking away moisture in his eyes.

"She was a good woman, although she spoiled him."

Loukas nodded. "So Marcus says."

"Ah. You know Marcus? I hear that young whelp is the one who ran over him. He should lose his commission over this. He never did well at controlling his impulses." Gaius' eyes narrowed. Inner storms threatened his poise, and he struggled to maintain an outward calm.

Loukas folded his hands and bowed his head. When he looked up, his eyes asked questions that didn't need words. "This incident may have been the cure for that. He's been here daily helping to take care of Julius. He'll probably be here this evening after his duty hours are finished if you want to see him."

"I'm not sure that would be a good idea. I'm not thinking fond thoughts of him." Gaius folded his arms and leaned against the building.

"I can understand how you would be angry. Indeed, he's angry at himself. I hope that, once you observe his changed behavior, you might find a way to forgive him."

"Forgive him? Forgive him! For annihilating my son in an act of pure stupidity? I might as quickly forgive the disease that stole my wife. You hope too much, Physician. I would sooner see him crucified."

Loukas nodded. "Again, I understand your anger. This, your only son, appears to be permanently disabled. If only Marcus hadn't been in a hurry to get to his destination, if only Julius hadn't run back into the street after something dropped, if only these two things hadn't happened at the same time. If only the past could be changed. But there is only the future, and only God knows what will happen then. Maybe Julius will be an invalid always, or maybe a miracle—"

Gaius snorted. "Miracle? Only children and fools believe in miracles. I do believe in the abilities of a good physician, but even that might not be enough."

Loukas chuckled. "I'm not a child, so I know what classification I must be in."

"What do you mean?"

"I mean that I have seen some unexplainable 'cures.' Especially when a certain wandering Jewish Prophet is involved. I saw Him touch a blind man and make him see, straighten a crippled woman's foot, and put his fingers in deaf ears and make them hear."

"Fakes." Gaius blew a short breath through disbelieving nostrils.

"Fakes?"

"People placed in the crowd to trick folks into believing in magic. I would have thought a physician would be smart enough to see through pretenders of that sort. Now, I'm sure I need to move Julius."

Loukas shrugged. "Believe what you will, Legate. I do advise that you wait a few days. Thus far, he hasn't been able to be active for more than a few minutes at a time without the disabling headache plaguing him. I hope that in a week or two, the swelling will go down and the headaches decrease."

"I'll grant that, but I will also be back on a daily basis to see my son." Gaius wondered if the physician would deny him entrance.

"I would hope so. You are welcome in my home, sir." Loukas bowed his head in farewell and turned back into the house.

Gaius watched the physician. An odd man. He seemed to know what he was about, yet believed in miracles. But then, maybe all Jews do. If he was a Jew. He didn't look much like the rest of them. Gaius' efforts to goad the physician were met without offense. *Well, we shall see what tomorrow brings.*

Chapter 36

Loukas took Marcus aside outside his home that evening when Marcus arrived to help care for Julius. "Have you seen Julius' father? He's in town." Loukas grasped his friend's elbow. "The legate came here to see Julius this morning, but he didn't stay long."

"I haven't seen him, but I have heard he's here." Marcus grimaced. "I also heard he'd like to see me hanging from a cross bar." He ducked his head and ran his fingers through his hair.

"I don't think he's anxious to see you. Yes, he's angry, and he said you should lose your commission over this. However, he indicated he didn't want to meet you, at least not here. I suggest you check to see who's here before you enter. I can tell everyone here to warn you away if he's here when you arrive or if he arrives when you are here."

"No. Whatever he hands to me, I've earned. I won't avoid him, although I won't seek him out, either. I'll ask his forgiveness, and if he takes my commission from me so be it." He sighed heavily, again running his hands through his hair. "What I did was so brainless. I was having such fun, racing the chariot through the streets. I used to laugh when people shook their fists at me if I nearly knocked them down. I injured the closest friend I have. He might never be right again, and I'll live with that for the rest of my life."

Marcus sat down on a rock, laid his head in his hands, and sobbed raggedly. When he stopped, he looked up at Loukas with red, streaming eyes. "I haven't even been able to ask God for forgiveness. I asked Julius, but he couldn't understand what I meant. How can I ask God when I can't even get forgiveness from Julius? I want him to hit me, knock me down hard and kick me, then say, 'That makes us even.' Instead, he treats me like I'm still his best friend."

Loukas laid his hand on his shoulder and opened his mouth to speak but shut it with a snap, his eyes widening and heart pounding with alarm.

Gaius stepped forward, his sword held in his right hand. He lifted it up, ready to slice through Marcus' neck. Loukas stepped forward between Marcus and Gaius. An odd look crossed Gaius' face, and he dropped the sword to his side.

"You would give your life to save this wretch?"

"I would. He's my friend."

Marcus pushed Loukas aside. "You will not. This is not your fight." He stood before Gaius, palms up. "Go ahead. You want to see me dead. Do it." His eyes were dry and steady, and he held his chin up, inviting the sword.

Gaius shook his head and sheathed his blade. "Just a test, Marcus. Just a test. You passed."

"A test?" Loukas asked, frowning.

"I heard your conversation. I wondered if Marcus was looking for pity as he used to do when he was young. I couldn't kill you, Marcus. I would turn you over my knee if you were still a youngster. Take a rod to your back, maybe even now."

Marcus released his breath. "With my blessings, sir. I wish someone would." Marcus sobbed and then knelt. "I'm sorry, Gaius. I'm so, so sorry. I wish it had been me instead of Julius."

Gaius knelt in front of Marcus and took the younger man's shoulders, tears in his own eyes. "We will grieve together, Marcus."

Loukas stood back watching the interaction between the two men, a sense of wonder washing over him. He remained silent, not wanting to intrude into what was happening. Marcus was finding a route to being forgiven. Gaius was a surprising man, not at all what Loukas feared. Nodding to himself, Loukas quietly turned and walked into the house.

Gaius spent most of the time at the physician's house and noted with gratitude the physician and the others' care of his son. Between them, someone stayed with Julius every moment, bathed him, and fed him.

His condition had deteriorated over the past two days, and now he couldn't leave his bed. He moaned, twisting and turning and grasping his head. The men bathed him, and at least one spent nights beside his bed. The young woman, who seemed to be the daughter of an older Jewish man whom Gaius assumed was one of the physician's friends, spoon fed Julius. She held his head up and stroked his throat, encouraging him to swallow. Loukas' wife brought fresh clothing and bedding when Julius wet or soiled what he had. The young woman whom Cyril seemed very much interested in—the physician's daughter, he was told—sat and told him stories of her homeland.

While he watched them each take such good care of his son, Gaius wondered if they were related to or working for Loukas. Surely no one would be willing to perform such tasks without pay.

Miriam often wept. Julius' infantile petulance when awake drove them all to distraction. Even Loukas grew impatient with Julius' whining refusal to take the medication provided to him. Gaius wondered if his son would survive a trip to Rome, and he made no move to make arrangements for such a trip.

Miriam knelt beside the bed watching Julius sleep. Marcus stood behind her.

Tenderly, she pushed Julius' hair back from the hoof-shaped crescent on his forehead. How she wished Jesus were here, but He was not. She bowed her head.

Marcus dropped to his knees beside her.

Miriam looked up, startled at first.

Cyril nodded in silent agreement and knelt on Julius' other side. Before Miriam returned to her prayers, Abba and Loukas knelt in the empty spaces around Julius.

As she prayed, eyes closed, her hand warmed and a tingling sensation filled her.

Gaius gasped, and Miriam opened her eyes. Before she could look to Julius' father, she caught the wild-eyed stares of Cyril and Marcus. "Did you feel anything just now? A warmth in your hands and a tingling?" she asked.

"I thought it was just me. You felt it, too?" Marcus asked.

"Yes I did." Cyril's eyes were moist.

"What does it mean? Do you know, Miriam? You are more acquainted with this praying stuff than I am." Marcus stood. "Does this always happen when you pray?"

"Not to me. Sometimes I feel God's presence, but not like this. Never quite like this."

Julius stopped his restless twisting and lay quietly on the bed. His hair lay in damp curls on his forehead, and Miriam again brushed his hair aside. "Look! Where the horse kicked him. The swelling is going down, and where it was dented, it's not anymore."

"It doesn't look as red, either," Marcus said, staring.

Julius opened his eyes, gazing around as his friends gasped.

"Why is everyone staring at me?" He sat up. "What are you doing here, Miriam?"

Miriam's eyes filled with tears. "You know me!"

Julius' eyebrows lifted. "Why wouldn't I know you?"

"Perhaps you don't remember, my friend, but you got kicked in the head by a horse." Cyril looked as though the sun had reappeared after being gone for years.

"You thought you were eight years old, and you wanted your mother." Marcus grinned happily.

Abba, still on his knees, stared with round eyes.

Julius' gaze fell on Gaius. "Father, what are you doing here?"

Gaius' mouth worked, his eyes watering. He gulped. "I heard you were hurt. I came to see you."

"Hurt? I'm fine. But I'm glad to see you." He looked around at the rest of them. "Why are you all gaping at me?"

Marcus blinked, then blinked again. He cleared his throat, his voice rough. "You have been in sorry shape for the last few weeks, my friend."

"I thought I dreamed it all. I had a headache, and then I felt cool hands touching me and a strange vibrating sensation. The next thing I knew you all started chattering and woke me up."

"We think maybe God used our prayers to heal you," Cyril said. "We felt the vibration too."

"Thanks be to God, and thank you, too. Look, it's dark. We need to escort Miriam and Micah home." Julius rose to his feet.

"Wait, Julius. I don't think you should go anywhere. You had a serious injury." Loukas grabbed his arm and pulled him back toward the bed.

"If God healed me, and I agree He must have, then there is no reason I should stay here. Let's go." He stood, looking around. "Anyone seen my sword and helmet?"

"We didn't bring them here. You'll find them in your quarters. Are you sure you don't feel dizzy?" Loukas asked, putting up a hand to touch where the indentation had been. "This is amazing. Truly amazing."

"Wait a moment, before we go anywhere, would someone please tell me what just happened?" Gaius demanded. "I saw a...a glow in this room. Like several candles. The air filled with a strange feeling. Somewhat like when lightning's about to strike close by. Then my son suddenly is normal. I don't understand."

"We have just had an encounter with the one and only living God, Gaius. He healed your son." Loukas lifted his hands toward the ceiling. "Praise be to You, Adonai Raphekha, O Lord our Healer."

"Let's be on our way. If I don't make it, I have you strong men to carry me the rest of the way." Julius clapped Marcus and Cyril on the back.

Marcus shrugged, still grinning as though his mouth were pinned to his ears. "Well, if that is what you want, I guess that is what we will do. You are the centurion, after all, and we are but worms who must do as you command." He bowed low, sweeping his hand across his body.

Miriam retorted with an impish smile. "Speak for yourself. I am no worm." She took Julius' left arm and Abba, with a laugh, took his right arm. Together, they walked into the front room, where Quinta and Joanna gazed in amazement.

Dropping Julius' arm, Abba broke into a psalm of praise and began stomping his feet in a dance, waving an invitation to the other men. "I will bless the Lord at all times; His praise shall continually be in my mouth...."

Miriam and Joanna clapped their hands, and Loukas joined in the dancing. Cyril, Marcus, and Julius watched the feet of the two men, glanced at each other, and then joined in the dancing. Gaius stood to the side rubbing his eyes.

Miriam opened the door and stepped outside, holding out her hand to Julius. "No betrothal this day, since it's the Sabbath, but your days of freedom are limited. Come, my husband-to-be."

Julius laughed and danced out the door. Abba, Cyril, and Marcus followed him, Abba singing a little out of breath.

Gaius strode forward and placed himself in front of Julius.

"Betrothal?" Gaius' brows drew together as he stopped Julius. Miriam held tighter to him.

"Forgive me. I forgot to introduce you, Father. This is my soon-to-be betrothed, Miriam, and her father, Micah." Julius flushed a dark red visible even in the moonlight.

"Aren't you forgetting something?" Gaius' voice went cold, his grip on Julius' arm tightening.

Julius cast a glance to Miriam. He closed his eyes, and when he opened them, he stared into the depth of hers as he spoke to Gaius. "Father, Eugenia was a childhood playmate. I never intended to marry her. I know she asked you about it, but I didn't think you took her seriously." He tilted his head, capturing her with a bad-puppy stare. "I promise. Nothing more."

"Never mind about Eugenia. She tired of waiting for you and married two years ago. I mean you forgot to ask your father about this arrangement." Hands on hips, Gaius still blocked Julius' way.

Julius' held breath exploded in nervous laughter. "Oh, I understand. Father, would you give me permission to wed this loveliest of women? It only took me six months to convince her father. How long will it take to convince my own?" He began walking again, Miriam tucked happily to his side. Abba, Cyril and Marcus stayed a few steps behind. Loukas walked close in back of Julius, as though still expecting him to faint.

Gaius grasped Abba's arm. "You and your daughter are Hebrews. Am I correct? You are citizens of a country that refuses to bow to Caesar. How long do you think it will be before issues confront our children if they marry? Rebellions arise daily in this land. What if we go to war with your people? How could my son make such a decision?"

Julius waved off Abba's answer. He looked down at the ground, and then up at his father, his gaze steady. "I hope it will never come to that. It would be a choice that would rip me apart, no matter which way I went. And it wouldn't matter if I were married to Miriam or not, because I have come to love these people and this land, too. My allegiance is sworn to Rome and you, but my honor would not allow me to fight against all of the Hebrews. Some of them, yes. Marcus, Cyril, and I recently fought some brigands who were Hebrew rebels, but even the elders here agreed that was necessary."

"You sought the approval of the Hebrew elders before fighting?" Gaius' lips tightened and he released his hold on Miriam's father.

"No. The conversation with the elders took place sometime after the fracas. I only wanted you to know they considered the action justifiable. If it comes to war with the Hebrews, Father, I will take the right action, or at least the action that seems right. I have no desire to shame you."

"And yet you would marry a Jew?"

Miriam gasped. Gaius' previous words hinted at his disdain for her people. She bit down on her lower lip to keep it from trembling. She loved Julius. She could not allow him to have to decide between her or his father. She would have to let him go.

But Julius, if Miriam could read the hold he kept upon her, had no such qualm. "I would marry this woman, Father. She owns my heart. I don't care what nationality she claims. And," Julius took a deep breath, "I worship her God."

Gaius walked with his head down.

Miriam longed to know what he was thinking.

He heaved a sigh and returned his gaze to his son.

"Very well. You have my agreement. When is this betrothal to take place?"

"The betrothal was supposed to happen the day I was run over. Now I don't know. It's up to Micah and Miriam's mother, Deborah."

Miriam smiled up at him. "It will not happen this day. The Sabbath day just began two hours ago, so perhaps tomorrow, just after sunset. Or after Ima recovers from seeing you again."

"Ima?" Gaius asked.

"My mother, sir," Miriam said. "Her name is Deborah, but I call her Ima."

Abba turned from where they walked. "We should find out soon, Mirie."

Leah, Amos, and Ima met them at the door.

"Julius!" Ima's hand flew first to her face and then to Julius' shoulders.

"Our God has done it again, wife. Behold the injured man." Abba pounded Julius' back.

Ima put her arm around Julius' waist. "Should you be walking so far? Come in. Sit down. Or would you rather lie down?" She turned to Abba. "What do you mean, 'God has done it again?'"

Julius hugged her shoulders. "Don't worry, dear lady. I'm much improved. And I want you to meet my father, the Legate Gaius Saturnius. My future mother-in-law, Deborah, and Leah, Deborah's sister, with her husband, Amos."

"Welcome to our home, Legate."

Gaius rubbed his forehead. "I don't understand. I thought Jews did not allow non-Hebrews to enter their homes."

Miriam's parents looked at each other and smiled. "We are happy to make an exception for the father of Julius," Abba said. "Our law also says we should welcome strangers.

They stepped aside and waved the group into the house.

"Thank you. I am honored." Gaius bowed to his hosts and entered.

"Now, Julius, tell me what happened?" Ima asked, her face alight with curiosity. She touched his forehead with a look of wonder. "Micah, did you not say there was a wound?"

"They all prayed for me, and I woke up."

"Oh, Ima, you should have been there. The presence of God was so strong in the room as we prayed. We all felt it. And then Julius woke, stood up, and all his injuries disappeared. The scars and the hoof print on his forehead, they faded away right in front of our eyes."

"I think this calls for a double celebration, do you not, wife? An offering of praise to God for this healing and tomorrow, a betrothal." Abba spread his arms around Julius and Miriam and pulled them close. "This time, Julius, don't go running out in front of a chariot. Exactly why did you do that, anyway?"

Julius frowned, scratched his head, and stared at the ceiling. "I don't remember. The last thing I remember is bathing before leaving for the ceremony."

"One of the gifts or maybe the bride price?" Abba asked.

Julius clapped his sides and looked down. "Oh, no, the gifts!"

"Don't worry, they're at our residence." Cyril smiled. "They were in a bag tied to your girdle, and I put them away. It didn't look like you would be doing anything with them for a while."

Julius put a hand inside the breast of his tunic and reddened. "I think I know what I went after."

"What?" Miriam turned to face him. "You look guilty. Confess."

"Your scarf."

"My scarf? You had my scarf?"

"Yes. Remember when you were running around looking for Loukas when your mother was at the last threshold?"

"Yes?"

"Remember how the wind blew that morning?"

"Oh, *that's* when I lost it. Later, Amos remarked on it, but I didn't remember losing it. I thought I had just forgotten to put it on." She held up one end of the scarf she wore. "This is a new one."

"I thought you had others. I know I should have brought it back, but at that time it didn't look like I could talk Micah into letting you marry me. The scarf smelled like your hair. I kept it close to my heart." Julius patted his chest and smiled down at Miriam, taking a step closer with a kiss in his eyes.

Miriam stepped toward him.

"Ahem." Abba scowled. "You are not betrothed yet."

Miriam and Julius started, and both took a step backward.

"Be here tomorrow, at sunset. Now, all of you go home. The past weeks have been wearying." Abba grinned as he shooed their family and friends away.

Chapter 37

Julius dreamed an earthquake struck Jericho. He had to find Miriam. The ground shook and something held him so that he couldn't walk, but he struggled to lift debris from her.

"Wake up, Centurion. You need to go talk to the tribune this morning and be back in time to get yourself betrothed. Remember, you spent most of the past couple of weeks sleeping. Come. Up, up, up." Cyril shook the end of Julius' bed.

Julius groaned. "You've really become a pain since you were emancipated. I think I'll change your name to Brutus."

"You can't do that. I'm not your slave anymore."

"Wait. Go back. Say that again." Julius sat up in his bed, grinning.

"That I'm not your slave?"

"No, that I need to be back in time to get myself betrothed. This is the day!" Julius jumped out of bed.

Cyril laughed. "I wondered how long until that reached your head. But then, your brain got scrambled, so maybe it takes longer for information to seep in."

Julius followed Cyril into the kitchen. "It's still dark out there. Why so early?"

"Marcus came by. His men patrol the road today, and since you're supposed to be escorted...."

"He mentioned that last night. All right. Warrior and Duros are about to get their exercise. I think I'll take Father along."

Julius and his father entered the tribune's quarters and saluted.

"Well, Julius, what a surprise! Last time I saw you, you didn't look so good. And Legate Gaius, I heard you were in Jericho. Seeing you must have been what Julius needed." Rufus stood up from his chair and returned the salute.

"It wasn't my appearance that healed him, Rufus." Father shook his head. "I'm still not sure I believe what I saw."

"What do you mean, Legate?"

Julius remained silent, wanting to hear what his father had to say.

Father shook his head. "I mean it appears the Jewish God healed him. If I hadn't seen it myself, I would say someone was dreaming or out of his mind." He clapped his hand on Julius' shoulder. "This man is ready to go back to duty."

Rufus' skepticism showed in his eyes as the rest of his face became carefully blank. "I would guess it was a trick of sorts, or perhaps a magician. There is a mystic now walking the wilderness, so I hear, who regularly does tricks like this."

Father shrugged. "Think as you will, Rufus. You saw my son, as I understand, a few weeks before I did. When I arrived and for the time I stayed there, he remained a child. Toward the end of that time he became worse, unable to stay out of bed for more than a few minutes, sleeping more and more. I feared for his life, but then the physician and several others gathered around his bed and prayed for him. He rose from his bed and became as you see him now, whole and without scars or swelling."

Rufus duplicated Father's shrug and bared his teeth in a forced-looking smile. "I don't know, Legate, and I guess it doesn't really matter. What matters is that we have the centurion back and just in time. He's been promoted to senior centurion in Caesarea, and he's to be there in three weeks."

Julius, silent until now, jumped as though he'd been stung. "Three weeks? But sir, that's barely enough time to...."

"It's enough time to get your gear packed and travel there, Julius. Remember, I told you about this a few months ago." Rufus scowled and sat down. "I was beginning a letter to the tribune there when you walked into the room. I'm glad I don't have to tell him you won't be able to perform your duties."

"Yes, sir." Julius felt the blood drain from his face. What would this do to the betrothal?

Father stared at him. "What is the matter, Julius? Are you feeling ill?"

"No, Father. I'm fine. Just considering...all that must be done in the short amount of time I have."

His father smiled and nodded, the look in his eyes saying more than words.

Rufus' eyes narrowed. He leaned forward, knuckles on the table. "Is there something you're not telling me, Centurion?"

"Do you remember that I requested permission to marry a Hebrew woman?"

"Vaguely. Was that part of the document I signed and gave to you to fill out?" His scowl evened out, shoulders relaxing.

"Yes, Tribune. The betrothal is this evening. I dread telling her parents I leave so soon."

"Your service to Rome comes before any wife, Centurion. This is not a move that you have authority over, and don't think Tribune Appius will grant an extension. He's not known for bending for much of anything. In particular not for marriages. He's not in favor of soldiers marrying, so if you're going to, you'd be wise to do it before you get there." Rufus picked up a sheaf of papers from his desk. "I'm sorry, Julius, but that's how he is."

Father extended his hands to Rufus. "We'll be going now, Rufus. It's been good to see you again, but now, as my son said, there's much to be done. I hope to see you again before I return to Rome."

Julius saluted with a fist to his chest, and he and his father turned to exit the tribune's quarters.

A soldier walked up to Julius as they stepped out of the building. "Sir!"

"Yes, soldier?"

"The contingent you arrived with...brigands attacked a couple of people on the Jericho Road, and the men went back to help. They'll come back after you as soon as they can."

Julius frowned. "How long ago?"

"Just after you went into the tribune's quarters, sir."

"Are there any other contingents that could escort us back to Jericho?"

"No, sir. The ones still here in town are on guard duty; the rest are out on other patrols."

Julius turned to his father, jaw clenched. "Any suggestions?"

"Why can we not go on our own?" Father asked. "We have good horses."

"The tribune ordered that no one travel without an armed contingent. Robbers and cutthroats prey on people traveling the road, especially Romans." The knot in Julius' stomach twisted tighter.

"If we can even get a half-dozen men to ride with us. Let's go back and talk to the tribune." His father turned on his heels, and Julius followed him back through the door. Father led the way back up the stairs to Rufus' reception area.

"We want to see the tribune again, Decanus." Father said, walking without stopping through Rufus' door.

"He left, Legate."

"Left?" Father whirled on the hapless decanus, who took a hurried step backwards, nearly bumping into Julius.

"Yes, sir, Legate, sir. He had an appointment with Pilate."

"Humph. And he'll be back when?"

"He…he didn't say, sir." The decanus' Adam's apple bobbed. "But usually he's gone for several hours when he goes to see the Prefect. I…I cannot disturb him there, sir."

Father growled at the decanus one more time and again turned on his heels, his cloak twisting like an angry white whirlpool behind him. Julius followed him back down the stairs, but not before he witnessed the decanus' sigh of relief to see Father's departing back.

Julius grinned to himself. His father had not lost his ability to terrify lesser men. He sobered as he thought about his problem. *What's going to happen now? Miriam's family won't be happy with this move. What if Micah won't let her marry me? And if I don't make it back to Jericho in time for the betrothal? That certainly will make them unhappy. What should I do, Adonai? I don't want to put my father—or myself—into danger by traveling that road alone. Tell me what to do, Lord, and I will do it.*

Wait.

The Voice in his head reverberated throughout his body. It was so plain Julius had no doubt. *All right, Adonai. I hear You.*

His father straightened, glancing around.

Julius wondered if he also heard the Voice.

Father removed his helmet and scratched his head. "You know, I was thinking we should just go and take the risk, but now I don't know if that would be the right thing to do. I mean, I changed my mind. Let's wait. Is there a place where we can get something to eat? Then we can go wait by the gate the troop will come back through."

"I agree, Father. I got the same message." Julius grinned at the startled look in his father's eyes. "There's a large marketplace next to the temple. I know where we can find food there."

Chapter 38

It was late afternoon before the contingent returned to escort Julius and his father back to Jericho. Julius led them down the road as fast as he could without winding the horses. When they walked into Micah's house, a palpable sigh of relief floated through the room. Miriam jumped to her feet and ran to Julius, stopping inches in front of him.

"Where were you? I wondered if...I thought you...." Her eyes looked pinched and worried.

Julius held himself erect, wanting but not daring to touch her. Not in front of her parents and his father. He smiled into her eyes and spoke to her alone. "I'm fine. We were delayed in Jerusalem. The tribune said—"

"Well, my soon-to-be son-in-law, you decided to join us. Welcome, Julius and Gaius. There is a ceremony to be performed here. Shelumiel, we need your services. Everyone, give us your attention."

Shelumiel stepped forward, one of his rare smiles illuminating his countenance. "My children, kneel here on this rug."

"Do you have the wedding contract?" Shelumiel's gaze rested on Julius.

"I do," Julius said, holding up a small scroll.

"Is it signed?"

"I shall sign it now in front of these witnesses," Julius answered with formality. He unrolled the papyrus, dipped the quill in ink, and signed the document. Rising, Julius walked to where Micah sat, handing him the contract with shaking hands.

After he read aloud the groom's promises to love, provide for, and protect his bride, Micah stood to present the scroll to Miriam. A tear strayed from one eye, and he brushed it away.

"Daughter, do you accept the terms of this contract?"

Miriam looked at the writing through tears that dripped on to the parchment.

"I do," she replied, voice shaking as badly as her hands.

"Groom, do you have the bride price and gifts?" Shelumiel's booming voice seemed to fill the room.

"I do."

"Then give the price to her father and the gifts to the bride." He paused as Julius presented a bag of coins to Micah. Julius lifted a jeweled necklace and gold earrings, bracelets, and anklets from a separate bag and placed them on Miriam, one at a time, accompanied by silence and punctuated with sighs from women in the room. When he finished, Julius again knelt and Shelumiel continued.

"Do you agree to never sell your bride?"

"I do," he said, his voice strong.

"Do you agree to never share her with other men?"

"I agree."

"Do you agree to love her before you love yourself, loving only God above her?"

"Yes."

"Do you promise to provide for her needs as long as you live?"

"I do."

"Do you promise to protect her with your life, if necessary?"

"I promise."

"Do you promise to be faithful to her, looking only to your wife to provide for your needs?"

"I do."

Shelumiel lifted a cup of wine. "Before the earth was, God is. If the earth no longer exists, God still will be. He brought forth Adam from the earth, and Eve from Adam. This betrothal again joins man and woman into one unit." He sipped from the cup and handed it to Julius, who followed suit.

"This man has promised to love, protect, and support his bride from now until death."

Miriam watched as Shelumiel accepted the cup back from Julius. Shelumiel brought it with solemnity to her, and she took a sip and handed the cup back to him.

Shelumiel placed it on the table next to her. "Do you, Miriam, agree to love Julius for as long as you live, honoring only God before him?"

"I do." Miriam couldn't stop her voice from trembling.

"Do you promise to be faithful to him and only him?"

"I promise."

"Will you care for him if he is injured or sick?"

"I will." *Although, Adonai, I do hope I won't ever see Julius so hurt again.*

"Will you stay by him whether rich or poor?"

"Yes."

"Will you honor and obey him in all things?"

"Yes."

"Will you go with him wherever he goes?

"I will."

Julius stepped in front of Miriam, lifting her to her feet. "Be consecrated to me, be betrothed to me, be my wife," he said, his eyes conveying his heart.

"I will."

Julius approached his bride with dancing feet, weaving first through the gathered throng. First Abba and then the other men jumped to their feet and followed him, encircling him and then parting to enclose Miriam in the circle. Reverently, Julius stepped to her and placed a veil over her face, thankful for Shelumiel's teaching. A shout of joy arose from men and women alike, and the dancing increased in fervor, individual men breaking away and showing off their skills, delighting the entire crowd.

When peace again descended on the throng, Abba raised a cup of wine.

"My daughter Miriam no longer belongs to me, but to her betrothed, Julius. They shall be one flesh and cling only to each other for as long as they live. They shall reserve their bodies to each other alone and no other. May their descendants be as the grains of sand on the beach."

With solemn face, Micah combined the cup from the first blessing with the cup of wine from the second blessing, handing one of the combined cups to his future son-in-law. After Julius drank from the cup, he handed it to his bride-to-be.

An hour later, Julius stood with his father, Micah, and Deborah. All guests but family had departed. Miriam scurried off with Leah to sew her new coins onto a headband. Amos stood by the door, staring up the stairway as though he could make Leah reappear sooner that way.

Julius shifted from one foot to the other and cleared his throat. "I had some news from the tribune today that could be upsetting. I've been transferred to Caesarea, and I must report there in three weeks." Julius blurted his news.

Micah's eyes widened and then narrowed. His face reddened, and Julius wished he could find somewhere to hide.

"Three weeks?" Deborah's hand flew to her mouth. "How can we arrange a wedding in three weeks?"

Julius pled with his eyes for Micah and Deborah to understand. "It would take almost a week on the road with Miriam and all the household things. Normally, I wouldn't worry about the household things. That would have been Cyril's job, but I freed him, and I don't know that he will want to go with me this quickly. He is betrothed to Quinta, and I'm sure he'll want to marry before leaving. If he decides to follow me at all."

He could feel the sweat soaking his tunic. "It's not likely the tribune in Caesarea will be willing for me to come back for a wedding. I'd have to go through the permission process again, and we'd need a bigger miracle than what we had before from what I've heard. Tribune Rufus tells me the tribune in Caesarea does not allow his men to marry. So, you see, we'll need to be married within two weeks."

"*Two* weeks?" Deborah and Micah chorused.

"I don't blame you for being upset. I am, too, but I have no choice as to when to go."

Micah looked as though Julius had struck him between the eyes with a large rock. "Yes, I can understand that. But we need time to think on this. Can you come back tomorrow? Surely there will be a solution in our minds by then."

Deborah turned to Micah. "Two weeks. That doesn't give us much time. We have to let our friends know. Maybe Amos would take word to those in Bethany, Jerusalem, and Capernaum?" She looked questioningly at Amos, who backed up one step, eyes wide.

Micah grasped her arm. "Wait, let's rethink this. People will talk about a hurry-up wedding. Surely it wouldn't hurt them to wait a year or however long it takes for him to be able to come back here. Caesarea is too far away." Micah rumbled like approaching thunder, and his brows drew tighter by the moment. "Why didn't you tell us about this before the betrothal? I never thought you would betray us so."

"I'm not betraying you, I swear it. The tribune informed me just today. Father, tell them I'm not betraying them." Julius turned pleading eyes on Gaius.

"It's true. I heard him, too." Gaius nodded.

"You didn't know about this before?" Micah demanded.

"No...well, yes, in a way." The perspiration now rolled from Julius' face. "Several months ago—"

"You knew months ago?" Micah interrupted, his countenance crimson. "And you did not feel it necessary to tell us?"

"The tribune only said that they wanted me in Caesarea in the future."

"You would take my daughter to the ends of the earth and not inform us? Tell me, did you not let me know this before because you knew I would forbid the betrothal and marriage? Did you think that by waiting until after the betrothal you would be safe? Think again, Roman. This betrothal is off!" Micah picked up the jewels on the table and threw them at his feet, spat on them, and ground them into the floor with his sandal. "Get out of here."

Julius gulped. "Micah. Sir. Please."

"Get out!" Micah picked up a jar full of flowers at his right hand and threw it at Julius, missing him by a fraction of an inch.

Julius bowed. "I'm going. Father?" Julius and Gaius made their way out the door, followed by Micah's eloquent curses.

Deborah grasped Micah's arm. "Now, Micah, you are thinking more about how far away Miriam would be and not about how impossible it might be for Julius to get permission to marry, not to mention permission for time off to come back for a week-long wedding."

"The betrothal is off."

"You will break Mirie's heart. You know it will."

"I will not talk about this. Good night." Micah stomped over to their bedchamber and jerked the curtain closed behind him.

Deborah sighed and walked outside. To her surprise, Julius and Gaius stood there, Julius sweating in the cool night air. Gaius talked quietly, holding Julius' shoulders.

She strode over to them and touched Julius on his arm. "Please, don't judge Micah too harshly. When he's had time to think this over, he will change his mind."

"I'm not judging him. Truly, Deborah, he is right. It was wrong of me to keep this probable move from you. Now I have lost my love, and it's my doing." Ragged breaths escaped his throat.

"You haven't lost Miriam, Julius. Nor will you. We'll go ahead with the wedding plans. Let me manage Micah. Two weeks is not much time to plan. Actually one week. Jewish weddings take a week, you know. We'll have to skirt Micah until he comes around, but he will. You might have to kidnap Miriam, though."

Julius stood staring at her, mouth open. "Kidnap?"

"It's an old Hebrew custom, dating back to the days when the tribe of Benjamin didn't have any women for brides. They stole virgins from the daughters of Shiloh. Even now, when you see a bride being carried to her wedding, they're carrying on the custom, although the kidnappings aren't involuntary anymore." Deborah gave him a sly grin. "At least not usually."

"Not usually?" Julius' eyebrows rose to questioning points.

"We can't tell Miriam. If she's smiling instead of weeping, her father will know something is going on."

Gaius chuckled. "Deborah, you are a wise wife and mother, and I suspect Micah is hard put to keep up with you. If you should ever want to divorce him...."

"Not even the vaguest possibility. Micah is perfect for me. It's just that this time, he is wrong. He isn't usually, you know. But by the time he realizes he is wrong, it will be even more difficult to prepare for this wedding."

"How will we prepare for this…this kidnapping? Where will we hold the wedding? What if he doesn't change his mind?" Julius shot his questions off like arrows from an archer's bow, not waiting for the answers to send the next one flying. "And even if Miriam doesn't know, how will you convince everyone else to keep quiet?"

Amos ran from the house at the same time that a prolonged wail from that direction made it obvious that Micah had told Miriam the news. Amos looked back over his shoulder.

"Deborah, why are you out here? Shouldn't you be comforting Miriam? She's distraught. Leah is arguing with Micah. They need you in there. And why are you still here, Julius?"

Deborah shushed Amos. "Gaius, Julius, go home for now. I'll meet you at Loukas' house tomorrow at the fourth hour. Don't worry, I'll handle this end, and we'll get this wagon on the way. Bring Marcus and Cyril."

"What wagon, Deborah?" Amos asked, looking around.

"Never mind, Amos. Wait here, I'll send Leah out, and you can go home. I'll be coming to see you tomorrow morning." She hurried into the house.

As Deborah walked into the house, Miriam ran to her. "Ima, Ima, tell me it's not true. Tell me Abba didn't cancel the betrothal. Tell me he didn't send Julius away. It can't be true. It can't!" Miriam's voice raised with each syllable until it became a high-pitched scream. Tears streaked her cheeks. Her new headdress with the coins sewn in even spaces across, bright beads between each coin, she held in her clenched fist. "Abba said I can't wear my headband. It's not true, is it Ima?"

Deborah threw a narrow-eyed look at Micah as she gathered a sobbing Miriam into her arms and held her tight. She murmured the comforting words mothers do. She could see Micah's anger melting before the hysteria of his cherished daughter, but she didn't intend to let him off easy.

Deborah escorted Miriam up the stairs to her bedroom, one arm around her shoulders. Miriam held her hands to her head and stumbled on the steps, shoulders shaking as she sobbed.

When she descended the stairs, Micah had disappeared, Deborah suspected into his shop, his hiding place when he wanted to think or pray. Leah came with arms held out, tears coursing down her cheeks, too.

"Sh, Sister. Come with me." Deborah led the way out the doorway and away from the house, too far for Micah to hear their soft voices. "The betrothal is *not* off."

"What?"

"Sh. Not so loud. I said, 'The betrothal is not off.' Micah will come to his senses and change his mind, but meanwhile, we will proceed just beyond his sight."

"But, Deborah, he will be furious. He was so angry this evening I thought he would explode. I've never seen him lay a hand to Miriam before, and he slapped her. Then he tore the headdress from her head."

"He slapped her? Micah slapped her?"

"Yes, but I don't think she even felt it. After he said the betrothal was cancelled, she shrieked 'No,' and then just kept screaming. And he slapped her. She stopped screaming but didn't stop crying."

"Never mind that now. We have a big job ahead of us. First, you must convince Amos to go along with this and not tell Micah. I'll be by in the morning at the third hour, and we'll go to Loukas' house to do our planning. And we cannot tell Miriam. It's her tears that will change Micah's heart."

Chapter 39

Deborah hurried along the way to Leah's house thinking what a disaster her own home seemed this morning. Micah had walked around the house with his head hung down, glaring, silent. Miriam refused to come out of her room and wouldn't eat. Amos and Leah waited for her in front of their door. Amos had his anxious face on. Leah looked frustrated. Deborah could guess they'd spent the morning, or maybe all night, arguing. She smiled as reassuringly as she could manage and suggested they start for Loukas' home.

"Deborah, are you sure Micah will change his mind? You know it is the father who must make decisions for their daughters. And we all heard him. He said the betrothal is off." Amos, despite his long legs, puffed as he talked and strove to keep up with Deborah and Leah while they trotted in the direction of Loukas' house. "Can't you slow down a little?"

"Amos, we've gone over this three times now. Micah will change his mind at any moment. We have only one week to prepare for the wedding. There is no time to dawdle." Deborah, out of breath too, threw a scowl in his direction.

As they approached the house, Joanna ran out to meet them. "What's wrong? Has someone been hurt?"

Leah wiped the sweat from her brow. "No one is hurt, but we do have an emergency."

"Come in. Loukas, we have more company," Joanna called when they got in the door.

Julius, Gaius, Marcus, and Cyril turned with Loukas to face them as Quinta walked into the room. Her face lit with joy when she saw Cyril, and she touched the coin-laden headdress across her forehead. Cyril's answering smile gladdened Deborah's heart even while she wanted to weep for Julius. It didn't look like he'd slept. His eyes were red and swollen. Dark circles and stress lines dominated his unshaved face, and his hair stood out at every angle from his head.

"Julius tells me Micah called off the betrothal. Deborah, surely that can't be true." Loukas' brow creased. "Micah was so overjoyed with his new son-in-law yesterday."

"That was before Julius announced he moves to Caesarea in three weeks." Deborah pulled the scarf off her hair and twisted it in her hands.

"Ah. Now I understand." Loukas nodded, glancing toward Quinta.

Deborah sat down on a bench. "Micah can't stand the thought of his only child being so far away. Miriam is inconsolable. But the betrothal is not off."

"You say the betrothal isn't off, but Miriam is upset. You didn't tell her?" Joanna's brows lifted.

Deborah shook her head. "No. It's her despair that will convince Micah. I hate seeing her in such anguish, but it's only for a few hours. Or at most, a day or two. The problem is we need to start planning and preparing for the wedding now." She took Joanna's hand and turned to Loukas. "The reason I wanted to meet here is to ask if you would be willing to allow Quinta and Cyril to be married at the same time, and to ask if we can have the wedding here at your house. I can't get our house ready without Micah becoming suspicious."

Loukas folded his arms across his chest. "I'm reluctant to sneak around behind Micah's back. I'm surprised you suggest it, Deborah."

Deborah swept her hand through her hair. "Don't you understand? Micah will want this wedding as much as any of us as soon as he gets past his anger. But if we wait until he wakes up, it could be too late."

"She's right, Loukas. We have much to prepare and purchase. The wedding garments, the veils, the litter, the house, the wine and food, and other incidentals by the score." Joanna ticked the items off on her fingers. "And it will have to be finished in one week."

Loukas lowered his head, paced, muttered, and looked skyward. After a lengthy pause, he stopped in front of Cyril. "I am a fool to ask this question, but would you agree to marry our Quinta so soon after your own betrothal?"

Deborah held her breath. She had not even thought that the young man would hesitate.

"Hmm." Cyril rubbed a hand along his jawline. "I'm not sure."

Julius all but pushed him to the floor.

Cyril laughed. "My future father-in-law asked a foolish question, but he is no fool. I have been ready to wed Quinta since the day I first saw her."

Quinta fell into Joanna's arms, a girlish giggle on her lips. "I am to be married in one week."

Deborah turned her attention to Loukas. "And so, Loukas, do you agree?"

Loukas hesitated. Then he nodded. "It's time. Let's get busy."

Time was slipping by them, with not enough hours to prepare. Deborah knew every moment must count. .

Joanna called for Meskhanet to bring food and watered wine, and she brought cushions to put on the floor around the table for everyone. As the group settled onto their pillows, the young Egyptian slave came to offer food and drink.

Deborah lifted her gaze and smiled as Marcus' attention fixed on the girl's graceful walk from one person to the next.

Loukas chuckled.

Marcus looked away, and his face flushed. "I'm a proselyte now, sir, but I'm not dead."

Loukas' chuckle turned into laughter, and Marcus joined in.

The rest of the group looked confused and curious, but neither Loukas nor Marcus enlightened them. Deborah, though, knew when a man was smitten, and Marcus might laugh, but inside, she knew his heart churned. "The weddings, my friends. We are here to plan for weddings, remember?" Her smile took the vinegar from her words. "The need to hurry will mean that we skip many of our beautiful wedding traditions, but let's keep as many as possible."

"For instance, if you're not waiting the usual year or so, there won't be time for Julius to build a house for Miriam, nor Cyril for Quinta. Where will you live?" Loukas asked.

Julius straightened. "Oh, no, I didn't think of that. I don't know. Obviously, we can't take them into the officers' quarters."

"Do you have anyone on your staff you can send ahead to find a house for you?"

"My staff? I don't have a staff, other than Cyril. There are several men under my command here. They won't be under my command in Caesarea, though, and I don't think Rufus would allow me to do that."

Loukas narrowed his eyes. "I won't allow my daughter to go unless there is a home for her. Usually, the bride goes to the house of her husband's father. But you won't be in Rome with Gaius." He folded his arms across his chest and sat back.

Julius grinned and looked to Gaius. "My father does have a house in Rome. I don't think it would be wise to take Miriam with me to Rome, though. My father is about as fond of the Jews as most Jews are of Romans. Just before the accident I wrote to him, telling him about Miriam and about my conversion to Judaism, a letter I doubt he received yet. I fully expect to be disinherited."

Gaius guffawed. "I should disown you, you insolent whelp. And the only reason you would be reluctant to bring Miriam to my home is that you fear I will steal her from you."

"You would choose Miriam over your own father and your inheritance?" Amos asked, eyes wide.

"And what is so odd about that, husband?" Leah grinned around the frost in her voice.

Amos flushed. Deborah doubted Amos would ever understand his wife's teasing.

"I chose the One God over the myriad of Roman gods, too," Julius replied quietly.

Amos' face paled. "Oh! This won't bring an attack on Jericho, will it?" Amos cast worried eyes on Gaius.

"I don't think so, Amos. I have some influence with Caesar Augustus, but I don't think even this would be reason enough for Caesar to declare war on you." Gaius' dry wit was lost on Amos.

Loukas cleared his throat. "Amos, stop worrying about the Roman army. We have enough to worry about with these weddings and the move." He sighed. "Now back to the problem of no place for our daughters to live. What do you intend to do about that, Julius? Cyril works for you, and so will go with you to Caesarea. I won't allow Quinta's wedding to proceed unless you provide a home for my only child."

"Sir, I honestly don't know. I wish I did. The best I can do is go talk to the tribune here and see if I can send an emissary to Caesarea to find a house for us."

"Julius, I'll go," Marcus offered. "I'll take my chariot. It should only take me a day to get there, a day to find a house for you, and a day to come back, if all goes well."

"Have you forgotten how to count, Marcus? If you left tonight, you would be three days into being considered a deserter before you return." Julius ran his hands through his hair, his worried frown deepening.

"There is another solution, you know." Gaius' amused tone drew everyone's attention. "I can go. I have four racing Arabians here with me. That's how I got here so quickly after hearing about the accident."

Julius' distracted expression cleared. "That would be perfect, Father. I'll send some funds with you. I have enough laid by that you wouldn't have to spend a single kodrantes."

"Well, there's one problem out of the way, or at least potentially solved," Deborah said. "Now there's another. I'm assuming Marcus will be one groomsman, but who will be the other?"

"Amos could." Leah's scowl dared Amos to object, but object he did.

"I hardly know this man, and he's a Greek. I'm not Greek. It wouldn't be proper."

"We know that, husband. But who else could? Loukas can't; he's the father of one of the brides'. Julius can't; he's a groom. Marcus should be Julius' groomsman. Micah not only doesn't know about the wedding still being underway, but he's also Miriam's father. Of course, if Cyril doesn't want you...." Leah glanced at Cyril.

"I would be honored to accept Amos as my groomsman." Cyril didn't smile, but his eyes twinkled.

"But, but, but," Amos sputtered.

"That settles it. Amos, consider yourself elected by popular acclaim." Julius clapped his hand on Amos' shoulder.

"But I—"

"Amos, we won't invite any of the Pharisees. They will never know," Deborah said. "Now just subside."

Amos yielded but scowled and shifted on his pillow.

Joanna tapped her fingers on the table. "With the weddings here, we might solve another problem. We aren't Hebrew, so Julius' friends may come here. Some people might refuse to come because the grooms are not Hebrew, but they would be the same who wouldn't want to come because of us. There is plenty of room in this courtyard for all who want to be here.

"I agree." Loukas nodded.

"Good. Julius' and Cyril's other friends should come," Leah said.

"What is the groomsman's role?" Marcus asked.

As the group plunged through the rest of the arrangements, even Amos lost his reluctance and showed some animation.

Chapter 40

By the time Deborah reached home, her anxiety over Micah and Miriam twisted her stomach into knots. An ominous silence filled the house when she walked inside.

"Miriam? Are you here?"

A muffled sound came from Miriam's bedroom, and Deborah ascended the stairs. Miriam, disheveled and slumped on the edge of the bed, raised dull, red-streaked eyes to her mother.

"Ima, why did my father cancel our betrothal?"

Deborah sat beside her. "Your father loves you, Daughter. So much that he can't stand the thought of you moving away from us. When Julius announced the move to Caesarea—"

"The what?" Miriam sat up straight.

"Ah, your father didn't tell you why he cancelled the betrothal?"

"No." Miriam's eyes flew open wide. "What move to Caesarea?"

"Julius said his tribune told him yesterday he must report to Caesarea in three weeks." Deborah placed her arm around Miriam's shoulders when they started to shake.

"No, Ima, that can't happen. I can't lose him. I can't. It will kill me." Her voice rose in hysteria, and her eyes flooded again. "Please, please, Adonai, not that. I'll never see him again."

"Have you been praying, Daughter?"

"Y-Yes."

"What has God said?"

"Nothing."

Thank You, Lord. "Have you talked to your father?"

"No. Oh, Ima, I can't talk to him. I won't be able to talk without crying. I've cried so much now my eyes are on fire. It would only make him angrier. I don't like for him to be angry with me." Miriam buried her face in her hands.

"Have you eaten yet?"

Miriam shook her head. "No. I'm not hungry."

"You need to eat something. Come, I'll fix you some fruit." Deborah stood and offered her hand to Miriam.

"No, Ima, I can't eat. My stomach would rebel." She raised her face from her hands and picked up a sodden rag, wiping eyes and nose.

Deborah walked across the room and picked up a fresh rag from the basket there. "Here, Daughter, this one is clean and dry. Give me that one. It needs washing."

"Ima, would you talk to Abba? He'll listen to you."

"What should I talk to him about? That he should go to the tribune and talk that Roman into letting Julius stay here? That he must change his mind and continue the betrothal? What makes you think he would listen to me if he won't listen to you?"

Miriam stared at the rag in her hands, and lifted it to her face. She shook her head and wept again as Deborah turned and descended the stairs.

That was difficult, Adonai. I want so much to tell her. Please, Lord, work on Micah's heart. I know he's angry, but he's hurting, too. I know him, and I know he's going to change his mind. If only he would do that now, everyone would feel so much better so much sooner. Please, hold us together, please.

Micah sat, head in hands, on the stool in his shop, resting his elbows on the workbench.

"A man must make the hard decisions for a family, Adonai," he murmured. "A man's family should not move away from him, should they?"

Silence. Cold silence, at that.

Tears coursed through the sawdust coating his face. *My wife won't talk to me. My daughter won't even look at me. Now You are also quiet, Adonai?*

He stood, wiping his eyes with the sleeve of his tunic. Pieces of sawdust made their way into his eyes, and he rubbed them angrily.

I still think I did the right thing. He reached for a skin of wine hanging on a hook on the workbench and took a long pull. He wiped his mouth with his sleeve and made his way into the house. Deborah should have been back from the marketplace a long time ago. She hadn't even made his breakfast this morning. Not that he was hungry, but still...Where was she? He pushed wearily to stand and moved toward the door.Deborah walked out from the kitchen as he came through the door from the shop.

"Where have you been, wife?"

Deborah glanced at him and set some fruit and bread at Micah's place at the table. "Upstairs talking to Miriam. Before that I went to the marketplace. Do you want a step-by-step description?"

Micah stepped backward as though she had struck him.

"Deborah...?"

His wife turned her back on him and ran into their bedroom, pulling the curtain shut behind her. Micah sank down and stared at the food on his table.

He had hurt his wife and his daughter, but he just couldn't allow Julius to take Miriam so far from him. She was all he and Deborah had. What of their grandchildren? He had dreamed of bouncing them on his knee.

With Deborah's healing, they had so much to look forward, to, but now, Miriam might never find a husband. She'd proved too hard to please. He'd been so willing to bend to her wishes. But not this time. *Not this time, Adonai. A father must be a father.*

Deborah sat at the table, her head in her hands. Wedding plans proceeded as smoothly as possible, considering the circumstances. The wedding clothes needed only finishing touches, the litter was nearly built. But here it was, the day before the wedding, and still Micah stubbornly clung to his pronouncement.

The three of them broke into tears at the slightest provocation. Miriam looked haggard. Her eyes, red and swollen, had deep circles under them. She nibbled on small pieces of fruit and drank the watered wine her mother brought to her room, but she hadn't descended the stairs since that day.

Micah spent his days in his shop. He seldom spoke. Every time he came into the house to eat, his eyes seemed glued to the stairway.

Deborah knew the circles under her own eyes must be pronounced, too. *How long, O Adonai?*

She rose to her feet, wrapping her scarf around her head. "I need to go to the marketplace. I'll return as soon as I can."

Micah nodded, saying nothing, brooding over a goblet of wine. He'd done too much of that this week. Deborah prayed for something she could say or do to change this gloom in the house by the time she returned.

When she stopped at Leah's house, they sat and talked in soft tones for a few moments as Leah sewed a few more bright flowers at the edges of Miriam's veil.

"Leah, I was so convinced I knew the mind of Adonai, but what if I'm wrong? What if Micah doesn't change his disapproval by tomorrow? If we proceed against his judgment, he could wind up hating me. I couldn't stand that. What can I do? I feel so helpless."

Leah gazed at her sister, and suddenly her eyes brightened. "What if you told him Loukas decided to proceed with Cyril and Quinta's wedding?"

"Just how am I supposed to know this thing? I'm only supposed to be going to the marketplace."

A knock sounded at the door, and Leah rose. Joanna stood in the doorway, a broad smile on her face. "I thought I would find you here. Shalom, my good friends. I have to tell you, my Loukas is without equal, the most intelligent man in all of Judea. We will move to Caesarea. Not for a few weeks yet, but soon after the wedding. As soon as he can finish with the patients now under his care."

"Oh, Joanna, I'm so happy for you. And so envious." Deborah rose to greet her. "I wish Micah would think of that, too."

"Oh, I think he will. You see, Loukas is paying Micah a visit even now to invite you to the wedding of Cyril and Quinta, but he will casually mention the move. I think perhaps it would be a good idea if you go home now." Joanna's eyes sparkled. "I'll go with you."

Deborah laughed and grasped Joanna in a joy-filled embrace. "That's so wonderful! First, though, we have to get something at the marketplace. That's where I told Micah I would be. Let's go."

When Deborah walked in the door a short time later with Leah and Joanna following, they found Micah beaming.

"Deborah, do you think we could prepare for a wedding by tomorrow?"

"Tomorrow? But Micah, you said..."

"Everything has changed. Loukas had the most wonderful idea. You see, they—he and Joanna—decided to go ahead with Quinta's wedding so she could go with Cyril and Julius to Caesarea. Loukas and Joanna will follow in just a few weeks."

Deborah widened her eyes and blinked at Loukas. "Oh, no! Loukas, who will we go to for medical help? There is no one else here we want for a physician."

"That won't be a problem, my love. You see, we will also move." Micah threw out his chest as though he thought of it himself. He turned and bounded up the stairs. "Miriam, you are getting married tomorrow. Ready yourself!"

A disheveled Miriam appeared at the top of the stairs. "What?"

"It's only one day until your wedding, Mirie." Micah pulled her into a tight hug.

"My wedding? To Julius?" Hope and suspicion mingled in her voice. "Tomorrow?"

"To Julius, yes." Micah held her at arm's length. Tenderness filled his voice. "I was so stubborn, Mirie. Will you forgive me?"

"Forgive you?" Miriam's eyes widened with realization as Micah led her by the hand down the stairs. "Tomorrow?" she repeated.

"Sit here beside me, Daughter." Deborah said. "This is a time when we must plan without panic. I'm sure Loukas and Joanna will help us." She winked at Joanna. "And Leah and Amos, too."

Miriam ran fingers of both hands through tangled locks. "I must look like a beggar."

Loukas grinned and patted her arm. "You do look a little ragged, child, but you can clean up after we leave. Miriam, what would you think if your parents moved to Caesarea?"

Miriam gasped. She looked at her father, who nodded and smiled, and at her mother. She threw her arms around her mother, then around her father. "Oh, Abba, this is the happiest day of my life."

"Please pardon Miriam and me. We need to have a mother and daughter conversation." Deborah winked again at Joanna.

"We have to go, too, because we have other people to invite." Joanna held out her hand to Loukas.

"And I have a son-in-law to tell. I'll be back soon." Micah trotted out the door before Deborah could catch him.

"Oh, no, what if he catches Julius getting ready for the wedding?" Deborah's heart pounded with panic.

"Don't worry. We came up with this idea last night, so Julius is prepared." Joanna grasped Deborah's arm, preventing her from leaving.

Miriam frowned in confusion. "What do you mean, 'Julius is prepared?' Prepared for what?"

Warmth flooded Deborah's face. "Uh, Daughter, I, uh...."

"She's trying to say your betrothal was never cancelled. But don't you dare tell your father." Joanna's eyes twinkled. "We have nearly everything in readiness."

"Ima?"

Deborah sighed. "Yes, it's true. You see, I knew your father would change his mind, but in order to still be able to have everything done before the wedding, we had to begin work last week."

"Why didn't you tell *me*?"

"I couldn't. Your face would give us away. If you had known, you would have walked around the house singing and smiling."

Miriam blushed. "Oh."

"We do need to tell a few more people now, ladies, so Joanna and I have to be on our way." Loukas bowed his head. "If you will excuse us."

"Thank you, my friends." Deborah pulled Joanna into her arms for a quick hug.

"And from me, too," Miriam said. "I promise I will pull my share of the load for the next day."

After Joanna and Loukas left, Miriam turned to her mother and Leah. "Would you two help me with my wedding clothes? I haven't even started on the veil, and the cloak hasn't been measured or hemmed or...." She stopped when the two women began laughing.

"The cloak is finished, Daughter, and the veil nearly so. Leah sewed until her fingers bled."

"But don't worry. I took care to bleed only on the floor." Leah held her bulging stomach as she laughed again.

Chapter 41

The next morning, a crisp blue sky greeted Julius. He stretched and grinned, rose and padded barefooted to his door to open it.

"Hey, you lazy servant, get up," he shouted toward Cyril's door. "There are things to do today."

"*I* am not the lazy one," Cyril called from the kitchen and then appeared in the doorway. "Do you think Marcus and Amos will have the litter ready in time?"

"He said yesterday all there was left to do was the canopy, so I suppose so."

"Did your father find a house?" Cyril placed dishes of pomegranates and cheese curds on the table and walked back to the kitchen.

Julius followed him. "Sorry, I meant to tell you last night. He returned yesterday evening. He managed to find us something somewhat better than a hovel. In fact, I don't think I've lived in a place such as he described since I followed Father to his battalion."

"We won't be living beyond your salary, will we? How much did this palace cost?"

"Mother gave me a tidy sum, but I always put as much of my salary away as I could. Father negotiated a good price. This place has been unoccupied for a time, but he says it's not in a bad state. We'll have to hire some servants or buy a couple of slaves to finish getting it in shape, though."

Cyril sliced a small slab of beef. "I thought Miriam didn't approve of slavery."

"She doesn't. But that's not to say I couldn't buy a couple of them and set them free, right? And maybe they would be willing to work for me for a time."

"My guess is they would be willing." Cyril grinned.

"So, when is Marcus supposed to be here?" Julius examined his pomegranate.

"In time for the wedding, I'm sure. Why are you so anxious? It's barely the first hour. We have all day to prepare. We don't kidnap our brides until after dark."

"And why are you so calm? Anyone would think this is your hundredth marriage."

"Will worrying change anything?" Cyril wiped a spill of red juice from Julius' side of the table.

"All right, then, you stay here in your calm little world. I will find Marcus."

"He has been hanging around a lot with Amos. Those two have become unaccountably thick. Who would have imagined this? One nervous Jew and one insane Roman."

"I need to know where to find Amos, too." Julius paced between the door and the table.

"At this hour he could be at home in bed with his wife, so I think Marcus is *not* with Amos just yet. I think you might find Marcus still in his bed, too."

"It's time they were up. There is much to do today."

"Like what? Get dressed? Do you want that white robe on all day so that it will be nice and dusty before the wedding? Breakfast is ready. Sit still and eat."

"Eat?" Julius looked at the food set before him and discovered he had a decided lack of appetite. "How can you think about eating?"

"It's easy. I don't want to faint in front of all those people, so I eat." Cyril demonstrated by placing a large curd into his mouth.

Julius heaved a heavy sigh. "My stomach churns. My head hurts. My hands shake. I think I might be getting sick." He put a hand to his brow.

Cyril laughed, holding his sides. "The mighty warrior, felled by a weak stomach in the face of matrimony." He wiped his eyes.

Julius tried to look indignant, but he lost the battle to an embarrassed chuckle. "You think I have bridegroom's disease."

"All the classic symptoms, I would say. Would you like for me to go get Loukas?"

"And have him laugh at me, too? I think not."

"Marcus?"

"That would be courting humiliation. Forget it."

"Then eat something, man. Trust me, it will help."

Julius sat down and put a piece of beef on the flatbread, put a bite in his mouth, and chewed with a decided lack of enthusiasm.

"This is dry. I don't think I want any wine this early, but is there some milk or juice of some sort?"

"We don't have any milk or juice, but I could crush some grapes. Or water. One of the slaves brought some water around this morning. Or watered wine."

"Water would be perfect. My mouth is so dry you'd think I just came off the desert."

"Another symptom," Cyril said, bringing them both a cup of water.

"Another symptom? Oh, you mean bridegroom's disease. So why aren't you afflicted with this disease?"

"I am, but my symptoms are manageable. I've seen this before. Remember when your cousin Lucius was about to get married, and you sent me to help him?"

Julius chucked. "I'd almost forgotten. I thought we would have to throw him in prison and drag him in chains to his own wedding. But I figured he was just being Lucius. He wasn't enthused about getting married at all. He had nightmares about having to settle down, even with the beautiful Julia."

"Well, according to others of your uncle's and father's slaves, it wasn't unusual behavior in a bridegroom."

"How about the brides? Do they go through this, too?"

"I don't know. I only talked to men about weddings."

"Ima, would you hate me if I changed my mind now?" Miriam's voice trembled, her eyes wide.

"No, of course not. I'll tell your father the whole thing is off." Deborah nodded, an understanding look in her eyes. "I'll tell him you decided you really don't love Julius, and you don't want to marry him."

"No, not that. I do love him, and I do want to marry him but not today."

"When, then?"

"I don't know, just not today. I'm not ready."

"Do you mean not ready because your veil isn't finished?"

"Yes, that's it. My veil isn't finished."

"Oh? Did Leah say she wouldn't be able to finish it?" Deborah raised an eyebrow.

"No, she said she could finish it this morning, but what if she doesn't?"

"What if she does?"

Miriam lifted her robe from a nearby chair. She held it up to the front of her and looked down at the brilliant white with jewels sewn onto the bright blue belt. "My robe...it doesn't look right, either. I...I think maybe it's too long. Or maybe it's crooked. I'm just not ready, Ima. My knees feel so weak. What if I fall down in the middle of the ceremony? What if I start crying?"

"What if I told you all brides feel this way on their wedding day?"

"They do?"

"Remember Hannah?"

"Well, yes, but—"

"How about Mary?"

"I can understand why Mary would run away, but she did come back in time for the ceremony." Miriam sighed. "I'm sorry she did now."

"So am I. But the point is, almost every bride is nervous and wonders if she's losing her mind."

"Ima, I'm scared. I want today to be tomorrow instead. Or better, next week sometime. Or next month. I just don't want today to be today. I can see why sometimes the bride shouldn't know when her bridegroom will come for her. She has a year or two to prepare, and after a while it must become just another Wednesday. Ho hum, he probably won't come today. But I know today is *the* Wednesday, and I feel so frightened."

"No, traditionally the bride doesn't know, although Mary must have, since she ran. Under the most hidden of conditions, though, it seems the word gets around even when it's supposed to be a secret. Now, come, Daughter. Either you marry today or Julius will have to leave Jericho without you, and you may never have another day to plan for a wedding."

Chapter 42

A cooperative full moon emphasized the deep shadows. Julius hugged the darkness, hurrying between buildings on quiet feet, followed by four other shadows, Cyril, Marcus, Amos, and a hired piper. The five men reached Loukas' home and threw a rope ladder over the surrounding enclosure. The piper played a low, seductive tune.

Cyril secured the ladder to a handy tree, and Julius climbed to the top of the wall. Marcus gave Cyril a leg up, and Julius helped him to the top of the wall. Cyril dropped to the ground and strode to where Quinta waited at in the courtyard.

Marcus handed the ladder to Julius, who lowered it to lean against the wall. Julius watched the couple and strained to hear their conversation.

Quinta's bright hair caught the moonlight.

"You are so beautiful." Cyril stood in the window and nuzzled Quinta's hair as he pulled her close.

Quinta whispered something to Cyril and then giggled into his tunic.

Cyril rubbed his thumb softly across her lips.

"Hey!" Julius whispered none too softly.

Cyril pulled himself away and helped Quinta climb the ladder.

Cyril followed her to the top of the wall, straddling it. He held her hands as she stretched her feet to the ground then jumped down behind her.

"Your seat, my lady," he said, bowing as he handed her into the litter chair. The men lifted the poles easily and trotted to Micah's home.

They came to a halt near the door. "Now," Julius whispered. In accordance with the prearranged signal, the piper began playing a love song, low, slow, and soft. Julius climbed the ladder to the roof. Miriam met him at the parapet, and he claimed the kiss he'd been longing for since the stolen kisses in the grove. Scintillating sensations ran through him, and they might have forgotten to finish the kidnapping if he hadn't heard Micah's deliberately heavy steps on the stairs.

"Who goes there?" he demanded. "Is someone come to steal my daughter from me?"

Miriam chuckled and pulled away. Julius helped her find her footing on the ladder then climbed quickly down after her. The piper's tune quickened, and one of the neighbors opened his door. The piper increased both the volume and speed of the song to call other neighbors out.

Cyril and Quinta, caught sharing a quick kiss of their own, broke apart. The two girls sat in the litter chairs, and Marcus with Amos in back, and Cyril with Julius in front lifted the litter again. With a joyous shout, they began their trek through the neighborhoods, winding here and there, laughing and calling people to join them. Other pipers joined along the way, along with a drum and a horn. The moon shone so bright no torch was needed, but a few people still carried them.

By the time they returned to Loukas' home, such a large throng followed the litter that Deborah wondered if it challenged the capacity of even this spacious courtyard. The men set the litter down and moved the chairs, the draped canopy of the litter now forming their wedding chapel.

Shelumiel stepped under the canopy, inviting the grooms to join him.

"My friends," he said, his resounding voice quieting the entire crowd. "We celebrate a beautiful wedding ceremony this night only one week following the betrothal." He scowled fiercely at the few who murmured. "Still your gossiping tongues. The reason for the wedding so soon is because the couples must immediately move to Caesarea after the celebration is finished one week from this day."

"Julius, Cyril, kneel here on this rug."

Leah, seated beside Deborah, placed her hands on her belly and grunted softly.

"What was that, Leah? Are you having a contraction?" Deborah asked in a whisper, glancing around. She placed her palm on Deborah's belly. The hardened muscles under her hand answered the question.

"I don't know," Leah responded just as softly. "Maybe the baby just chose this moment to stretch."

Deborah shook her head. "No, I don't think so, but maybe he will postpone his entry into this world for another hour or so. Usually the first baby comes slowly." She hugged Leah's shoulders and turned back to face the ceremony.

"Let us proceed with the marriage." Shelumiel invited the crowd to be seated with a wave of his hand. He pronounced the seven blessings, raising a cup of wine and taking a sip after each one.

"Praised are You, O Lord our God, King of the Universe, Creator of the fruit of the vine.

"Praised are You, O Lord our God, King of the Universe, Who created all things for Your glory.

"Praised are You, O Lord our God, King of the Universe, Creator of man.

"Praised are You, O Lord our God, King of the Universe, Who created man and woman in Your image, fashioning woman from man as his mate, that together they might perpetuate life. Praised are you, O Lord, Creator of man.

"May Zion rejoice as her children are restored to her in joy. Praised are You, O Lord, Who causes Zion to rejoice at her children's return.

"Grant perfect joy to these loving companions, as You did to the first man and woman in the Garden of Eden. Praised are You, O Lord, who grants the joy of bride and groom.

"Praised are You, O Lord our God, King of the Universe, who created joy and gladness, bride and groom, mirth, song, delight and rejoicing, love and harmony, peace and companionship. O Lord our God, may there ever be heard in the cities of Judah and in the streets of Jerusalem voices of joy and gladness, voices of bride and groom, the jubilant voices of those joined in marriage under the bridal canopy, the voices of young people feasting and singing. Praised are You, O Lord, Who causes the groom to rejoice with his bride."

After the glasses had been passed to the brides and grooms and back to him, Shelumiel set the two glasses on the table beside him.

"Mozeltov!" Shelumiel shouted, and the crowd repeated the shout. The music started up once more, dancing broke out among the men, and singing filled the air with joy.

As the men danced past, Leah gasped and gripped her abdomen again, and Deborah turned to her sister. "Should we find a room aside?"

"No. I want to see this marriage through."

"How much do these pains hurt?"

"I've had worse headaches, but usually headaches come on slow. These are sudden, and I guess the surprise makes me catch my breath."

"From now on, whenever one happens, you reach over and touch my elbow. I want to know when the pains become regular and close together."

"Do you think he will be born today, then?"

"I think so, but sometimes women will have a false start once—or more than once—before the infant decides it is the right time."

Loukas left to lead the two couples out of the main hall to their respective rooms for their first alone time while the merriment continued. The servants set out food and wine, and the seven blessings were repeated before people began eating while they waited for the grooms and brides to return.

Leah, instead of touching Deborah's elbow, grasped it hard with both hands, her face reflecting the pain she felt. Gritted teeth stopped the cry in her throat. Deborah turned to her, nodding. "Let's go find a room"

"This way," Joanna whispered from behind Deborah. She led the way toward a bedroom on the roof of their house.

Julius glanced around the elaborate room, thinking Miriam must like the tapestries and jeweled lamps. Joanna and Loukas provided them with this room for the week remaining before the move, and Julius' heart filled with gratitude for the extras they delivered.

"A beautiful room, is it not?" Miriam said, running her hand along the embroidered cover on the elbow-high bed. She lifted her gaze to his, drew an audible breath, and flushed a glowing red. "It is not too late for you to reject me."

"Reject you?" Julius shook his head. "Did I hear you right?"

"Yes." She dropped long lashes over her eyes. "Another man has seen me." Her eyes flew open. "I have not known a man, but one tried…." Her voice faltered.

"I knew. It makes no difference to me, except that I am glad he didn't hurt you."

She smiled, such a small tilting of her lips. "I feared…."

He shook his head. "No. Even if he had succeeded in his attempt, it would not stop my love for you. You are the perfect woman for me. Nothing could change that, not even the cruelty of Brutus." Staring into her eyes, he took her small, soft hands in his rough ones, making slow circles on her palms with gentle thumbs. He raised one hand and then the other to his lips, kissing, and then softly nibbling the fleshy edges of her palms. Taking a deep breath, he gritted his teeth and stepped back.

"I know this hasn't been an easy week for you, my love, and this week and next week will be strenuous, too. If you want to postpone our, ah, our consummation until even after we reach Caesarea, I will understand."

Miriam pulled his hands behind her back. Then she locked hers behind his head. With a slow step forward, she molded her body to his.

"No, I do not wish to postpone anything. I've dreamed of your kisses since that evening on the hill and longed for the feelings I felt then. You made me quiver from head to toe. You made my heart pound so hard I thought it would burst from my chest. It's your duty as my husband to fill me again with those feelings."

Julius' arms tightened, and his lips lowered close to hers. "I certainly don't want to be accused of failing my duties," he whispered against her mouth before he kissed her.

Cyril stood in front of Quinta, perplexed. She stood in the middle of the room, wringing her hands, tears flowing down her cheeks.

"What is it? Have I done something wrong?" He swept his hands through his hair, wanting so much to touch her, but afraid to.

"No, no, you do nothing wrong. It is only that…that, I do not know what to do. And I am afraid this…this consummation will hurt. My friend Aliah is newly married, and she says it will hurt, and I do not want to hurt. She would not say what, but I think it must be bad enough to make blood."

Cyril maintained his distance, his hands stretched toward her. "Ah, now I understand. I wish I could tell you that our first time of making love will not hurt, but it will. It will only hurt for a moment, sort of like a hard but quick pinch, I'm told. I don't really know, since I'm not a woman. I will be as gentle as I can, my sweet bride. I promise." He approached her with slow steps and tilted her chin up. He kissed her trembling lips gently. "Or I can wait, Quinta, until you're not afraid."

Quinta's eyes flooded again, and she hugged Cyril fiercely. "You are the best man who ever existed, my husband. I do not wish to deny you anything."

"You aren't denying me anything. Postponing isn't denial. We will wait."

"Will they not be waiting for, for the sheets from the wedding bed? My friend, she say they look to see if the bride is a virgin and that blood shows that she is."

Cyril looked around the room. The only thing sharp seemed to be the edge of a lamp, and he used it to cut his thumb, dripping a few drops of blood on the sheets.

"That should satisfy them. You may relax, my love." He pulled her close and kissed her, gently at first, intending to stop there. Her mouth opened to his kiss, and his excitement rose. His lips worked hers with passion. Quinta caught her breath and pulled back. Her eyes were wide, pale irises nearly hidden by dilated pupils.

"I think I am understanding. Do that again." She pulled his mouth down against hers again, then put both arms around his waist and pulled him tightly to body. Her hands slid down his back.

"My own, my love, if you want me to stop, that's not the way to do it." He breathed her name and leaned down to kiss her again.

Chapter 43

A cheer rose from the crowd as Julius led Miriam into the courtyard. Cyril and Quinta emerged a moment later, and more cheers erupted.

Cyril glanced around. "Where is Amos? I wanted to give him my thanks for being my groomsman."

Deborah grinned. "He'll no doubt be out shortly, carrying his son."

"His son?" Miriam cried. "Leah had her baby? She was sitting beside you just a few moments ago."

Deborah laughed. "A few moments? That was over an hour ago, and this little boy was in a hurry."

Julius' cheeks burned, and he grinned.

A smiling Amos entered the courtyard carrying a small bundle. "Behold my son," he shouted, lifting the infant high in front of him.

Several of the men pushed in toward Amos, admiring the red-faced and crying babe and pounding Amos on the back. He handed the baby to Deborah and returned to the room where Leah awaited.

Julius' mother-in-law carried the child around for the women to ooh and ah over. When everyone else had had a chance to admire, one of the men in the back of the room came forward. Deborah looked up into the Man's face. Her eyes widened.

The Man took the child and blessed him. "Tell Leah and Amos this child will be a leader of My followers one day. They must guard his steps carefully and keep him from the snares of the evil one."

"I will tell them, Lord." Deborah bowed.

Julius watched as Jesus approached. The Man bowed his head to the bridal party.

Miriam gasped, and her eyes widened. She dropped from her throne to her knees before Him. "Lord, our celebration is honored to have You here."

"I'm happy to be here." He reached down and lifted her to her feet.

"Lord, thank You for healing my mother. I will bless Your Name forever."

Julius' breath caught in his throat, and he, too, left his elevated seat and knelt at Jesus' feet. "Lord, You should take my throne."

"The only throne I want is in your heart, Centurion."

"In my heart? I don't understand."

"A throne is where a king sits. If God is the King of a man's heart, the kingdom will be found wherever that man is." Jesus grasped their hands with His. "Your life will not be easy. You will have challenges to face in this marriage. But if you remain with God as your King, your burdens will be easier to carry.

Epilogue

"This has been a memorable, week." Miriam said as she greeted Julius at the door. "It was difficult to pack early in the morning before people began coming, and then I would have to sit still all day. Just think…tomorrow morning we leave for Caesarea. Ima and I packed everything I need to take. Do you need help packing up your things?"

Julius took time for a deep kiss that left them both breathless before he replied. "Uh, what were we talking about?"

"Packing." Miriam giggled.

"Oh, yes, packing. There's nothing left to pack. Cyril did it all before the wedding. All I had to do at the end of the day was join you on our thrones."

"It was fun being kings and queens for a week, wasn't it?"

"You, Quinta, and Cyril got to be two queens and a king. Rufus wasn't about to let this new groom off during my final week here." Julius pulled her close, intending another kiss, but Miriam ducked her head.

"Were you able to get the request for Marcus' transfer through?" She held his hand as she turned to enter Lucas' courtyard.

"I put the request in, but we won't know for quite a while if he gets to go to Caesarea, too."

"You've been friends for so long. Won't it seem strange not to have him around?"

"Yes, but I have you and Cyril. Marcus is the one who will be lonely, I'm afraid. I'm a little concerned about him. Cyril and I are his closest friends, perhaps his only real friends." Julius' brow furrowed as he followed her into the house.

"He did get introduced to the other proselytes, and they seemed to be a very welcoming bunch. He might be all right."

"I'm afraid they won't know how to take him. He tends to put strangers off with his prickly humor. That's part of the reason I'm trying to get him transferred up to Caesarea with me."

"I haven't seen him the last couple of days. Do you think maybe he's off sulking somewhere?"

"It could be. I hope he hasn't gone off anywhere without leave."

"Without leave? Marcus wouldn't do that, would he? He could get in trouble." Miriam sat on the edge of the fountain wall and patted the wall next to her.

Julius sat at her side and slipped an arm around her, nuzzling her neck. "I hope not, but it wouldn't be the first time. It's been a couple of years since he decided to make an unauthorized jaunt, but he's done it before."

Miriam put her hands on his chest, slowly moving them upward. "Maybe you should go find him."

"I checked all his favorite haunts before I came here and didn't find him. He was off duty today. I saw him this morning, and he was acting a little strange."

Miriam lifted her eyebrows. "Strange? How?"

"Well, he just keeps staring off into the distance. And he loses track of what's being said in the middle of a conversation. It's just not like him to act so distracted."

Sometime later, a knock sounded at the door. Julius looked up from his place at the table as Meskhanet brought the basket of loaves toward where he and the rest sat. She detoured to the entrance, lifted the latch, and swung the door open.

"Come," she said, leading the visitor inside.

"Well, Marcus, what brings you here again this day?" Loukas asked. "Meskhanet, please bring another cushion and set another place at the table for our guest."

Julius met Miriam's eyes, one eyebrow arched, and nodded.

Marcus' gaze followed Meskhanet's graceful form as she performed the requested tasks.

Made in the USA
San Bernardino, CA
06 November 2013